Dangerous Games

Dangerous Games

Danielle Steel

W F HOWES LTD

This large print edition published in 2017 by
W F Howes Ltd
Unit 5, St George's House, Rearsby Business Park,
Gaddesby Lane, Rearsby, Leicester LE7 4YH

1 3 5 7 9 10 8 6 4 2

First published in the United Kingdom in 2017
by Macmillan

A CIP catalogue record for this book is available
from the British Library

ISBN 978 1 51007 016 5

Typeset by Palimpsest Book Production Limited,
Falkirk, Stirlingshire

Printed and bound by
T J International in the UK
Printforce Nederland b.v. in the Netherlands
Ligare in Australia

To my wonderful children,
Beatie, Trevor, Todd, Sam,
Victoria, Vanessa, Maxx, and Zara,
May those you trust never disappoint you
  or destroy you,
Live in honor, love honestly,
Be true to yourself, and be kind to each
  other.

I love you, always,
Mommy/DS

Come not between the dragon and his wrath.

★

Time shall unfold what plaited cunning hides.
—WILLIAM SHAKESPEARE, *KING LEAR*

CHAPTER 1

It was nearly four in the morning when Alix Phillips ran for cover as gunshots rang out. A fruit-canning factory had been shut down in Alabama, putting thousands out of jobs. The union had been trying to stop the shutdown for months, and finally violence had broken out in the town, out of desperation and frustration. Most of the factory workers were African American, some of whose families had worked there for generations. There had been looting and destruction in the town and surrounding area all night, and two young men had been killed. The riot police had been called in from nearby cities, and the acrid smell of tear gas was everywhere. Alix was reporting from a live feed, and had to abandon the spot where she'd been standing, as Ben Chapman, her cameraman, grabbed her roughly by the arm and forced her to leave. He nearly had to drag her to get her away from the scene, as troops narrowed in on the area, and flames exploded the windows as looters set a building on fire. She had just been saying on her broadcast for national TV that nothing like it had been seen since the riots in L.A. in 1992.

'Are you fucking crazy?' Chapman shouted at her, as they took refuge behind a building around the corner, and National Guardsmen and riot police thundered past them. Ben and Alix were wearing their press badges around their necks and had been on the scene all week. Alix's face was smudged with soot, and her eyes were watering from the tear gas heavy in the air. 'Are you trying to get killed?' They had been working as a team for four years, and got along well, except in moments like this.

To her own detriment, Alix Phillips would put herself on the front line of any battle, riot, demonstration, or dangerous situation in order to bring the reality of it to their viewers. Ben loved working with her, but they'd argued about it before. Her fearlessness made for award-winning footage, and the network loved it, especially at a time in broadcasting when few reporters were willing to take the risks she did. It was in her DNA. But there were times when reason had to win out, or should have, and with Alix it never did. Once she was in the heat of a story, she was blind to all else. She'd been a TV news reporter since she graduated from college seventeen years before, and at thirty-nine had made a powerful reputation for herself, reporting from every hot spot on the planet. She covered the news abroad and in the States, on special assignment, and the producers loved her because she never turned anything down, and her brilliant editorials and assessments were known around the world. She was a legendary reporter whom everyone admired, and was a household name. Working with her was a privilege Ben enjoyed, except when she went too far and put their lives on the line. He was a brave man, but not foolish. But nothing stopped Alix, she was passionate about every story.

Ben was forty-two, and had been in the military until four years before. He had been part of an elite Navy SEAL team, which made him well suited to the kind of assignments Alix preferred, and he had signed on enthusiastically to work with her. Other more cautious cameramen had turned the opportunity down. She was healthy, extremely fit, headstrong, honorable, courageous, afraid of nothing, and very smart. Her stories were flaw-lessly covered, and his talent with a camera in his hands was equal to hers as a reporter. Their producers and audiences loved them. They were the perfect combination and complemented each other. Both were known for their professional integrity and in-depth stories. They had been all over the Middle East together, had covered mili-tary takeovers and civil wars in South America and Africa, natural disasters, coups d'état, and a number of important political exposés in the States. Trouble of any kind was their specialty, and they made it riveting to watch with his images and her words and presence on the screen. Ben always teased her that if there was a disaster somewhere in the world, Alix would find a way to get there, and risk her hide and his, just as she had already done several times that night in the Alabama riots.

They heard an explosion a few minutes after they'd taken cover. Alix dashed back out before Ben could stop her, and he followed. He was as zealous as she was, but he felt it his duty to protect her too, which she ignored whenever possible.

'Are you ever going to ask me if I think it's smart to go back out or if we should wait?' he complained when he caught up to her. They were both tired and hadn't slept more than a few hours in days.

'Of course not.' She grinned at him, and ran alongside a group of soldiers who had been sent to reinforce the riot squad. But in spite of the hazards, he liked working with her. They were combat buddies and partners in crime. He was six feet five with powerful shoulders, and in remarkable shape. She was a foot shorter, with a lithe, athletic body and long blond hair, and she liked to think she was as physically capable and tough as he was. She trained at a gym every day when they were at home in New York, and she loved to box. But twenty years as a Navy SEAL and sheer size made Ben the stronger of the two, inevitably, whether she admitted it or not. She was beautiful when she cleaned up, but was perfectly at ease in combat clothes, covered in grime. She didn't care how she looked when she was working. All that mattered was getting the story, whatever it took.

The riot went on until seven in the morning, when all the rioters and looters had been rounded up and taken to jail. The fires continued to burn white-hot and weren't put out for several days. The small factory town remained under military control when Ben and Alix left and got on a plane to New York in Birmingham, after driving fifty miles in their rented car to get there. The town they'd just left had almost been destroyed, and because of the factory closing, most of the locals were now unemployed and on public assistance of some kind, and many had already lost their homes. It was a sad story, and Alix had blamed local government in her broadcast for providing so little support and being so ill prepared to quell the riots and looting before they got out of hand. The mayor was said to be corrupt, although she implied it but didn't say it, and the town was bankrupt. The region had been declared a disaster area on the morning after the riots began. She was pensive and quiet as they flew back to New York. It was hard to imagine such extreme poverty in the United States, but they had seen it before. And it tore at her heartstrings when she saw the kids, barefoot and in clothes that were ragged and too small, and many homeless now as well.

'What are they going to do now?' she said softly, glancing at Ben, as the flight attendant served their lunch in business class. Due to the hardships of their work, the network paid for them to travel business class whenever possible. It was one of the perks they both enjoyed about their job.

'Go on unemployment, or move away, if they

can,' Ben answered seriously, remembering the poverty they'd seen there. It upset him too, although they had seen far worse things in the wars and horrors they'd covered together around the world. It helped that they were both unencumbered, neither of them with someone waiting for them at home, and Ben assumed they'd be back on the road again in a few days. They usually were. A new dire situation would happen somewhere and they would be sent there. It was not unlike his life in the military with the SEALs. Ben had been defending the people and principles he believed in all his life.

Alix came by her talent and courage honestly. Her father had been a famous British journalist and had been killed by a bomb in Ireland while covering a story, when she was a child. She remembered him only dimly, but from everything she knew about him, he had been a wonderful man. Her mother, Isabelle, was French. Alix had grown up in London, gone to college in the States, and once she decided to stay there to work in TV news for a major network, her mother had moved back to the small town she came from in Provence. She had been a good mother, and never interfered with what Alix chose to do. Alix loved her fiercely and visited her whenever she could, which was never often enough.

Alix's college years in the States had been turbulent and stormy. A romance in her sophomore year had led to the birth of a daughter a year later. The baby's father had been a year younger, a sweet boy who was passionately in love with Alix and tried to match her courage when she decided to have the baby, much to his parents' dismay. They were cool Bostonians from a wealthy banking family, and their dreams for their son did not include an illegitimate child, nor marriage to an unknown girl from London, from what they considered an insignificant family, no matter how bright Alix was. And her dreams of following in her father's footsteps as a journalist did not please them either, although Wyatt thought she was amazing. Despite his parents' protests, they were married less than a month before Faye was born.

The delivery was easy, but everything that came after wasn't. Wyatt's parents cut off all financial support, and Isabelle came from London to help them with the baby, although she wasn't thrilled with Alix's decision either, but young love had prevailed over reason.

And three months later, the unthinkable happened. While vacationing with friends in Nantucket, Wyatt was killed in a boating accident, and Alix became a twenty-year-old widow with a three-month-old infant. Still in shock over Wyatt's death, Alix and her mother attended the funeral in Boston, where they realized that Wyatt's family had told no one about their son's marriage or his child, and Alix and her mother were treated like unwelcome strangers. A somber conversation with

Wyatt's father the day after the funeral made clear that his family wanted no contact with Alix or their granddaughter in the future. They considered her nothing more than a youthful mistake he had made, and they felt no bond to mother or child. They wouldn't even look at their son's infant daughter.

Alix went back to London with her mother then, and after a month of long, tearful discussions, Isabelle convinced her to go back to school and leave Faye with her in London. Alix was torn, even as she boarded the plane to go back to school in the States to finish her junior year. And once there it became obvious that it had been the right decision, and her mother had been wise.

A year later, with near-perfect grades, Alix graduated with honors and got an extraordinary opportunity in network news in New York. She was on her way. She went home to visit her mother and daughter whenever she could, but she was deeply immersed in her demanding job for several years. Isabelle moved back to France then, to Provence, and took Faye with her, while Alix accepted every challenging assignment they gave her. She could never have achieved the early years of her career with a baby to care for, and Faye thrived with her grandmother. She was five when Alix finally decided to bring her to New York, which was challenging, but she wanted her daughter with her and felt ready to cope.

They managed, Faye spent summers with her grandmother in France, and a nanny cared for her in New York while Alix traveled for her job. It wasn't ideal, but it worked. And Alix and her daughter had in common that they had grown up without their fathers. It created a special bond between them, and Faye worried fiercely about her mother when she saw her on TV when she was away or on assignment. Isabelle had never complained about Alix's chosen career, but Faye did, all the time, and accused her mother of being irresponsible and trying to get killed.

'I don't have a father. What will I do if something happens to you?' she said angrily.

'You'd go to live with Mamie,' she said, referring to her mother in Provence. Faye's paternal grandparents had never made contact again in nineteen years. Alix had always thought they would eventually, but they never did. Faye didn't exist for them. She remained an embarrassment they chose to deny, with no sentiment for their late son's only child.

'That's not good enough,' Faye would say to her mother in a fury about the dangers of her job. 'I need you too. Not just Mamie.'

The truth was that Alix and Faye needed each other, but Alix loved her career too, and was determined to stay in it. And when Faye left for college, Alix felt free to take tougher, longer, more dangerous assignments than ever. Every fiber of her being came alive on those assignments. Faye was proud of her but upset about it too. It was a constant battle between the two women.

Faye was nineteen years old and a sophomore at Duke, and she knew that if there was a war, an uprising, or a terrorist attack somewhere, her mother would wind up there, drawn like a moth to flame. And the network she worked for took full advantage of her willingness to leave at the drop of a hat, and go anywhere they sent her. Anyone who knew Alix was acutely aware of the fact that nothing could stop her. If there was trouble somewhere in the world, Alix had to be in it, just as she was now. And because of the way she'd grown up, Faye was fiercely independent too. She was as determined as her mother. She wanted to go to law school after college, and Alix was sure she would, and she could afford to send her now. Her job as star reporter for a major network paid her well. But her work wasn't about money for Alix. Her career was her passion, she loved what she did. She found each assignment new and exciting, and she was the consummate professional. Like her father, Alix was a journalist to the core, and she liked being a war correspondent best of all. She and Ben had that in common, which was why they worked well together, on the toughest assignments the network could give them.

Alix never talked about her personal life or her past. Ben had been startled to learn a year after they started working together that she had a child. Her willingness to risk her life in the line of duty had never suggested to him that she had a family at home. And in fact she didn't. All she had was

Faye, and her mother in France. In that sense, she and Ben were very much alike. In his case, he was divorced with no children, and she knew he had parents and three brothers somewhere in the Midwest, whom he rarely saw. He had nephews and nieces, although he saw little of them, and said that he and his family had nothing in common. They thought him an oddball for leaving home and joining the SEALs. He said that the military had been his family for many years. He had strong moral values and a need to protect those around him, but he had no close personal ties Alix was aware of. And when she had questioned him about why he left the SEALs, all he said was 'It was time,' and clearly didn't want to talk about it. Like Alix, he was an intensely private person. They were there to do a job together, and that was what they did, like two soldiers of fortune, bringing the truth to their viewers, and shedding light on treason, betrayals, and crimes against humanity around the world. Above all, Alix believed in exposing evil deeds and shocking events, and so did Ben, whatever the risk to them to do so.

'Did you have time to call Faye?' Ben asked casually as they flew back to New York. He liked hearing about her, and he thought Faye a bright, interesting young woman, like her mother, willing to stand up for her ideals.

Ben had left home more than twenty years before, and had been divorced for fourteen years. He never talked about his ex-wife, and Alix correctly sensed he didn't want to, so she didn't ask. They were each entitled to their memories and secrets. They were colleagues, not lovers, and had become friends working hard together.

'I did,' Alix said about calling Faye from Alabama. She tried to call from wherever she was.

'How is she?' he inquired.

'Pissed, as usual,' Alix said, grinning. Faye still hated it when her mother went on dangerous assignments, and this one was. 'I think she'd like me to cover baking contests, dog shows, and county fairs.' He laughed at the idea. Faye never failed to remind her mother that she and her grandmother in Provence were all she had, and accused her of being selfish. As a result of the constant reminders, Alix had taken out a hefty life insurance policy for her, as her own father had done for them. It had allowed Alix to get a decent education, and her mother to take care of her full-time while she was still at home. But even though she pretended to be cavalier about it, there was no question that being a single mother weighed on Alix heavily at times. Not enough to make her change her life or give up her job. She couldn't at this point, and didn't want to. But she felt guilty whenever Faye complained.

Alix and Ben talked intermittently through lunch, and then Ben watched a movie on his iPad with his headphones on, and Alix put her seat back, covered herself with a blanket, and went to sleep.

Ben woke her as they approached JFK. He always

said that she could sleep in a ditch, standing on her head, and she woke up and put her seat back up just as they landed on the runway. She looked surprisingly rested and refreshed.

'Are you going to your place?' Ben asked as they gathered up their things. She was still wearing army surplus fatigues and combat boots and an old camouflage jacket that was frayed and had seen better days. She had an entire wardrobe of combat clothes she wore for work, unlike any of the other women Ben knew.

'No, I think I'll go into the office and see what's on my desk,' she said vaguely. He always told her she was a workaholic, and she could no longer deny it. The evidence to support his theory was overwhelming, and she looked lively and full of energy as they stepped off the plane, and headed toward baggage claim. She was tireless, which drove him crazy at times, when he was tired himself. She never was, or at least it never showed. They knew the airport well, and had spent far too many hours there, waiting for delayed planes to take off. Ben had expected her to say she was going to work. He knew that she'd sit at her desk for several hours, eventually take a shower at the office and put on more of the same clothes, and in the end not bother to go home, and stay till all hours. She hated going home to her empty apartment. He couldn't wait to get back to his own apartment in Brooklyn and sleep on clean sheets in his comfortable bed that night. The thought of it was sheer heaven to him, after four days of bad motels and catnaps in the back of a car. Alix didn't care where she slept, or if she did, and didn't need much sleep, which was an advantage she had over him and most people.

Women glanced at Ben as they walked through the airport. He was a powerfully built, tall, handsome man, but in spite of that, Alix had always been indifferent to his charm. She loved working with him, but had never been interested in him as a man, and they knew each other too well. They had seen each other in lots of unpleasant, terrifying, awkward, and embarrassing situations. And Alix knew instinctively that it would have spoiled everything if they'd ever gotten involved. And he had expressed no interest in romance with her either. They both liked their relationship just the way it was, uncomplicated and entirely based on work. They were well matched to work together in every way. Many teams the producers put together were a lot less compatible than the two of them, and some fought all the time and hated each other offscreen. Some of the battles behind the scenes at the network were legendary, but not between the two of them. They'd become fast friends right from the beginning and still were.

They each picked up their suitcase off the moving belt. Alix managed her own with ease. Ben no longer offered to help her, he knew she wouldn't have let him anyway. Alix prized her independence above all, and took pride in taking care of herself.

They took separate cabs into the city and she headed for work, curious about what she'd find. And when she got there, she discovered, as she always did, a mountain that had sprung up on her desk while she was gone. Notices, memos, copy they wanted from her to go with her stories, fact checking, edicts from management that had been circulated around the office while they were away. By late that night, she had gotten through most of it. She was too tired to go home by then and stretched out on the couch in her office and fell asleep. She woke up before the others came in the next morning, took a shower, put on jeans and a sweater from her suitcase, poured herself a stiff cup of coffee, and was back at her desk when Felix Winters, her senior producer, walked in.

'Did you sleep here?' Felix asked her wryly, knowing the answer before she nodded with a grin.

'Of course.'

It didn't surprise him. He was pleased with their coverage of the riots, she could see it on his face. He rarely said it, but he liked almost everything she did. He wasn't lavish with praise but had deep respect for her.

'Bring your coffee to my office and let's catch up,' he said, and she nodded and promised to be there in a minute, as an assistant producer stuck his head into her office. They had a breaking story to put on the morning news ahead of everything else, and he wanted to let her know. An earthquake in Afghanistan had killed thousands of people. She wondered if she and Ben would get sent out on the story, and headed to Felix's office.

Alix and Felix both kept a close eye on the monitor on his desk while they chatted. The videos and live coverage from Afghanistan were awful, with bodies piling up in the streets and people crying, and buildings turned to rubble, with people trapped inside them.

'It looked nasty in Alabama. I was worried about you,' he said with obvious concern.

'We were fine, but it was ugly. They sent the troops in too late. It was out of control by then.' The senior producer was distracted as she said it, and he nodded, looking pensive. 'What's up?' She knew that expression on his face.

He hesitated for a minute before answering with a sheepish grin. 'One of my crazy hunches. Don't ask me why, but I saw a photograph of the Vice President yesterday. It's bothering me.'

'You've never liked him,' Alix reminded him with a smile.

'True. He just seems phony to me. And for a guy who plays holier than thou and claims to be Mr Clean, I don't like the company he keeps. And where did he get all that money so fast?'

'He married it,' she said with an ironic expression. 'That's one way to make easy money.'

'Sometimes not so easy,' Felix quipped, and she laughed. 'I don't know. Something about him always seems wrong to me.' She had heard it before.

16

'Who was he with in the photo you saw?' she asked with interest. Felix had good instincts, but he had his share of pet peeves too, and the Vice President had always been one of them, although he'd had a dignified career, and the right connections, the late senator Bill Foster being his closest friend. Foster was considered a political icon, and they were planning a presidential campaign together when Foster died. But Felix didn't like Tony Clark anyway.

'He was with a state gaming commissioner. And every time I play golf in D.C., I see him with some lobbyist or other, and none of the ones people respect.'

'That's not against the law,' Alix teased him.

'I know. Wishful thinking. I always hope we'll catch him doing something illegal one of these days. But he's too smart for that.'

'Or too honest,' Alix said cautiously. She had no strong feelings about the Vice President one way or the other. Tony Clark was smart, rich, and successful, and impressively connected socially and politically. He played the game well. Too much so to risk it by doing anything foolish, in her opinion. But Felix never agreed. He thought him overconfident and arrogant.

'Do me a favor, sniff around your Washington contacts and see if anything turns up. You never know.'

'Hope springs eternal.' She laughed at him as she left his office and then turned to ask him, 'Are you sending us to Afghanistan?'

17

'I'll let you know,' he said, watching the monitor intently as she left, and she thought about his dogged search for malfeasance by the Vice President. She never agreed with him on that, but she'd check her sources anyway, to humor him. He was her boss after all, and sometimes he was right. Not this time, though. She was sure. Felix just had an issue with him. It was visceral, he couldn't stand the guy.

She was watching the morning news from a monitor on her desk, when Ben walked in an hour later. He looked fresh and rested, but so did she, after a few hours' sleep on her office couch. Work always invigorated her, and Ben guessed correctly that she hadn't bothered to go home.

'Are we heading for Afghanistan?' he asked her, as he lowered himself into a chair across from her and glanced at the monitor on her desk.

'Felix hasn't told me yet. He's on a witch hunt for the Vice President again.' She smiled at Ben. 'He wants me to check it out.'

'Clark's a busy guy,' Ben said of the Vice President, looking unimpressed. 'And I've never liked him either. Something about him always rubs me the wrong way. But I think he's clean. He's too smart and ambitious not to be.' He agreed with Alix about that.

Vice President Tony Clark was in his early forties, had previously been divorced from a wealthy socialite, had married a much younger woman in his second marriage four years before, and had

18

two very young children. They were the picture-perfect vice presidential family. They even had a golden retriever named Lucky. His young wife was the heiress to one of the biggest fortunes in the country, and her father had been the largest donor to the last presidential campaign. Tony Clark always seemed to have it easy, and even when things went wrong for him, he always landed on his feet shortly after.

Clark had been on the fast track to run for the vice presidency with Senator Bill Foster, a childhood friend. It had been an obvious pairing due to their lengthy connection. Foster had all the charm, wit, political expertise, charisma, connections, and intelligence to run a fantastic campaign to win a presidential election in a few years and take Clark with him, until Foster was murdered during his second senatorial campaign. Bill Foster's father was one of the most famous kingmakers in Washington, and they were an important political family. His widow's brother was a senator from Connecticut. Foster knew the right people, but Clark had the money. Not his own, but he had access to big campaign donors. Together they would have been an unbeatable team. Instead, after Foster's death, Clark took a year to reinvent himself, and emerged as one of the hottest tickets of the hour with another senator who had the inside track to the White House. Tony Clark married his current wife two years after Foster was assassinated.

Clark was an important presence in the lives of Foster's widow and two children. He and Olympia Foster were occasionally seen together in public, and he had been a strong emotional support system for the last six years. Since her husband's death, she had been reclusive and had almost disappeared. She had been the perfect mate for Foster, and his staunch supporters were as much in love with her as they had been with him. As she thought about it, Alix wondered what had happened to Olympia. It had been months since her name had even been mentioned, although it was known that she and the Vice President had remained close friends. Faye had once sent her a fan letter and gotten a warm response. Olympia Foster was a lovely person, and like others, Alix had always thought there was something Kennedyesque about her. She had the same kind of dignified elegance and shy grace as Jackie. And like Jackie, she had survived her husband's tragic death, shot by a random assassin while she was with him, which made the public sympathize with Olympia even more.

'How do you two feel about curry?' Felix stuck his head back in the door and asked them both. Alix looked disinterested but Ben said he liked it.

'Are you ordering lunch?' Ben asked him.

'No, there's a scandal in the high-tech world in India. I'm sending you both to New Delhi tonight. You're on a nine P.M. flight,' he said matter-of-factly. 'International check-in at seven,' he reminded them.

'I'd better get home and repack my bags,' Alix commented, forgetting their conversation about the Vice President. There were no clean clothes left in the bag she'd brought back from Alabama. And she wouldn't need combat gear in New Delhi. She needed summer dresses and sandals.

'He doesn't waste a minute, does he?' Ben said after Felix left, looking hesitant about flying to India that night.

'It sounds like a good story,' Alix commented, trying to be positive about it. She loved her work, sometimes more than he did. And he was tired after Alabama. She wasn't.

'They're all good stories when you're doing them,' Ben Chapman said honestly.

'I'd better get going,' Alix said as she stood up. She had a thousand things to do to prepare for another trip on such short notice. And they both knew that they would have to attend a long briefing about the Indian story that afternoon, if they were leaving that night.

She hailed a cab outside the network building a few minutes later. She thought about the assignment in India as they sped downtown, and made some notes to herself of things she wanted to research for the story. She thought of her daughter and was going to call her before they left.

Alix got out of the cab in front of her battered building in the East Village, and went inside to do her laundry and pack her suitcase. Despite Ben's momentary fatigue and apparent lack of enthusiasm,

21

she was excited to be going to India that night. What she did so well was in her blood, and still made her heart race after all these years. And anyone who knew her knew that was never going to change.

Alix was back at the office three hours later, with her packed bag. She had brought summer clothes for the climate in India, and some respectable-looking dresses in case she had to meet with government officials or interview important people in connection with the story. One of India's most influential, richest men was at risk of going to prison, and the story was hot. Felix briefed her and Ben on all the information they had, and asked her to stay back to talk to him alone for a few minutes. He had been a reporter years before, and had risen through the ranks at the network, so he understood the job she did. He had aged visibly from the constant pressure he was under, and he relied on Alix and a handful of others to keep their ratings high. He kept a tight rein on them to make sure nothing slipped. His strength was ferreting out stories and having his investigative reporters cover them before anyone else knew about them, and he still had a sharp nose for sensing a story in the making. And Alix was at the top of his list of those who did that best. She never let him down.

He handed her a thick manila envelope across his desk. 'I'd like you to take a look at that on the flight, and do a little research on it from Delhi if you have time. I know you think I'm nuts, but it's on the subject of the VP. He may be clean but I smell a rat somewhere, or some money changing hands. Let's check it out.'

Alix raised an eyebrow with interest. She loved doing research projects for him, and even if she didn't agree with him, a lot of the time he was right. He had a sixth sense for the news like no one else. She glanced into the envelope and saw assorted photos of Tony Clark.

'Just take a look,' he said to her, 'and see if anything rings a bell. I still have this crazy gut feeling that he could be taking bribes from lobbyists or even someone else. Maybe I'm wrong, but humor me and sniff around. He's turning up with some of the less trustworthy lobbyists in Washington with a fair amount of regularity. Not officially, but informally, as "friends." His people claim it's coincidental when they're questioned about it. I don't buy that. He's always where the money is, and he doesn't do anything unless there's something in it for him.'

Clark was adept at staying below the radar and leading an exemplary life, but occasionally there was something about him, even to Alix, that seemed too good to be true. And she had to admit that he was a lucky guy, had made a fortune, and married well twice. In Felix's opinion, it couldn't all be fortuitous, smart investments in the stock market and his wives' money. He was a very rich man in his own right, and hadn't been at the beginning of his career. So where did it come from? That question had gnawed at Felix for a long time. No one had ever accused the Vice President of improprieties, but Felix always wondered how he had gotten what he had. Experience and the instincts of a once-great reporter himself told Felix that there was something there. He just didn't know what. But it was more than just the Midas touch or blind good fortune. And Felix just couldn't seem to let it go. He had provided Alix with a number of recent photographs of the VP in various places, with assorted people, for her to study.

'I'll take a look,' Alix promised. She was more interested in Clark's political ties than his fortune. He had powerful connections, and high aspirations. Clark's relationship with Bill Foster didn't seem like an accident to her either. Foster would have been the perfect ride for him, straight into the White House, even in a secondary position, which Clark didn't seem to mind. He had become close to the current President only after Foster died. There always seemed to be an agenda with him. And now he was the Vice President. 'I don't like him much myself,' Alix admitted to Felix. 'But he doesn't strike me as a guy who'd do something stupid or dishonest, like take payoffs from a lobbyist. He's always got an eye to the future, and I think he's got big plans for the long term, like running for President himself in four years, after the President's second term ends.' He had just been reelected. Everyone was waiting for Clark to throw his hat into the ring of presidential hopefuls, but he hadn't so far. It was early days yet, for another couple of years. And Felix wanted to keep a close eye on him to see just how far he went.

'You're probably right. But he's been seen with three of the shadiest lobbyists in D.C. recently, having dinner, playing golf, supposedly they're all just pals. I just want you to explore quietly, use your connections, and see some people about it when you get back. You can check out the pictures now, while you're away.'

'Any idea who you want me to see?' she asked him. 'Off the top of my head, I don't know anyone close to him.' And as soon as she said the words she thought of Olympia Foster, but decided instantly it was a ridiculous idea. She had been out of the loop for six years, but she and Clark were still close friends. Alix thought she might learn something if Olympia Foster would talk to her. In the first year after Foster's death, Clark had been constantly seen with Olympia and her kids, after supporting her through the funeral. Photographs had shown her brother, the senator from Connecticut, on one side of her, and Clark on the other. Alix suspected that Olympia was likely to know more about what Clark was up to than anyone else, although Alix didn't expect her to divulge any secrets, if there were any. But people talked to Alix easily. She was disarming, and good at what she did. She had a warm, informal style which made everyone open up to her, and was why Felix had chosen her for the assignment, unofficially so far. He knew that if anyone was capable of it, Alix would come back with the story, if there was one.

'I'll read the material, and make some calls from New Delhi, if I have time. I have a few contacts in D.C. who might be helpful. It's a small town, with a lot of talk,' she said, looking thoughtful. She wanted to call Foster's widow herself and see if she could get in to see her. It would probably get her nowhere, but it was worth a shot. Alix had always admired Olympia's dignity and courage, and it would be interesting meeting her, if Olympia was willing. She never gave interviews, but she might agree to spend an hour with her, to talk about her husband's legacy.

Olympia had written a book about her husband after his death, and Alix had read it and enjoyed it. It had extolled his virtues, explained his political positions in depth, and talked about his dreams for the future of the country. If what she said was accurate, it made it an even greater loss for America that he had died. The book was intelligently written and very coherent, although colored by the deep love of an adoring, grieving wife. She had wanted to honor her husband posthumously, and she had, nobly and with great eloquence. The book had sold over a million copies and been a huge success.

Alix stood up after the meeting with Felix, with

the envelope of material on Tony Clark in her hands, and he wished her luck with the story in New Delhi. He didn't think they'd be there long, but firsthand reporting on the scene would make it more interesting for their viewers and keep the ratings high. Felix lived for that.

Alix was thinking about Olympia Foster as she walked back to her office, where Ben was waiting for her with his bag. They had to leave for the airport in half an hour.

'Did you get fired?' he teased, and she laughed.

'Not yet. I'm working on it.'

'Just to remind you, I like my job, and I'd hate to have to get used to a new partner.' He glanced at the envelope she put into her hand luggage. 'Homework?' She nodded.

'Tony Clark. Felix still thinks he smells a rat. Or, for now, a mouse. He's hoping for a rat.'

'And you've been assigned to be the rat catcher?' Ben asked with interest.

'If there is a rat. That remains to be seen,' Alix said with a smile. She liked working with him too.

'That should keep you busy,' Ben said and flipped through a magazine while he waited for her. All he had to do was follow her and catch the stories on film, the heavy lifting was all hers. She called Faye before they left the office, while he went to get coffee for them both. She wasn't sure if she'd get her daughter or voicemail, and was pleased when Faye picked up. Once they were in New Delhi, it would be harder to find the time.

'I saw the rest of the story in Alabama.' Faye sounded angry when she said it. 'You're still trying to get yourself killed. You're lucky no one tried to shoot you. They're going to get you one of these days, Mom.' She was resentful. Alix knew it was based on fear. Fear of losing her mother.

'It wasn't as bad as it looked,' her mother tried to reassure her, but Faye knew her better.

'It was probably worse. It's hard to believe that kind of thing can still happen today. It was all about racial discrimination under the cover of the factory owners crying poor.' Faye, as usual, got the point, she had grown up with the stories Alix covered, and she always tried to explain them to her. It had made Faye cynical at an early age, which Alix sometimes regretted, but she dealt in the real world, and her daughter was a very bright girl. 'So where are you off to now?'

'I'm leaving for India tonight. It's a business story, so you can't complain about this one being dangerous. I'm covering a high-tech scandal, and a big-deal tycoon going to jail. Fascinating, and tame.'

'I figured you'd be covering the earthquake in Afghanistan,' Faye said with an edge to her voice. 'I'm sure they'll send you to some war zone soon.'

'That's not all I do,' Alix reminded her.

'You do enough of it. You lied to me, you told me last year that you were going to stop doing stories like that. You've been in five war zones since then.' Faye always kept track, much to her mother's chagrin, and she was right.

'I have to go where they send me, Faye. It's part of the job.'

'Why couldn't you be something normal, like a teacher or a nurse, or a weather girl on TV?'

'My legs aren't good enough to be a weather girl, and I don't wear miniskirts.'

'Don't be so sexist, Mom,' Faye complained.

'Sorry. I don't want to report on the heat in Atlanta, or the snow in Vermont, or tropical storms in the Caribbean. I'd die of boredom.'

'So you play commando. You're going to get killed one of these days, Mom.' There was silence for a moment, and Alix didn't know what to say. She could be right. It was how her own father had died.

'What's new at school?' Alix changed the subject to distract her, which didn't always work.

'Nothing much. I got a C in chemistry.' But she got As and Bs in everything else, so Alix wasn't worried about her grades. She had been an outstanding student all her life. 'I talked to Mamie yesterday. She said for you to call her sometime.'

'I keep meaning to, but I haven't had time,' Alix said, feeling guilty. She didn't call her mother often enough. Isabelle was gracious enough not to complain, and Faye called her frequently, which helped. 'She's going to Florence and Rome on some kind of art tour. She wanted me to come too, but I can't.' They talked until Ben reappeared with the coffee and pointed to his watch. They had to leave in a few minutes, and Alix nodded.

29

'I'll call you from New Delhi,' Alix promised, and meant it, although they both knew it might not happen if things got too busy there. 'I'll be back in a few days.'

'Before you head out to somewhere else. Try to stay out of trouble, Mom. I love you.' She said it with feeling, and tears filled Alix's eyes for a minute. It hadn't been an easy road for them, but they had come through it and loved each other, and Alix knew that Faye was proud of her.

'I love you too, sweetheart. Take care of yourself.' They hung up then, and she took a long swig of the hot coffee and smiled at Ben.

'How is she?' he asked, with interest. He knew how much Alix loved her daughter and worried about her too.

'A C in chemistry, but other than that fine.' He smiled in response. He had no room for family, since traveling the globe for the network wasn't conducive to lasting relationships, or even temporary ones. His love life was hit and miss, and consisted mostly of pretty women he met but never got a chance to date, or one-night stands. There just wasn't the time or opportunity for much else. It suited him most of the time. He had never had the urge to remarry, nor had Alix. She always said that marriage wasn't on her list of goals, for the same reason, and she was leery of getting involved with men who would complain about her work or try to convince her to change her career. Giving up her job, even with the risks, was a sacrifice she wasn't willing to make for any man. And she knew from experience no one wanted a girlfriend or a wife who was dancing around land mines in Iraq, or riding in a tank up a mountainside in Afghanistan to meet with terrorists. And Faye wasn't wrong, one of these days she might get killed. So she made do and for now, the occasional chance encounter, her work, and her daughter were enough to satisfy her.

Losing her own father to a bomb at an early age had marked Alix more than she realized. She was afraid to get too close to any man, for fear she would lose him, or herself. Her job kept her from leading a normal life and didn't challenge her childhood scars unduly. The death of Faye's father shortly after her birth had reinforced Alix's fears of losing someone she loved. The only two people Alix allowed herself to love and be close to were her mother and her daughter. There was no room for a serious man in all that. Ben suffered from the same thing, for different reasons but with the same effect. Being a Navy SEAL had suited him perfectly, and this was a close second. In some form or other, he needed to challenge himself and take risks every day. It was a habit for him by now, after the SEALs. And with Alix, as her cameraman, he could count on facing danger constantly. Ben always said that in some ways what they did was like playing Russian roulette. Neither of them was afraid of dying.

'Ready to roll?' he asked her easily, she picked up her bag and wheeled her suitcase out of the office, while he carried his own, with his camera equipment in a heavy bag over his shoulder. They were used to traveling as unencumbered as possible. They left the office and went downstairs to find the town car waiting for them to take them to the airport. Despite his initial reluctance, they were both happy to be on the road again. Ben looked pleased to be heading out with her. This was what they were good at. And in Ben's eyes, Alix was the best.

'I don't think I could live any other way anymore,' she said honestly, as they pulled away from the curb into New York traffic. 'I don't know what people do who stay home all the time and have the same routine every night.'

'It's called having normalcy,' he said in a quiet voice, thinking about it. Something he knew he'd never have, and didn't want.

'I don't think I'd be good at it,' Alix said thoughtfully.

'Probably not,' Ben agreed with her. The way they had both lived for years was all they knew and all they wanted, and what they were best at. And if they died in battle, they were willing to accept it. It was what they had signed on for, with full knowledge of the risks they took. She smiled at him, as the driver wove through the crowded streets and they headed for the airport. They were like two birds who had been freed from their cage and were heading for open skies again, and it felt great to both of them.

CHAPTER 2

They stopped at Heathrow Airport in London at nine A.M. local time on their way to New Delhi, and Alix did some shopping, while Ben went to get a haircut and a neck massage. They had both slept on the plane and did a lot of their living and minor chores in airports, where they spent more time than anywhere else, and they saw all their current movies on planes. They were on a noon flight to New Delhi.

Alix had looked at the photographs and read the material on Tony Clark on the first flight, and found it very interesting. She could see why Felix was doggedly suspicious of him, but there was no evidence to indicate that Clark was taking money from any lobbyist. More than anything, he seemed to be socially involved with some of the most powerful lobbyists, and a few of the more questionable ones, but he hadn't done anything tangible one could put a finger on to suggest that there was an exchange of favors, or that he was being bribed to meet their needs. Lobbyists served a useful purpose, to keep politicians informed of the needs and activities of the industries they represented, so the elected officials could endorse and pass laws accordingly.

From what Alix could glean from Felix's research, Tony Clark's connections were intriguing, but for now it was no more than that. But she was still planning to make some calls to check it out when she got back. She had some good contacts on the Hill who liked to talk, and she wanted to hear what they had to say about him before she took it any further and reported to Felix. She had a feeling that her producer was being premature or overzealous. Maybe the Vice President was setting something up for the future but hadn't committed any improprieties yet, or broken any laws. There was absolutely no proof of that, no matter how slimy he seemed. And Clark was no fool. He was not going to jeopardize an impeccably orchestrated career, and wind up destroying everything he had built. Of one thing Alix was sure, however innocent he looked, he was a very calculating man, and would do nothing that could injure himself. So he would bear watching, and some snooping wouldn't do any harm, but she suspected there was nothing anyone could nail him on, and her instincts were usually pretty good.

She studied the photographs again intently, and only one stood out to her. Clark was engaged in what appeared to be a serious conversation with a lobbyist who had been accused of paying bribes to politicians, but it had never been proven, and he hadn't been charged with anything. The lobbyist had worked for a state gaming commission at one time.

She and Ben talked about it as they had breakfast in the airport, after his massage. She had just bought a pair of boots at one of the high-end shops. It was the first time she'd shopped in months.

'I agree with you,' Ben said over coffee. 'If nothing else, Clark is a hell of a smart guy. He's not stupid enough to risk everything he's set up for himself, by taking bribes from the lobbies. That's just not going to happen. I think Felix is barking up the wrong tree if that's what he thinks. Tony Clark is just never going to step over that line. And he was so close to Bill Foster. It didn't get cleaner than him. He would never have associated with a crook. They'd be in the White House today if Foster hadn't been killed.' The motive of the gunman had never been determined. The killer was a Syrian national with a stolen passport, and he'd been shot by security before he could be questioned. There was no reason for Foster's murder, other than an act of individual terrorism. The Syrian government had denied any connection to him or responsibility for his acts. It was just a senseless tragedy, and Clark was devastated by it too.

'I guess it can't hurt to ask around about Clark,' Alix said off-handedly. 'I'm going to call some of my Washington sources when we get home. Who knows? Maybe he's doing something else less direct than taking money. Maybe he's just trying to line up campaign funds for the future, if he runs for President in four years. That sounds more like him. Connections and money. Big money for his campaign. Clark never strikes me as sincere, and he's all about his own image and PR. But there's no law against that. He's a politician through and through. Foster was an idealist, and something of a visionary. They were a good combination. The realist and the dreamer.'

'Or the schemer and the dreamer,' Ben said with a grin.

They boarded the flight to New Delhi. Ben read a book for the first part of the flight, and Alix watched a movie, since she had already done her homework for Felix and all the prep work for their interview in New Delhi. She was interested to meet the tycoon who had gotten himself in trouble, and the intrigues of the scandal read like a modern-day TV series. He was one of the richest men in India, and had done things that were highly illegal, and made billions more. He'd gotten caught on a minor detail, and the whole house of cards had come tumbling down. Once he was exposed, people he had done business with were denouncing him all over the place. He was liable to be sent away to prison for a long time, like Bernie Madoff, who had bilked people out of billions in the States. Alix had covered that story too. Large-scale crooks were not unfamiliar to her, and made fascinating interviews.

They both slept for the last part of the trip, got

to their hotel at two A.M., and were up early the next morning for their meeting with the man they had come to see. He was currently under house arrest, and when they were ushered into his palatial home, he greeted them with total aplomb and ease. He didn't even look worried. Alix saw instantly in the first moments of their conversation that he was entirely ego driven, and completely without remorse. He was a textbook sociopath. She had met many in her line of work, dictators, politicians, successful heads of corporations, criminals. It was a special breed, and no one was more seductive than a sociopath, which was how they got people to do what they wanted.

The interview was interrupted by a sumptuous meal at midday in his white marble dining room, served by an army of servants. He was fascinating to talk to and he would have gone on all day if they'd let him. But Alix knew she had all she needed by the end of lunch. More would have been superfluous, and Ben was satisfied too that he had all the footage necessary to illustrate the story and the man.

For two more days Alix and Ben met with people he had done business with and also those he had cheated, as well as government officials and legal experts who explained the consequences of his actions. No one in India seemed to have any doubt that he was going to prison, although the tycoon who had committed the crimes had no doubt that he would be exonerated. He seemed to believe that

he was smarter than everyone else, and he probably was, but he had been caught nonetheless.

At the end of three days, they had completed all
the interviews they needed and concluded all their
business. They were leaving the next morning, and
that night Ben made a reservation at a fabulous
restaurant for dinner. 'We owe it to ourselves,' he
said as they walked into the Dum Pukht, with its
lavish blue and silver dining room and crystal
chandeliers. The food was exquisite. The concierge
at the Leela Palace, where they were staying, had
recommended it to them. And occasionally in
foreign cities an evening like this was a perk they
both enjoyed.

Alix had bought a pale blue sari for herself that
afternoon, and another for her daughter, and some
brightly colored bracelets she knew Faye would
love. For once they were in a place where there
were actually pretty things to buy. Most of the
time, with the kind of stories they covered, that
wasn't the case. She and Ben were both pleased
with the piece, as they discussed it over dinner. It
wasn't edited yet, but they had sent the rough cut
to Felix digitally, and he was thrilled and praised
them both for a job well done and an outstanding
interview. He knew he could always count on
them.

'They say that India is the most romantic country
in the world,' Ben said to her when they ordered
cognac after dinner, and Alix smiled at him.

'So I hear. The last time I was here, it was for

38

a flood that killed eight thousand people. This story has been unusually civilized.' She looked relaxed and pleased. 'I'm sorry you have to waste the romance of India on me!' she teased, and he grinned at her. She had seen him eyeing beautiful Indian women in the streets and at the restaurant that night.

'I was just thinking that too. But I'd rather be having dinner with you than the guys I've worked with. Having dinner with a bunch of Navy SEALs isn't too romantic either. And the canteens we ate in never looked like this.' She laughed at the vision.

'Don't get used to it, it's not likely to happen again anytime soon.' Most of the time she and Ben were in combat zones, in filthy clothes, sleeping in miserable accommodations, or in military trucks or the back of Jeeps. 'I was just thinking how strange it is that our subject is convinced he won't go to prison, and everyone we talked to in any kind of position of authority says it's a sure thing. Do you think he was just bullshitting us, or himself?' Alix asked him. But she also knew it was the nature of sociopaths to believe themselves above the law.

'Denial is a wonderful thing,' Ben said as they finished their drinks. The meal had been superb, and in comparison to New York, surprisingly cheap, so neither Ben nor Alix felt guilty about their expense accounts. They were entitled to a little extravagance once in a while. 'I think he genuinely believes he won't go to prison. He's convinced he's smarter than everyone else. You heard what he said,' Ben reminded her. He always listened closely to the interviews while he filmed.

'I figured that was just bravado for the media and for me.'

'I don't think so. I think he means it. He's in for a surprise, or who knows, maybe he can bribe his way out of it, but it didn't sound like it to me. There's been too much collateral damage from what he did, although he doesn't see it that way. So where do we go next?' She had spoken to Felix after he saw the rough of the interview and asked him the same question. He said he thought they'd be home for a few weeks. And he reminded her that he wanted her to do the checking he'd asked for about Tony Clark, since there were no pressing stories at the moment. He still thought there might be a story there, even if Ben and Alix didn't agree. But he was their boss, and they had to do as he said. 'I wouldn't mind a couple of weeks in New York,' Ben said as they left the restaurant to go back to the hotel. 'I feel like we're almost never there.'

'We aren't. And I'd like to catch a weekend with Faye, if she's not too busy. I could fly down to Duke.' She hadn't seen her daughter in two months.

'You're lucky you have her,' Ben said quietly, in a tone Alix had never heard him use before. They never talked about personal things while they were at work, but it was a beautiful night under a full moon in an exquisite place, and she had made

40

some effort to dress for dinner and so had he. It took them out of their normal work context, and made them feel more like ordinary people, a man and a woman having dinner, even if they were only friends and worked together.

'You've never wanted to have kids? It's not too late,' she commented to him in response to what he said.

'I think it is,' he said after the slightest hesitation. If he had been an interview subject, she would have pressed the point, but she didn't, even though she had heard a catch in his voice and wondered about it.

'I had Faye when I was twenty, still in college, and I was in no way prepared for what it entailed. We got married barely a month before she was born, and he died in an accident three months later. His family wanted nothing to do with me or Faye. And eventually I left her with my mother in Europe, went back to school, and got a job in New York. I left her with my mom for five years. It sounds simple now, but it wasn't then.' She had never told him the circumstances of her marriage and Faye's birth before. And he looked impressed by what she'd said. 'I could never have managed without my mother's help. It worked at the time, but that kind of thing leaves scars. All things considered, Faye has been amazingly mature and forgiving about it, and my mother was great with her. With no father and an absentee mother, she could be a lot angrier at me than she is. All she

41

complains about is my work. She wishes I was a "normal mom," but that's never been in the cards for me. My mother was a stay-at-home mom, and she was good at it. I would go nuts if I tried. On the positive side, what it's done, I think, is set an example for Faye to go after what she wants, do what she wants to do, and fight for what she believes in. Maybe that's not such a bad thing, even if I wasn't around all the time. I brought her back from France, where she was living with my mother, when she was five, it wasn't easy, but we made it work. She's a pretty cool kid.'

'So is her mom,' he said admiringly. 'I'm always in awe of people who have jobs like ours, still manage to have kids, and don't screw them up totally. What were your parents like?'

'My father was Sir Alex Phillips, the British journalist, who was killed by an IRA bomb when I was a little kid. My mother is French and an amazing woman. If I'm a halfway decent mother, it's because of her. She always encouraged me to do and be whatever I wanted. I'm sure it drives her crazy that I followed in my father's footsteps, and we know how that turned out, but she never complains. And if anything ever happens to me, I know she'll be fantastic with Faye. My mother is in her sixties now, but she's busy and happy, she travels, sees friends, and doesn't expect me to fill her life. She's a remarkable woman, and Faye is crazy about her. In some ways, she's closer to her than she is to me. They have a special bond.'

'I loved my grandmother too. She was a big, heavyset, cozy woman who was sure I could do no wrong, was a genius, and she was a wonderful cook. She was very proud when I joined the SEALs. The rest of the family thought I was wasting my time in the military. They wanted me to go into the family printing business. It just wasn't for me. It's amazing how important grandparents are in our lives, and the support they can give us,' he said, sounding nostalgic as he reminisced.

'I never had any grandparents,' Alix confessed easily. 'Mine died before I was born, and both of my parents were only children, so it was just my mom and me, which is why it's slim pickings for Faye too. All she has is me and my mom.'

'It sounds like she's doing fine. Both of my parents came from big families, and I haven't seen any of them in years. And I hardly ever see my brothers. We have nothing in common. They still live in Michigan, and "have normalcy," as you put it. It's hard for them to relate to me, after the SEALs and what I do now. And harder still for me to relate to them. I feel like I've landed from another planet when I go home, and that's how they treat me. They're all married and have kids. My ex-wife and I were childhood sweethearts, and she went back to Michigan after the divorce. She's married and has kids now too. I'm the only renegade in the bunch.' Alix sensed that there was more he wasn't telling her, but she didn't want to pry.

43

'Sometimes that's not a bad thing to be,' she said kindly.

'I'm not sure they'd agree,' he said as they walked into the hotel. It had been a nice evening and they were both feeling mellow.

'I can't imagine ever giving all this up. Can you?' she asked him.

He shook his head in answer and laughed. 'No. But I can't see you dodging mines and bullets forever either. We'll have to do something tamer one day.' Although they had enjoyed the assignment in New Delhi, which had been less rigorous than what they were used to.

'Not yet,' Alix said firmly. 'I'm not ready to sit at a desk, and I'm not sure I ever will be. They'll have to bury me first,' she said with fervor.

'Hopefully not. Not on my watch anyway.' She was a handful and a challenge, but he loved the work. She kept him busy chasing after her and trying to keep her out of danger. 'You need more than one Navy SEAL to keep you out of trouble.'

She thanked him for the enjoyable evening, and they both went to their rooms. She was already packed to leave the next day. And early in the morning, they took a flight back to New York. It was late when they arrived, and this time she went home, and told Ben she was going to stay home the next morning to make some calls.

'About Tony Clark?' She nodded, and waved as she walked into her building, and he went on to Brooklyn. She texted Faye that she was home, and got no response. She was probably busy studying or out with friends. Alix wasn't worried.

In the morning, Alix looked at the list of calls she wanted to make to her contacts in Washington. But there was one person she was going to try to see first. It was gnawing at her and had been for days. She had looked her up on the Internet and was surprised to find her number easily. Alix wondered if it was a home or office number, but she dialed it anyway, and a woman answered who sounded efficient and businesslike.

'Jennifer MacPherson,' she said clearly. Alix asked if it was Olympia Foster's office, and the woman on the line confirmed that it was. Alix said she wanted an appointment with her, and didn't identify herself by the network, but the woman on the phone had recognized her name and asked what it was about.

'I'd like to speak to her about her late husband,' Alix said quietly. 'I'm an avid fan of her book.' She could hardly say that she wanted to see her to ask if Tony Clark was a crook. And she hoped that the book would be an effective way in. Her assistant took down Alix's contact information and said she would let her know if Mrs Foster was available, which meant if she wanted to see her. It was all Alix could do for the moment. She couldn't force her way in, and she had no other access, so she had to be able to get past the palace guard, in the person of Jennifer MacPherson, who sounded formidable, and none too friendly to Alix.

When she hung up, Alix sat thinking for a minute about Olympia, and wondered if she would agree to see her. And then she made the other calls to Washington, and interestingly, no one seemed surprised that she wanted to know about Tony Clark and his ties to various lobbyists. No one seemed surprised by the question, but they said they had no information about him, though two said they had wondered about him too. All of them promised to see what they could find out, and said they would get back to her. It intrigued her that several of her legitimate political contacts had doubts about him too. Maybe Felix wasn't wrong. All she could do now was wait to hear back from them, and prod them if they took too long to respond. But the question had been asked about Tony Clark's activities. And she had reached out to Olympia Foster, as a close friend of his, although Clark's name was never mentioned. She had started the ball rolling, the rest remained to be seen, and where it went from there. You could never tell where it would lead once you started asking questions. The answers were almost never what you expected, which was part of the fun of her job. There were new surprises every day. How could she ever give that up for a 'normal' life and ordinary work?

CHAPTER 3

Alix had given Olympia Foster's assistant her cellphone number as the best number to reach her on. Three days later, no one had called, and Alix didn't want to be rude and push. She knew that Olympia would have to be handled with kid gloves, if she even got the opportunity since the word on the street was that Olympia never talked to the media, or very rarely. And Alix didn't know it, but Olympia's assistant had strongly advised her not to meet with her. Alix was a member of the press after all, and an investigative reporter for a major network. And she was known to be both aggressive and seductive with her subjects. Jennifer didn't trust her at all.

'But you said it was about the book,' Olympia said, hesitating. She knew who Alix was and had always admired her news coverage on TV. She was intelligent and thoughtful and respectful of her subjects, even if she got them to admit to some amazing things. But Olympia had nothing to hide.

'She said she's "an avid fan" of your book. She didn't say it was *about* your book,' Jennifer said precisely, 'and that's what she's saying to get through the door, to soften you up. That doesn't mean it's true.'

'What else could it be about?' Olympia looked mystified.

'You never know with the press. It could be about some scandal the public doesn't know about yet.'

'I've never been involved in a scandal, and neither was Bill,' she said calmly. It sounded innocent to her, but she was famously naïve, and Jennifer had spent a dozen years protecting her, even when the senator was alive. And she had doubled her efforts to shield Olympia once he was gone.

But in spite of everything Jennifer said, Olympia decided to see Alix. She wanted the opportunity to talk about her second book, another one about Bill. This one was subtler, and less about his activities than about his philosophy about the role of government in the future, in a changing world. She hadn't had much support for it so far, and it didn't have a publisher yet. They wanted to see the finished book and make sure it wasn't too repetitive of the first, nor too theoretical. She had used the first book as a way to stay locked up in the house for three years, correcting and editing and fine-tuning it, and now she was doing it again. Her children were upset that she had become a recluse, and thought she should get back in the world again. They were worried about her. But Olympia was still determined to carry Bill's message to the world. It had become her sacred mission.

Josh and Darcy, her children, had already told her that she had used every possible excuse not to return to the land of the living, and this was only prolonging the process. They thought she should get out more, see old friends she hadn't seen in years, find some activity, get a job, or even go back to school. They reminded her that their father had been gone for six years and they considered her new book yet another way to extend her period of mourning and make it her way of life. She insisted that wasn't the motivation behind it, but the result was the same, whatever her reasons for writing the book. Jennifer thought the kids were right, so a conversation with Alix about a second book about Bill Foster didn't sound like a good idea to her. And who knew what Alix really wanted, or what she would say?

Olympia listened to Jennifer's objections politely, and made the call to Alix herself. Alix was busy at the office and had just come out of a meeting when she answered the blocked call. She heard the distinctive, gentle voice at the other end, and recognized it immediately, and was stunned.

'Ms. Phillips?' Olympia said with her careful diction and smoky voice. 'Olympia Foster here. I believe you called me about my book. I'm actually working on another one now. It's not finished yet, but I hope it will be out in about a year, if I find a publisher for it. It's a little more esoteric than the last one, but Bill had such wonderful ideas for the country's future. I couldn't do them justice in the last book, there was so much to say.' She was obviously very anxious to talk about the book.

'Of course, I understand,' Alix said, bumbling over her own words for a minute, which was unlike her. But it seemed extraordinary that she was talking to Olympia Foster. It had been so easy, and now here she was. 'Would you be willing to meet and talk about it?' Alix asked respectfully. She didn't want to tell her that she didn't want to talk about her late husband, but about Tony Clark. She figured that might be more fruitful in person. What she needed now was to get through the door. She could deal with the rest later. Alix realized that her heart was beating faster at the prospect of meeting her, which seemed ridiculous, even to her. But Olympia had become an icon of sorts, a symbol of the good wife, carrying the eternal flame for her late husband, who had died a martyr's death. Her name was spoken with compassion, in hushed tones with deep respect. She was more than just a widow now.

'I'd be happy to meet with you,' Olympia said quietly. 'I've always admired your work. Your coverage of the news, particularly from war zones, is truly remarkable. You're a very brave woman.'

'Thank you,' Alix said, blushing. She felt like a kid, in awe of Olympia. Olympia seemed like a gentle person, was eight years older than Alix, and had a kind of ethereal mystique. She had become a legend.

Two days later, Jennifer opened the door of the

townhouse to Alix with a stern look. Alix had worn a gray skirt and sweater and high heels, and her long blond hair was pulled back in a neat ponytail. She looked sleek and well put together, and she smiled at Jennifer when she walked in. The assistant remained chilly and subdued. Alix could sense that Jennifer didn't approve of her being there, but clearly Olympia had made the decision, and Jennifer had to live with it, like it or not.

She led Alix into a small den, which was handsomely furnished with English antiques, and asked her to wait. She returned a few minutes later, and had Alix follow her upstairs, which she did solemnly. There was an odd sense of being in hallowed halls, and the house was very quiet. Almost painfully so. Alix knew that the Fosters had lived in Chicago and Washington when he had been senator, since he was from Illinois, and Olympia and her children had moved to New York after he died. She had lived there for the past six years, but the house looked as though she had lived in it longer. Alix followed Jennifer into a room that seemed like a shrine to Bill. It was lined with books, and there was a handsome antique English desk that had been his. His trophies, mementos, and photographs of him were all over the room, and there was a portrait of him over the fireplace. His presence and spirit were palpable in the room.

Olympia got up from the desk where she'd been working and walked toward her with the smile that Alix remembered so well. It was both shy and warm at the same time, and she invited her to sit down in a comfortable chair under the gaze of the portrait. The room wasn't depressing as much as fascinating, since everything in it appeared to be his or about him. It was where Olympia spent all her time, and where she was the most comfortable. All his most cherished possessions were around them, and photographs of him, with her, with the children, at the Senate, during his campaign, and her book to honor him was on the coffee table with his photograph on the cover. And Olympia herself was discreet, gracious, soft-spoken, and as ethereal as Alix had always thought her. There was something very vulnerable about her.

Olympia offered her coffee or tea, which Alix declined, and Jennifer left them a moment later with a severe expression, and disappeared reluctantly. Olympia saw no need to keep her there. Having seen Alix so often on TV gave her a false sense that they knew each other, and she was friendly and warm as she sat down in a chair facing her. They chatted for a few minutes about nothing in particular, and Alix admired their surroundings, and said the portrait was a wonderful likeness of him. She noticed from the date under the signature that it had been painted after he died, obviously commissioned by his wife.

Alix understood now why Olympia had stayed out of public sight. She was steeped in her memories, and continuing to mourn her husband as though he had died yesterday. Her eyes were sad and serious, and you could see the immensity of her loss in them. She had aged slightly in the past six years, but hadn't changed significantly. At forty-seven, she was still beautiful, and looked younger than her age. And Alix suspected she would have looked even more youthful if her eyes weren't two deep pools of pain.

She was wearing a simple black sweater and black skirt with black stockings. Eventually, Alix began to carefully approach the reason she'd come. She claimed to be interested in Olympia's latest book about her husband, and felt like a liar for it. Finally she brought up Tony Clark. 'The Vice President and your husband were very close,' she waited to hear what Olympia would say.

'Yes, they were,' Olympia said gently, as Alix watched her dark blue eyes. She had dark hair she wore to her shoulders, and porcelain white skin, which was flawless and almost translucent. She looked as though she hadn't left the house in years, which Alix hoped wasn't true. Everything about her seemed delicate and sad.

'Tony and Bill grew up together in a suburb of Chicago, Lake Forest,' Olympia explained. 'They went to school together, and Harvard, and they always stayed close. Bill was always more involved in the political scene because of his father, but Tony wanted to get into politics since he was a boy. He moved to New York after Harvard to pursue his political ambitions there.' And Clark had, in fact, been one of New York's senators before becoming Vice President. 'He's been incredibly kind to me and my children since . . . ever since Bill . . .' Her voice drifted off for an instant, and Alix nodded that she understood, so she didn't have to finish the painful sentence referring to when he'd been killed. 'He's my son's godfather, and has always been like an uncle to my children, especially now.'

'How are they, by the way?' Alix asked politely, curious about the children and how they had fared. They were in their twenties now, Alix knew.

'They're leading interesting lives,' Olympia said with a smile. 'Josh is twenty-four, has a degree in agriculture, and is working on an organic farm in Iowa. He's a real Midwesterner, like his dad, and he loves living close to his father's roots. And Darcy is twenty-two, in Zimbabwe, working with an organization to assist the locals in the village where she works. They're planting crops and bringing water and building plumbing in the village. They're both doing what they always wanted to do. We encouraged them to do that.'

'Do you think either of them will want to go into politics one day?' Alix asked, and Olympia shook her head.

'I don't think there's any chance of that. Neither of them is attracted to public life, and they learned the high price you pay for that. They've chosen other paths.' Alix wanted to ask her what she was doing, other than writing about her husband six years after his death, but didn't dare.

'And very noble ones,' Alix added. 'I have a daughter who's a sophomore at Duke. She wants to go to law school after she graduates. She's very interested in women's rights, and she talks about doing work in the Middle East at some point. They all seem determined to make the world a better place nowadays. I don't think I was that altruistic at that age.'

'Neither was I.' Olympia laughed. 'I went to law school too, but I was interested in more prosaic subjects, like antitrust and tax and business law.' Alix knew she had also championed women's causes while her husband was a senator. But she hadn't been active in any of that in recent years, and had retired from her legal practice when her kids were young and her husband got busy in politics. She had been a devoted wife and mother and had given up her own career.

'I have to admit,' Alix said cautiously, leading her back to the subject that had brought her here, although it sounded unrelated, 'I'm intrigued as to why the Vice President seems to be appearing at so many fundraisers supported by lobbies and why he seems to be engaging with well-known lobbyists. I wondered if you could shed some light on that, since you know him so well.' Olympia looked surprised by the question, and hesitated before she answered.

'I'm sure it's more of a social involvement than anything more meaningful,' Olympia Foster said easily. 'The Vice President has friends in every sector, and is greatly admired by everyone in Washington.' That was not entirely true, he was known to be an abrasive guy, although very smooth. But Alix didn't argue with her. 'I'm sure he doesn't want to offend anyone. The lobbies serve a useful purpose, and he's a great help to the President, reaching out to everyone. He was a tremendous help to Bill, with all the people he knows. They were a wonderful team, just as he is with the President now.' She proceeded to extol his virtues then, and it was clear to Alix that she wasn't going to get anything useful from Olympia. She was his biggest fan, and a devoted friend. She was almost as dedicated to him as she was to Bill. 'I really don't think there's anything to be concerned about in his being on amicable terms with some of the lobbyists. I suspect it's more coincidental than anything else.'

'Do you think he's going to run for President?' Alix asked her.

'I have no idea,' she answered, smiling at Alix. She had been charming and gracious throughout, and when she stood up, Alix took it as her cue to leave, and thanked her for her time and openness with her.

'It was a huge honor to meet you and spend time with you,' Alix said warmly, glancing at the portrait again on the way out and noticing that the eyes followed her, as the artist had intended. It was an artistic technique Alix had never liked and in this case had an eerie quality to it. 'I was one of your husband's biggest fans. He would have made a wonderful President.'

'Yes, he would,' Olympia said sadly, as Jennifer materialized and led Alix down the stairs after she and Olympia shook hands, and Olympia said she had enjoyed speaking to her too.

Alix hailed a cab to go back to the office when she left the house, and she had gotten nothing from the interview. She wasn't sure if Olympia was protecting Tony Clark, was unaware of his activities, or was telling the truth. According to Olympia, he was an extroverted person with a lot of friends in every sector. But Alix didn't buy it. It was too seamless and too pat and sounded more like a party line. She was almost beginning to wonder if what Felix thought was true. No one could be as innocent as Olympia claimed Clark was. She had said several times that he was beyond reproach, although she felt sure that many people were jealous of him. He was an easy target for it.

She was still in the cab on her way back to the office when Olympia picked up the phone in her study and called the Vice President. She got through to him immediately, as she always did. His instructions to his staff were clear. Any time Mrs Foster called, whatever he was doing, except if he was with the President, she was to be put through to him immediately. He was permanently on call to her, in case she had a problem of any kind. He had spoken to her the night before, and was surprised to hear from her again so soon.

'Hello, Olympia. Something wrong?'

'No, not at all. I had a visitor this morning I thought you might be interested in. Alix Phillips. She just left a few minutes ago.'

'From the news? What did she want?' He sounded suspicious, and wished Olympia hadn't let her come to the house. There was no reason for her to do so, no good could come of it, and he didn't like the idea of the press preying on her, and in her home.

'She actually came to talk about my book, but she mentioned you at the end. She was curious about your being seen socially with some of the lobbyists recently, and if you're going to run for President. I told her I didn't know about your future plans. And I assured her you have a million friends, and it means absolutely nothing if you're seen with some of the lobbyists socially.'

'Perfect answer,' he said, sounding somewhat relieved, but he wasn't happy that Phillips had asked the question, even if Olympia had given her the right answer. 'As it so happens, I play golf with several of them. There's nothing more to it than that.' He sounded jovial as he said it, and faintly amused. 'Are you sure she came over to talk about your book?' he asked, more practiced than she was at fending off the press, and suspicious of the reasons for Alix's visit. 'It sounds like she was much too interested in me.' He wasn't pleased but didn't want to sound critical of Olympia. He knew how sensitive she was.

'You came up in the conversation, but it's not why she came here. And she didn't mention you again after that. She loved the first book.' Olympia sounded pleased.

'No, she wouldn't mention me again. She's too smart for that. Just be careful of her if she calls again. These reporters are insidious, and she's very good at what she does. You need to be careful. There are wolves out there, waiting to pounce on you. And after what you've been through, they're too much for you.' He reinforced her vulnerability and not her strength. 'I don't want you hurt by them.'

'She wouldn't do that. She seems like an honorable person. I've always admired her interviews,' she said in defense of Alix.

'She's a reporter,' he reminded her. 'There's nothing honorable about that. She'd eat you alive if it served her purposes for a story. The press are no one's friends. I'll call you tomorrow, and I'll try to come up for dinner sometime next week. Stay away from the press in the meantime. You don't need that headache, and neither do I. Bill would expect me to protect you from them,' he assured her.

'I think it was fine,' Olympia said calmly, and he didn't argue with her about it, but he wasn't as sure. There had been inquiries in Washington too. He'd been warned about them. He had even decided to cancel his golf game with one of the major players on the lobby scene that week as a result. He didn't want the press putting their spotlights on him, even for a game of golf, or misrepresenting it in some way. He realized now that he would have to be more careful. And it had never occurred to him that they might try to see Olympia to seduce information about him from her. The press were a clever lot, especially the Phillips woman. She was too smart for her own good. He wondered who had put her up to it, her producers, or if it had been her own idea to visit Olympia. But one thing he was sure of, it had not been to talk about her book. That had been a ploy that had worked, he just hoped not too well. As long as Olympia had said what she'd reported to him, he wasn't too concerned. But he didn't like Alix snooping around. He had a profound hatred and distrust of the media. Olympia should have, but she didn't, she was sheltered and naïve. And the relationship they shared was a private matter between them.

Olympia had been shattered when Bill was killed, and Tony had stepped in. She was closer to Tony than to her own brother, whom she'd never gotten along with and who had a tedious, jealous wife Olympia liked even less. Olympia had been vulnerable and lost as never before after Bill died. Everything had happened so suddenly, and she was so traumatized initially, and Tony had been there for her. He and his wife had separated and divorced right before Bill died. Tony Clark could easily envision a future with Olympia once she recovered, which would serve both of them. She would be the ideal political wife, and his ambitions for the White House hadn't died with Bill. He had laid the groundwork for it for a year, and broached the subject with her when he thought the time was right. He had no children of his own, and he made time for her whenever he could. Tony visited her in New York at least once a week, sometimes even if only for a short time. And he spent hours on the phone with her every night.

A year after Bill's death seemed like the propitious moment to ask her to marry him, and he told her he thought it would be a wise decision for both of them, and would even benefit her kids. He was divorced, she was widowed, and she needed his help with her life and the kids. There were countless issues to handle over Bill's estate. Their being together made sense in every way.

She had promised to think about it, and he told her that he thought Bill would have been pleased to know she was in good hands. And there was no question in his mind, she had been an important part of Bill's campaigns. She had a luminous quality that people were drawn to, and a goodness that shone from within. Bill had always jokingly called her his secret weapon and said he couldn't lose an election married to her. Tony had big plans and the presidency in his sights, and he wanted Olympia at his side as his wife, not just as a friend. Her children loved him, and becoming the stepfather to his best friend's children showed him as a compassionate, responsible, loving man to the voters. He couldn't lose. He was sure Olympia would see the value of a shared future too.

He had been certain she'd accept, and was stunned and devastated when she turned him down. She told him regretfully that it felt like a betrayal of Bill, and she wasn't ready to move on yet, and maybe never would. But more important, the one thing she ardently didn't want was to be a political wife again. What had happened to Bill had convinced her that she never wanted to be a target for that kind of insanity again. She wanted no part of a political life, or the spotlight on her family and marriage. She said that was over for her, she couldn't survive another tragedy like what had happened to Bill. And she knew how much Tony's political aspirations meant to him, he had pursued them all his life, and she couldn't rob him of that. But for herself and her children, she wanted to be out of the political arena and the public eye forever. She had been adamant about it, and wanted to remain friends, but nothing else. Tony was in no way prepared for that, and stepped up his efforts with subtle pressure, convincing her that she couldn't manage without him, and that venturing out on her own was fraught with risk. She became more and more isolated and reclusive, as he became her only friend, but it still didn't push her into marriage with him.

He had spent a year trying to convince her that a joint future was the right idea, to no avail.

Olympia remained firm that she wouldn't marry again. And Tony knew he had to remarry, to ensure success in a campaign. So he married Megan after a brief courtship, and she got pregnant on their honeymoon. She wasn't Olympia, but she was very young, very rich, and had the right image for his political career. She was a beautiful girl, and their babies were evidence of his being a family man, which would get him votes. Everything Tony did was carefully calculated.

Olympia was the woman he had wanted to marry and could never have. She remained tantalizingly out of reach, and yet agonizingly close to him, and he spent all the time with her he could, without drawing attention to how close he was to her. Megan understood and didn't object. She felt sorry for Olympia after what had happened to her, and thought her a tragic figure and not a threat. And Tony wanted to keep it that way. The press meddling in their close relationship could only create problems for him, which he wanted to avoid at all cost, and had so far. He saw Olympia now as the holy woman who would bless his campaign one day. She had become totally dependent on him, and Tony had full control over her and advised her to remain in seclusion, which gave him more influence over her.

Alix Phillips spending time with Olympia was everything he didn't want. He looked worried and displeased when he got off the phone. He wasn't angry at Olympia for seeing Alix, but he was furious with Alix for manipulating her into a meeting, which was very definitely *not* about her books, no matter what Olympia thought.

'How'd it go?' Felix asked Alix when she got back to the office after seeing Olympia, as he popped two antacids into his mouth. He'd had a stressful morning, and his stomach had been a casualty of his career for years. Alix had given him five hundred rolls of Tums for Christmas as a joke, and he said it was his best gift.

'It was nothing. She's a lovely woman, and loyal to the core, to Bill Foster and to Tony Clark, to both of them. She claims that the Vice President is just a friendly guy and nice to a lot of people, but he has no involvement with the lobbies and never did. I think she believes that, but I don't. I asked her if Clark was going to run for President and she told me she had no idea. I think she might know but even if she did, she wouldn't tell me anyway. And she's not in touch with the real world. She's living in a tomb, and hasn't been to Washington since her husband died. She's writing a second book about him, and she acts like he was killed yesterday. I honestly think she doesn't really know what's going on, with Tony Clark or anyone else. Tony Clark is her closest friend. She sees him as some kind of saint, right after Saint Bill. I'm following up on some other leads in Washington, but other than the sheer pleasure of meeting her, she's a wonderful person, but she's a waste of time as a source of information about the Vice President.'

'I figured that might be the case, but it was worth a shot,' he said, looking dour.

'Yes, it was. I think he has bullshitted her into believing anything he says. He's a very convincing guy, and I get the sense that he's the only close friend she has. Her kids have both left home, so he's all she's got for company and emotional support.'

'Funny he didn't marry her. She would have been great for his career, and given him just the boost he needed to put him over the top,' Felix said thoughtfully.

'I don't think she'd have married him. I got the feeling she wants nothing to do with politics anymore. She blames that for her husband's death. And I can smell that Clark wants the White House, at any price.' He hadn't admitted it publicly yet, but it was clear.

'So can I,' Felix said, and popped another antacid into his mouth as he left. What Alix had said to him was all true, that Olympia was a useless source of information and under the spell of Tony Clark, but she was glad to have met Olympia anyway. Alix felt desperately sorry for her. All Olympia had left was the shadow of her former life. And Tony Clark as her only friend.

CHAPTER 4

A week after Alix's visit with Olympia, she was working on several stories at her desk. A sex scandal involving a congressman who had just resigned, a nuclear threat from North Korea, the Supreme Court reviewing issues surrounding abortion, and one of the Southern states was resisting same-sex marriage again. She and Ben had been in New York for almost two weeks. She glanced at the monitor on her desk, as she always did, and instantly noted a banner with a news flash cross the screen. She stopped writing for a few minutes, and watched scenes of rioting in Tehran. All of the protestors were women.

An extremist sect had put pressure on the Iranian government to tighten the rules again, after a long period of détente when women had had better jobs and educational opportunities, and conditions in Iran had improved markedly for them. Now the old regulations and ancient traditions were being enforced, and educated women were being pushed out of the workplace and many had recently been fired from their jobs. The women weren't having it and were staging mass protests. The scenes Alix saw on the screen were of women being dragged away, forced into police vans, and taken to jail. And a young girl had been shot during a demonstration that morning. As soon as the regular broadcast resumed, Alix picked up the phone on her desk and called Felix in his office. He had just seen it too.

'Things look hot in Tehran,' she said bluntly. They had shown a photograph of the girl who had been killed. She was twenty-two years old, had been a teacher, and was said to be much loved by all. She had become a symbol of the protest and women's rights the moment she was killed.

'Looks like it.'

Things had been relatively calm there for some time, and now there was chaos in the streets. This kind of news was Alix's stock-in-trade, and the kind of story she did best and gravitated toward.

'What are we waiting for?' she asked him.

'I want to see where it goes,' he said quietly. Felix always appeared unruffled and unimpressed, even if his nerves were raw. His wife had left him five years before, after a twenty-year marriage, and said he was married to his job and didn't need her. She left him for a college professor at Dartmouth she had met on the Internet. They were still living together five years later, and Felix was alone. He had no time for anyone in his life, only news stories about everything that went wrong in the world. He hardly ever saw his kids, the people who worked for him had become his family, and he had an unfailing instinct for which stories mattered, as their ratings showed. Their nightly broadcast was in the lead by a mile, but it came at a heavy price, to all of them in the business. Those who worked hardest had no private lives. It was the nature of their jobs, and a given for all of them. 'What are you working on right now?' he asked her.

'The congressman in the sex scandal. I talked to his wife on the phone yesterday. There's nothing out of the ordinary about it, you don't need me to cover that. The Supreme Court reviewing decisions about abortion. Resistance in some Southern states to same-sex marriage, North Korea, but that seems to be calming down, and I'm waiting to hear from a guy at the National Rifle Association who plays golf with Tony Clark.'

'Anything new there?'

'For the moment, it looks like Olympia Foster could be right. He just has a lot of friends.'

'Do you believe that?' Felix sounded surprised, as she heard him crunching the antacids he ate like candy. He had tried them all.

'No, I don't, but I've got nothing to go on except my gut for the moment,' she said honestly. 'I think there's something there, but maybe not enough.'

'Yeah, me too.' He had a feeling the Vice President was dirty, but he wasn't even sure why he did. He was too close to the money, suddenly too friendly with a number of people in important lobbies, and a few who had dubious reputations, and his public image seemed too picture-perfect to be real. But it was a long shot, guessing that he was taking bribes from any of the major lobbies. Maybe he wasn't, but something about him never seemed right to Felix. They might never be able to prove it, or come up with the goods on him, if there were any to get. Clark was a clever guy and not likely to leave an incriminating trail. But if he was going to declare his candidacy for the White House in the future, it was important to Felix to turn up whatever they could, if there were illegal activities in his present or past. Alix shared the same view. The public had a right to know. But the immediacy of the riots in Tehran took precedence over all that now. Tony Clark could wait, and since the protestors in Iran were mostly women, and one of them had been killed, Alix was chomping at the bit to go.

'What do you say?' she asked Felix, and he knew what she meant. He had been pondering whether or not to send her to Tehran when she called. She was quick. The story had broken only in the last hour. Alix never wasted any time. Local reporters on the scene were covering it for now, and they'd been using footage and live feeds from the BBC, which Felix never liked. He wanted his own people there.

'I'm not sure. They may subdue the protestors while you're still on the plane.' It was a fine art deciding when to send a crew and when to wait. He didn't want to miss an important story, nor waste money, manpower, and time. 'My gut says let's give it another night. That'll tell us more,' he said, hesitating.

'It's a long flight, and a lot can happen in one night. Let's not wait too long,' she said sensibly.

'We'll get you an emergency press visa today, so you're ready to go if things get worse. You can't leave before that anyway.' It sounded reasonable to her. And she knew they'd get one for Ben too. He showed up in her office that afternoon, looking antsy and bored. They were like firefighters on call, always waiting for flames to erupt somewhere in the world.

'Think we'll go?' he asked her, and she shrugged in answer. She'd been tying up loose ends all afternoon, just in case.

The NRA lobbyist who played golf regularly with Tony Clark had called her and had nothing relevant to say. He'd known the Vice President for a year, and said he was a great guy. He said Tony just wanted to keep his finger on the pulse of what was happening, he wanted to stay informed. There was nothing more to it than that. A lobbyist for the drug companies had said the same the day before. They all liked the Vice President and said they considered him a friend. She wondered if he was just lining up powerful contributors for his next campaign. There was no law against that.

Some of them didn't actually qualify legally as lobbyists since they didn't spend the requisite 20 percent of their time lobbying for a single client, which was the standard for federal lobbyists, according to the law. If they spent less time than that, or didn't work for a single client, technically they weren't lobbyists, so weren't regulated by federal law. There were lots of gray areas as to who was a lobbyist and who wasn't. And Tony seemed to spend time indiscriminately with the official lobbyists and the informal ones. None of her research about the Vice President had been fruitful so far, and Felix's hunch had gone nowhere. There was no evidence, or even a hint, that money had changed hands for Clark's benefit. Maybe they were trading favors, or he was laying the groundwork to cash in later on. For now, she still didn't know, but her antennae were up.

She filled Ben in on that, while they watched another news bulletin from Tehran. Things were calming down. Another protest had been quashed that afternoon without injury or death.

'It doesn't seem to me like we'll go,' Alix said after the bulletin, Ben looked disappointed and left half an hour later. He was on call, and Alix went back to work.

She didn't bother to pack a bag when she went home, and tried to call Faye, who didn't pick up her phone and sent a text from the library later on. Like her mother, she was diligent about her work. Her strengths were English, history, and economics, and she was thinking now about going for a combined MBA and law degree after she graduated from Duke, and she had time to figure it out. Also like her mother, Faye kept her eye on her goals. She wanted to get her combined MBA/JD at Harvard, if she got in, which didn't surprise her mother at all.

Alix went to bed early after watching the news. Nothing had changed, but Felix called and woke her at four A.M.

'They just shot and killed two young women. The police are claiming that other protestors did it, but someone got it on their cellphone on video. The police killed them. Pack your bags. I just called Ben. We've got you on a nine A.M. flight, you have to leave the city at six. Someone from the office will bring you your visa and Ben's, and some cash for travel, in an hour.' He had taken care of everything. All she had to do was pack and send a text to Faye.

'Don't you ever sleep?' she asked him. An assistant producer could have done it for him, but Felix was obsessive about the job. His ex-wife hadn't been wrong.

'Not if I can help it,' he commented to Alix about his sleeping habits. He treated them all like his children, even though he was only ten years older than Alix, and looked twenty years older. Being bald and overweight didn't help. He lived on a diet of doughnuts and Chinese food, which contributed to his constant indigestion and heartburn. There were some things even antacids couldn't help, coupled with the stress of the job. He always felt that their lives were in his hands, and sometimes he was right. 'Have a good flight.

We'll bring you up to date when you land, and tell you who we want you to interview. Get as high up in the government as you can, if they'll talk. And cover your head, we don't want you in jail, and wear your press badge at all times, Ben too.' It was like getting instructions from a father before she left for camp, and she smiled as she hung up. Ben called two minutes later and sounded excited.

'We're on the road again.' It had been obvious to Alix since they started working together that he preferred being anywhere in the world, under any conditions no matter how dangerous, to being at home. It reminded him of being in the SEALs when they were sent on a mission, and he'd been on some tough ones in his day. He thrived on the adrenaline rush he got from it, and at times so did she, and knew it about herself too. She had nothing to stay home for now, with Faye at Duke. She could be gone all the time if she chose. 'I'll meet you at the airport at seven. Felix said they'll drop off my visa with yours, and our money.'

'He told me that too.' She was wide awake now, they both were. The two of them were off to war again, covering crimes against humanity, in this case against women. They were the defenders of peace, justice, and human rights, for all. Sometimes it felt like a noble cause and at other times a job.

'One of those girls they shot last night was sixteen years old,' Ben said, sounding moved by it. He had a soft heart, softer than Alix's at times. 'She was just a kid,' he said emotionally.

'Not in her world,' Alix said, which they both knew was true.

She went to pack after that, in her small rolling bag. They had no idea how long they'd be gone, which was usually the case, or where they might be sent afterward. They might be gone for weeks or even months. But at least Alix knew Faye was fine at Duke. She didn't need to feel guilty about being gone anymore, although she had for years. She was on her own time now, guilt-free, or should have been. It was something Ben didn't need to think about either, with no girlfriend, no wife, no kids, and a family he never saw, and hadn't in two years. He was free as a bird.

One of the assistant producers brought her their visas and cash right before Alix left for the airport with a car and driver. She was ten minutes early for check-in when she got there, and Ben was waiting for her, with a look of excitement in his eyes, and a cappuccino in his hand for her.

'You've got the visas?' She nodded confirmation.

'And the money.' She handed him an envelope with his, and they checked both their bags in, and went to the lounge to wait for the flight to start boarding. There was a TV on in a small room in the lounge, and they watched the latest news with a cluster of businessmen. The riots in Tehran had gotten worse, and Alix was anxious to get there, and so was Ben. She had a head scarf in her purse that she wore in Muslim countries. Going bare-headed was a mistake she never made, and she had a chador in her suitcase, just in case, to cover her clothing to her ankles, and she knew to put the scarf on when they entered Iranian airspace and not wait till they landed. She'd done it all before many times.

She wanted to make calls as soon as they heard from Felix when they got there, to set up interviews for the broadcast. In addition, she was going to try to get interviews with the families of the three girls who had died, but her priority was the men in government who were making the decisions that had affected Iranian women severely, reversing an earlier trend toward modernism, which was over now, if they continued to follow the demands from the extremist religious sector. The men in power were claiming they had no choice. The religious faction made the rules, and they had to be followed, and the women protesting would have to comply, just like everyone else, or go to prison or be killed.

The current government had been moderate till now, and they didn't seem happy about the changes either, but the religious leaders had to be respected, whether young Iranian women liked it or not. It was always a problem in countries with powerful or extremist factions in the Middle East. The women in rural and more remote areas were even more subjugated to ancient rule than those in the cities, where they knew a freer way of life now and didn't want to lose it. But Felix had told Alix he wasn't interested in the broader spectrum, and wanted her to focus on the female protestors in Tehran, which was what she intended to do.

They boarded the plane at eight-thirty, and they took off on time for the first flight to Frankfurt, where they had a layover for many hours, and finally boarded the flight to Tehran. There were only three movies offered, one of them a Disney film, and the others were PG and of no interest to her or Ben. Alix caught up on research material she'd printed out at home. Ben slept for most of the flight, as he'd gotten too little sleep once Felix woke him, and he had to do his laundry and pack. He was always less organized than Alix when they left on an assignment on short notice. She was the master of fast exits at the drop of a hat. Ben always forgot something vital at home. She used a checklist she had developed over the years, which left nothing to chance, just like her broadcasts. She was meticulous about detail.

She covered her head with the gray scarf she carried, when they announced they had entered Iranian airspace, and they were among the first off the plane and through customs. Their papers were in order, the officials were pleasant to them, and they had no problem. They took a cab to the Laleh Hotel, and checked in to the small rooms that had been booked for them side by side. They had slept in one room before in emergency situations. Alix didn't mind and wasn't shy, you did what you had to in a crisis. But their accommodations were pleasant at the hotel. They called Felix when they got to their rooms, and Alix started making calls as soon as he gave her the list.

She already had some of the numbers they needed. She got lucky on her third call and learned that government officials had assigned two people to speak to the international press about the situation. It was clear that the government wasn't pleased with the light the events cast on them. They were proud of having relaxed the rules for women in recent years, and they weren't happy to rescind them, nor about the casualties that were mounting in the riots. Another young woman had been killed while they were on the plane, this time trampled by fellow protestors when they ran from the police who threw tear gas at them. The increasing tension and violence were getting worse, and had an ominous feel.

Ben and Alix showered and changed and ate a light meal before they went to their government appointments. The interviews went well, although Alix was aware that they were being fed the party line, but there was nothing else they could do.

They met with the families of two of the dead girls later that afternoon. They spoke English, and the interviews were heartbreaking. All had been respectable, educated young women who didn't want to see their country return to the dark ages, and were willing to lose their lives to protect the freedoms they believed in and felt they deserved. Their families were bereft by what had happened.

Ben and Alix approached the protest area with

caution that night. Ben shot film from the edges of the crowd, and their press badges gave them access, but even Alix was careful as she observed the restless crowd. Things were at a standoff for the moment, with neither side relenting nor on the offensive since that afternoon, but she knew it could change in a minute and become violent again. She gave the protestors a wide berth, after interviewing a few of them with a Farsi translator they'd hired. She and Ben agreed on an escape route if they had to retreat quickly, but he stayed close to her as he always did, at the ready to grab her or protect her if needed. His old military skills were instinctive, and he had assessed the best possible exit plan when they arrived.

They stayed with the protestors till after midnight, and there were no deaths that night. Alix and Ben went back to the hotel, and returned to the scene early the next morning. She had listened to the call to prayer being chanted at sunrise, and as always was struck by the mysterious beauty of the Islamic world, yet what was happening in Tehran was a terrible step back in time for the women of the country. It was hard to understand the contrast in a land that could be at the same time both so appealing and so harsh. It was a conflict that touched her to the core, and she expressed that in her broadcast, which Ben recognized instantly as an award-winning piece. Alix was always more modest and never saw what he did, she was just doing her job, but what she said on air went straight to the heart of the matter and the key human issues. And she spoke eloquently about it.

Nothing much happened for the next week. Like an old-fashioned infantry war, the protestors and government troops alternately advanced and retreated, gained no physical ground, and resolved nothing. Another young woman was killed, kicked by a horse when the riot police on horseback attempted to move the crowd. It was a senseless death like the others and proved nothing, except her willingness to die for a cause she believed in. She was a twenty-five-year-old woman with three young children. Alix interviewed her husband, who sobbed the entire time Ben filmed him, while he clutched his children in his arms, and the girl's mother and sisters wailed in the background. It illustrated perfectly the senselessness of battle, and the loss of young life. In order to defend her rights as a modern woman, she had left three little children motherless, and her husband and family and all who knew her brokenhearted. Ideologically it made sense and was a worthy battle, but humanly it didn't, and the government understood that too.

At the end of the week Alix and Ben had spent there, the government agreed to appoint a panel of eight women from among the protestors to meet with officials, and try to find a resolution with them, which they would then present to the religious leaders, hoping to reach a compromise that would satisfy everyone to some degree, even if not completely. It was a tremendous victory for the brave women who had protested and honored the five who had lost their lives. The government didn't want the battle to go on forever either, and Alix was sure there would be more eventually, if the agreed-upon compromises were not perfectly implemented, but it was a start, and an attempt to bring normalcy back to Tehran.

'Do you think they mean it?' Ben asked her when they went back to the hotel after the announcement.

'I do. Whether they can convince the religious leaders is another story. But I don't think the government wants to go back to the dark ages either. It's a tough situation, they have to respect their religious leaders, and want to have a modern, functioning country at the same time, and women here have always been well educated, and an important part of their workforce at high levels at various times. They don't want to lose that again.' It had been a good reminder to her for the past several days of how lucky she was.

They ordered room service in her room, and when they got there, she pulled off the head scarf she had worn since they arrived, which concealed her blond hair. She was tired of wearing it, and couldn't imagine living with it every day, let alone being fully veiled and covered, like women from strict religious families. There had been several among the protestors. It was such a different world from the one she and Ben lived in. There was a wonderful museum and university, and the prayers chanted throughout the city five times a day seemed mystical and exotic and reminded Alix of how unfamiliar life was here.

They called Felix, and he told them to stay another day, to get video coverage of the women going to the meeting with the government officials to conclude the story. After that, they could return to New York, and he praised them for a job well done, from all aspects. They had gotten the human interest side, the breaking news at the protest, and some excellent interviews with government officials. He couldn't have asked for more. They'd been there by then for eight days of nonstop work, Felix had had their one-week visas extended, and they were both tired but pleased with what they'd done, and thought the compromise meeting with the government and the protestors might actually work. The women claimed to be militant, but Alix had the sense that they would back down to some degree. They couldn't go on forever, and the loss of five women for their cause was enough.

The protestors were planning to stay in place until the meeting the next day, but a few had already disbanded and gone home to their families and children. Ben and Alix took a walk that afternoon, on the first break they'd had since they arrived. When they stopped for coffee, she told Ben that there was someone she wanted to call before she left.

'You have friends here?' He looked surprised. He knew she'd been to Tehran before on assignments, but didn't think it was more than that. She shook her head in answer to his question.

'Not really. I met a man here once, years ago. I was introduced to him by a BBC reporter who said he was a useful contact. He's well connected and discreet, he seems to know everyone, and stays below the radar. He's half Saudi and half Iranian, so he has connections on both sides of the fence, so to speak. He helped me out once, getting some info I couldn't get through official channels. He seems to know everything that goes on here. I thought I'd give him a call.'

'About the protests?' Ben asked her, intrigued by what she was after. Alix always took her stories to another level, and dug deep into the layers, even when she didn't need to. It was what made her so good at her job. She was relentless in her search for the truth, and not just what she was told. They had what they needed, but apparently she wanted more.

'You never know what turns up,' she said to Ben. 'I just thought I'd see if he's still around and what he knows. You can't tell, we might get another story out of it. People come through here. He's a smart guy, it might be a good investment.'

Ben grinned at what she said. 'And how do you list that on your expense sheet for the network? "Bribes"?' Although he thought it was a smart thing to do. She was right, you never knew what might come of it.

'I usually list it as "drivers" or "translators."' She smiled at him. 'It's a legitimate expense, even if it looks bad on an expense sheet. I've gotten some great leads from unorthodox sources before, particularly in this part of the world.'

'You won't get an argument from me.' He looked amused and impressed.

She called the source from the phone in her room when she got back to the hotel, and Ben Tarik Saleh answered on the fourth ring. She had almost given up when he did. She gave him her name, and he recognized it immediately from their previous transaction, and he greeted her like an old friend and asked about her family, which told her that he didn't trust his phone, nor did she. She knew the rules of the game. She was a pro, and he certainly was, with connections on all sides of some shady lines, and information for sale.

She asked Tarik if he wanted to have coffee with her, and he suggested his aunt's house, which was how they had met before. He used it as a code name for a coffee shop he frequented, one of several locations where he met the people who paid him for what they wanted to know. Alix looked pleased when they hung up. They were meeting in an hour, although he had mentioned a time three hours later. She knew the drill for that too.

'You're seeing him tonight?' Ben asked when she hung up, since he had been in the room and heard her end of the conversation, and had been fooled by the time she confirmed.

'No, in an hour. I'd better get going, it's pretty far from here.'

'I'll come with you,' he said instantly. 'You shouldn't go alone.' She had the last time, but knew it wasn't smart, but she'd had an unfamiliar cameraman with her and didn't want him to know where she was going, or why. She didn't object to Ben's offer, and they left the room a few minutes later. She put her scarf back on, they hailed a cab outside the hotel, and Alix gave the driver the address.

It was near the Tehran Grand Bazaar, with lots of traffic and confusion and people milling everywhere. The noise level was incredible. It took them nearly the full hour to get there, because of all the cars on the road. The coffee shop was a hole in the wall they wouldn't even have noticed if it hadn't been their destination. It was one of the few coffee shops also open to women. Alix recognized it immediately. Ben walked in behind her and sat down at a table near the front, while Alix walked to the rear of the small restaurant, where she saw the informant waiting at a table for her. He looked casual and indifferent when she sat down, as though he saw her every day.

'Thank you for meeting me,' she said, as his eyes scanned the restaurant and passersby. He seemed satisfied that nothing was amiss, and had realized that Ben was with her, and didn't care. She had three bills neatly folded into the palm of her hand, which brushed his under the table so quickly that no one would have noticed. She had just paid him the equivalent of three hundred dollars in local currency for whatever he had to say. It was a lot of money in Iran, and she knew that he would tell her if he wanted more for some piece of vital information he had to share. He had been fair with her before, and his leads had been reliable and fruitful.

'What are you looking for?' he asked her, sipping the coffee he had ordered, and he ordered one for her. He was somewhere in his early thirties, and looked like a poor man, which she suspected was no longer the case, since he had been selling information for years. He had good government contacts, according to the reporter who had introduced them, and had never been caught. She suspected he must have been related to someone higher up. Being half Saudi and half Iranian, he had contacts in both worlds and had lived in Tehran for years, moved around a lot, and had managed not to draw attention to himself by allying himself too closely with any side of the local tensions. Saudis were not overly welcome in Iran.

'I'm not sure,' she said in answer to his question. 'Anything you know here that might make a good story for us. Has anyone come through Tehran who shouldn't have?'

'Not recently. Maybe six months ago,' he said, thinking about it, narrowing his eyes as he took another sip of the strong coffee and she waited, not sure what she expected to hear. 'Your Vice President,' he said in an undervoice so no one would hear him. His lips barely moved, and then he lit a cigarette and blew smoke in the air. 'No one knew he was here. He's been here before, but not in a few years. He used to come often, a long time ago. He has Saudi friends, he meets them here. It's complicated but he knows important people, they make it possible for him. He comes very quietly.'

Alix was stunned to hear this, and it had been so easy. It almost didn't seem true, but she believed the information, and Tarik had been a trustworthy source before. 'Was he here on an official visit?'

Tarik shook his head. 'Not this time. The last time, yes, maybe two years ago. He used to come more often, eight or ten years ago. He meets with four Saudis, important men. They're the biggest exporters of oil in Saudi Arabia, related to the royal family. In the old days, he came every month, then less often. Now he is more careful. I can ask if he meets them anywhere else. Maybe Dubai. Is that what you wanted to know?' he asked her, and she nodded, trying not to look as surprised as she was. Coming to Tehran was not easy for an American, but clearly Tony Clark knew the right people to make it happen. With enough money, anything could be done, even here. She realized that he probably flew in and out on a private plane, undoubtedly provided by his Saudi 'friends.'

'I think it is.'

'Meet me here tomorrow at six o'clock, and I'll see what else I can find out. If he does business with them, they pay him a lot, many millions. Money is no problem for them.' It would explain some of the fortune Tony had amassed if he was

86

being paid by the Saudis. Even good investments wouldn't account for it, but Saudi oil money would. Alix had just never expected him to be involved in that. Taking bribes from lobbyists in Washington would have been one thing, but making oil deals with the Saudis was an enormous piece of information. 'See you tomorrow,' Tarik said as he stood up and left some coins on the table. She followed him onto the street without further conversation, and Ben got up and met her. Tarik picked up a bicycle he'd left outside and took off, and Ben and Alix walked down the street and hailed a cab. They were in the taxi before she said a word to him. She looked distracted as she thought about what Tarik had said. It was a shocking revelation, and confirmed her suspicions that there was something 'off' about the Vice President that she and Felix Winters couldn't put their finger on. Maybe this was it. But then, where did the lobbyists fit in? Or was Clark on the take from everyone, trying to amass money for a presidential campaign? Or was it all just greed, or all of the above? And he had married big money too.

'Get what you wanted?' Ben asked her quietly.

'I think so. I'm not sure. It was a good idea,' she said vaguely, and stared out the window on the way back to the hotel. She was thinking about Olympia Foster and that she had no idea what she was dealing with. If this was true, and the Saudis were paying Tony Clark, he was a major crook of massive proportions, and had convinced Olympia of his innocence.

She wondered if Bill Foster had known, or even suspected, what Clark was doing. But Alix knew Olympia would never tell her if he did. She was protective of them both. And Alix doubted that Foster was in on Tony's deals, if there were any. Foster was too clean for that. Alix had no concerns about Bill Foster. No one had ever been worried about Foster having dubious income from unknown sources, or misdeeds. He had died as he had lived, lily pure, with an untarnished reputation.

Alix went to bed early that night and said nothing more to Ben about what the informant had told her. They filmed the women going to the government meeting the next day, concluded the story, and were back at the hotel in the late afternoon. She told Ben then that she was meeting Tarik again in the same place. He didn't seem surprised, and they took a cab to the same coffee shop, and followed the same routine as the day before. Tarik looked like he was in a hurry this time. He said he had a meeting across town in an hour, and traffic was bad.

'He's been meeting the Saudis in Dubai,' he told her immediately. 'He stopped doing business with them four years ago when he became Vice President. Now he wants to start again.' Probably preparing for a presidential campaign in two or three years, Alix guessed but didn't comment. The President had just been elected for his second term, so Clark had to make plans now, and put money in his coffers. 'The money they pay him goes into Swiss accounts. Those accounts aren't safe anymore, so your government can probably find out if they know what to ask. He met two of them in college at Harvard, brothers, and they remained friends. He's been doing business with them for many years.' He slipped her a tiny piece of paper then, with their names on it. 'He won't come to Tehran again, it's not safe for him. He only came to see them once privately since he's been Vice President. I think they will meet in Dubai more often. He wants to make a deal with them.'

'Was a man named Bill Foster ever part of it? William Foster? Did he come with him?' She hoped not, but she had to do her job and ask. She couldn't protect anyone in her quest for the truth.

'No, he always came alone. My source is sure of that. And I've never heard that name. But your Vice President is a hard businessman and wants a lot of money from them. And then he will owe them what they want later on, when he's President. He has said he will win next time for sure. Is that true?' He was asking her for information now as a quid pro quo.

'I don't know,' she said honestly. 'He could, with the right running mate and enough money behind him.' He had a pretty wife and young family, and he carried the aura of Bill Foster with him as his best friend, even if he didn't have Foster's charisma. Elections had been won with less. He had been careful not to offend anyone as Vice President. And if he had the important lobbies behind him, he would be bought and paid for and owe his soul to some very important people before he ever won the election. But with their weight and money in the scale, they might just tip the balance and win the election for him. It was a frightening thought given what she knew now. He was totally corrupt if the rumors she'd heard in the States and what Tarik said were true. Alix was suddenly afraid that he would win. It was a travesty to the memory of Bill Foster and all he had stood for. She couldn't help wondering again how much Foster had known, if anything. He couldn't have suspected or he'd never have groomed him as his running mate, and what a disaster that would have been, and was now. The thought of it made her feel sick. 'I think he could win,' she said to Tarik. 'That wouldn't be good, to have a corrupt President in the White House, owned by the Saudis.'

'It's what they want,' he warned her. 'He's dealing with important men, and it would give them a lot of power in the States.' That was precisely what was wrong about it. A President who had been heavily subsidized by the wrong people. 'He went to them,' Tarik added. 'He needs money, a lot of it. He knew where to go. I have to leave now,' he said. 'It was nice doing business with you again.'

She slipped the equivalent of another three hundred dollars into his palm then, and he was pleased. They'd had good dealings before. It had been a long time, and he'd been surprised to hear from her again. He was happy he could find out the information she wanted. He liked to think he was an instrument of world peace. It made what he did seem nobler to him. But whatever his motives, Alix was satisfied. Now she had to figure out what to do with the information and where to go from here. She needed to think about it, and wanted to discuss it with Felix when she got back to New York. They were leaving the next day.

She followed Tarik out of the coffee shop again, and he took off on his bike. Ben joined her on the street and they went back to the hotel in silence. He could tell she didn't want to discuss what she'd heard, and she looked shaken by it. She trusted him, but at first she didn't even know what to say. It was hard to wrap her mind around, even for her.

They went for a walk after dinner, and Alix finally said something to Ben.

'According to my source, Tony Clark was paid off by the Saudis for years, that's where all the money comes from, paid into Swiss accounts. He stopped when he was elected Vice President, and now he's trying to make a deal with them again, probably to help finance his next campaign.'

'That and the lobbies?' Ben looked shocked. 'He's a busy guy.' He was pleased to have confirmation that his assessment of Clark had been right. Underneath the smooth exterior, he was a bad guy. 'What are you going to do with the information?' Ben asked her, as Alix thought about it.

'I don't know. I'll tell Felix, but I'm beginning to wonder if we should report this to some government law enforcement agency. This is a big deal.'

'Yes, it is,' he confirmed. 'I've got good contacts at the CIA. This is up their alley. They have special teams for this. Something like this belongs in the hands of the National Clandestine Service, and will ultimately end up in the hands of the DNI, Director of National Intelligence, or the DO, the Directorate of Operations. The CIA reports to them, on something as important as this. You can't hang on to information of this nature just as a story. It's a matter of national security if what your source said is true. Do you trust your source?'

'Yes, I do, but someone should check it out. Like the CIA or the FBI. If we hang on to it for a while, while we try to get more info as proof, is that obstruction of justice?' She looked worried, and he thought about her question for a minute.

'It could be. I'm not sure. Felix will know what to do better than I do. You've got one hell of a story on your hands here. It sounds like a ticking bomb to me. And since it's international, with the Saudis involved, this will go to the CIA, not the FBI.'

'Yeah, it sounds dangerous to me too.' She looked unhappy about it. 'I wish I knew how much Bill Foster knew, and if he did. His widow will never tell me the truth. She's too invested in protecting them both and I doubt she knows anything about this. But Foster was a smart guy. It's hard to believe he didn't know, or at least suspect something. But I don't think he'd tell her. And she won't tell me what she does know.'

'Do you think he was on the take from them too?' Ben asked her.

'No, I don't. Not for a minute. But I wonder if he suspected something. He was such a straight, honorable guy, I can't see him being part of something like this.'

'Neither can I,' Ben agreed. They had no problem believing it of Clark, though.

They were both lost in thought for a while after they talked about it, and walked back to the hotel in silence. Alix was exhausted by all the possibilities swirling around in her head. And every time she thought about it, she had more questions and fewer answers. She could hardly wait to talk to Felix about it as soon as they got back to New York. She hoped he would know what to do, and she thought that Ben was right, and they should go to the CIA or whichever agency was appropriate. She had never dealt with anything as major and sensitive before, where national security was involved, and someone as high up in government as the Vice President. And what would happen after a government agency like the CIA got involved, she had no idea. But of one thing she was certain, the Vice President was corrupt, and had been for years. The big question now was how much Bill Foster had known. Alix refused to believe he had been part of it, that just didn't seem possible. At least she hoped not. But whether Foster knew or not, what she had just learned about Tony Clark was huge.

CHAPTER 5

Alix went into the office an hour early the morning after they got back from Tehran. She knew that Felix would be there, and she wanted to talk to him about the information she had, so they could decide what to do about it. The story was too important to give up, but it could also be too big to keep from government agencies, since the Vice President was involved.

Felix was happy to see her, and was thrilled with her coverage of the riots in Tehran, and he thought Ben had done a great job as well. It was award-winning reportage, which wasn't unusual for her. And after they talked about it, she hesitated for a moment, and he could see she had something else to say.

'Something wrong?' He sensed a major issue on her mind.

'Journalistically, no,' she said cryptically. 'Morally, yes. I called an old source I have in Tehran. I haven't contacted him in years. Interesting guy, he has friends and contacts in high places, and he comes up with some very good stuff. He knocked me flat on my ass when I was there. Tony Clark has been meeting with four major Saudi oil guys

94

for years. He says his sources tell him Clark was being paid into a Swiss account, in the days when those accounts were kept secret. We might get lucky on that now, or the right authorities might. He says Clark stopped doing business with them four years ago, which coincides with when they won the election, but he's back now. He was there six months ago on an unofficial secret visit, and he's meeting the same Saudis as before in Dubai. He wants big money, probably for his own campaign, and if they give it to him, they're going to own him body and soul if he gets to the White House. It's a hell of a great story, but there's more than that involved. National security, corruption, the Vice President is a crook if any or all of this is true. And God knows who else he's taking money from, and what he'll owe them. If this is true, the possible future President of the United States is up for sale.'

'What about Bill Foster? Was he in on it? Did you ask?'

'According to my informant, Foster never went to Tehran, and he never heard his name. I wonder how much Foster knew, or if he didn't suspect it before he died.'

'Foster was nobody's fool, he must have had an inkling of something. Who would know about that?'

'His wife said that Clark had no connection to any particular lobbyist, so she sure isn't going to admit that her husband knew about payoffs from Saudis. I don't think she knows anything, and maybe Bill Foster didn't either. Clark is very smooth, and if the money was going into numbered accounts in Switzerland, how would anyone know? It explains the money he's made in the last ten years, which has never shown up in the financial statements he discloses, but crooked money wouldn't. He always claims that the money he's made is due to his Midas touch with investments. If he sold out to the Saudis, that explains it better than lucky wins on Wall Street.' Felix sat silently at his desk for a minute, thinking about it, and then looked at Alix intently.

'I had a call from one of my own sources while you were gone. I didn't want to put it in an email, or tell you on the phone. He says that a friend of his who works for one of the big gas lobbyists told him that they've been paying Clark under-the-table campaign money, against bills they want him to push and sign if he wins, and with them behind him he might win. And if he's taking money from them, he may be taking it from other sources too.'

'Jesus. He hasn't left anyone out, has he?' It was all so much worse than they'd suspected. And if the case against him could be proven, he would end up in prison after being removed from the vice presidency, never mind losing the next election. 'What do we do now? Ben thinks we should contact the CIA, and let them pursue it. Their connections to investigate are a lot better than ours.' Felix nodded. He didn't disagree with her, but the story was too good to give up just yet. He wanted to see what else they could find out, and then go to the CIA.

'What if we hang on to it for a few more weeks and see what turns up?' Felix suggested. 'I can call more of my sources. Then we can hand the CIA the whole story, or close to it, and they can take it from there.'

'And if they find out we're on to something?' She looked worried. She did not want to anger the CIA.

'We tell them we wanted to be sure. And the one thing I'd hate like hell about this whole damn thing would be to find out that Foster was part of it, and knew what Clark was doing or was implicated in some way. He died a hero. I don't want to see that go down the tubes, and find out that he and Clark were in it together. But it could happen, you never know.'

'I don't think he was,' Alix said quietly, and more than ever now, she wondered what his widow knew and what she was hiding, if anything.

'Let's give it two more weeks and hand it over to the CIA then,' Felix said, making a rapid off-the-cuff decision. He was a newsman above all else, and this was just too big a plum to hand over, especially given what Alix had discovered in Tehran.

'I'll agree to that,' Alix said. 'But no longer. I have a kid to support, and I don't want trouble.'

He nodded, looking serious, and started making phone calls to sources he had in Washington the minute she left his office. She had already exhausted hers.

'What did Felix say?' Ben asked her when she

got back to her office, and he saw her worried expression. Sitting on the story for two more weeks made sense newswise if they could crack it wide open and hand the CIA a done deal. But if they couldn't, it would be difficult to explain to the CIA why they hadn't come forward sooner. If nothing else, it made them look uncooperative, and sometimes they needed the CIA's help.

'He wants two more weeks to see what else we can find out before we hand it over.' Ben nodded, and was worried about her. With something of this magnitude, the boys in charge of clandestine operations and national security didn't screw around.

'Are you going to try to see Olympia Foster again?' Ben wondered out loud.

Alix shook her head. She had given up there. 'It won't do me any good. She won't tell me anything, and I doubt she knows anyway. No one could guess what he's up to, and on such a major scale. He's gone straight to the lobbies with big money who need presidential help. And if he makes a deal with the Saudis, he'll have everything he needs, not to mention his wife's money. He's got his ducks set up, all in a row.'

'I guess it won't hurt to wait two more weeks. He's not going anywhere, and he has no reason to suspect people are looking over his shoulder. And even less for him to suspect you know he's planning to meet the Saudis in Dubai.'

'This is starting to make me nervous,' Alix admitted to him. 'There are some very heavy players in the game. They're not going to like our exposing him, and neither will he. This could get ugly,' she said to Ben and he nodded. She was right. She had covered big stories before, and even an exposé of a major Mafia boss many years earlier, but this was even bigger. And the implications were enormous. Tony Clark had been setting this up for years. Alix wondered if he had been taking bribes all along, and now with a presidential campaign in sight, he had something to sell them if he won. He could endorse all the bills they wanted.

By the end of the week, one of Felix's sources had come through for him. A lobbyist for gaming interests confirmed confidentially that he had paid Clark a huge amount, and in exchange for immunity, he would be willing to testify. He didn't want to go down for Tony Clark. Felix was waiting to hear from one other major lobbyist, and would then be willing to go to the CIA. But they came to him first.

A week after Alix got back from Tehran, two senior operations officers of the CIA Clandestine Service showed up at the network and asked to see Felix. He looked surprised when they walked into his office a few minutes later, but was pleasant and appeared to be relaxed as he snuck three antacids into his mouth at once.

'What can I do to help you, gentlemen? Coffee?' he suggested. They declined and dismissed the offer as they sat down, and the most senior member of the team spoke first. His name was John Pelham, he was a senior operations officer of the National Clandestine Service. They were on the front line on critical international developments, terrorism, and military and political issues. It was an elite corps to protect national security interests, and they reported directly to the Director of National Intelligence, the head of the CIA, and the President.

'You've been doing some serious digging into the lobbies and the activities of the Vice President.' He came right to the point. 'We want to know why. Is it some kind of witch hunt designed to make the Vice President look bad and discredit him, or do you have a lead we should know about that you're not sharing with us? I don't think I need to remind you what that's called.' Neither man had smiled since they walked in, and Felix felt like a fool for being effusive with them. It was time to play it straight.

'We've had a couple of leads,' he said honestly, 'and played a hunch, but that's all it was at first. We didn't want to be irresponsible and start an avalanche on bogus information. We've been trying to ascertain if it's real, before we wasted your time with it.' He was backpedaling as fast as he could.

'That's our job, not yours,' Senior Officer Pelham reminded him in an ice-cold voice.

'Not always,' Felix responded. 'We'd drive you crazy and lose our credibility if we came to you with every lead we get.'

The officer conceded nothing. 'And just exactly what have you turned up?' He was angry at the senior producer for not coming to them sooner, but there was often conflict between the media and government agencies. This wasn't the first time. And it was why he was here. He wanted their information and their sources.

'I think this is a serious situation, and I trust our informants. As of yesterday, I have a lobbyist willing to testify in exchange for immunity,' Felix volunteered.

'Testify to what?' the senior officer said tersely. 'And it's up to us to agree to immunity, not you.'

'I'm well aware of that, but we've done the legwork for you here,' Felix said lamely. His stomach was on fire.

'If that's what you want to call it,' Officer Pelham said sourly. 'So what are you telling me?'

'I can't prove it to you, but we've been told that several large payments have been made to Vice President Clark, in exchange for favors if he wins the next election, or can get a bill pushed through for them during this administration.' It didn't get clearer than that. 'It would seem that he's getting payoffs from two major lobbies.' He reeled off which ones and Pelham didn't react.

'How are they paying him?' the senior operations officer said, frowning. He didn't like what he was hearing, at all, nor that the network had kept it from them while trying to break the story on their own.

'That's up to you to figure out, we don't know.'

'Is that it?' Pelham asked him, and Felix sighed.

'Unfortunately not. I had a reporter in Tehran a week ago, covering the riots for women's rights. An informant who's given us reliable information before told her that Clark is in negotiation with several major Saudi oil dealers for a deal with them, and apparently he's done business with them before, before his vice presidency, and he's looking for money now. He's planning to meet them in Dubai.' Pelham looked incredulous at what he had said.

'We'd like to speak to the reporter. Is he here?'

'It's Alix Phillips, our top reporter, as I'm sure you know. She's never given me a bogus tip yet, and she trusts her source.'

'I can't believe you've been sitting on this for God knows how long,' the operations officer said in a fury.

'What would you rather have, an unverified hot tip from some crackpot that may be worth nothing and send you on a wild goose chase, or for us to check it out before we call you? Personally, gentlemen, in your shoes, I'd rather have a clean tip than a rough guess. We were going to call you in a few days, but what I'm giving you is straight up.' Felix went immediately on the offensive, and they didn't look happy about it, but what he said made sense.

'Our officers are more experienced at verifying information like this than your reporters.'

'I think they did a pretty good job anyway, and for the record, Bill Foster's name came up in none of this. There is nothing to suggest he was involved or implicated in any way. We asked.'

'We'll check that out,' Pelham said grimly. A political hot potato had just landed in his lap. For Felix and the network, it would be a major coup that would send their ratings skyrocketing. For the CIA, it was a potential disaster that could seriously impact or impair the current administration. It was not good news to them. 'Who else knows about this?'

'No one yet. The sources I used, which I can't disclose to you, Alix Phillips, our reporter, and her cameraman. She did the investigative work herself, both in Tehran and here.'

'Is she here?'

Felix nodded, buzzed her from his desk, and asked her to come in. He didn't say why, and she was startled to see the two men with him, but she knew why they were there as soon as he said they were with the Clandestine Service of the CIA. Ben had explained all of that to her on the flight back from Tehran.

They questioned her thoroughly and made notes while they did, and then stood up and said that they would be back in touch if they had more questions, and that they expected Felix, Alix, and the network to cooperate fully with an investigation. Both Alix and Felix assured them that they would, and reiterated that this had not been an attempt to usurp the CIA's role in national security, but to make sure the story was real. Pelham didn't comment but told them that they could reveal none of this to anyone for the moment, nor release the story. A full investigation would have to be undertaken by the CIA. And then they left, and Alix looked at Felix nervously and sat down in a chair.

'What do you think is going to happen?' Alix asked.

'I don't know. You did their job for them. I'm sure they just don't know what to do with the information. This is not good for anyone. And if they can corroborate the story, they'll have to indict Clark, which looks like shit for the sitting President. I just hope Bill Foster doesn't go down in flames with them posthumously, he doesn't deserve it.'

'I hope they can prove he wasn't involved,' Alix said sadly, thinking of his wife and children.

'A lot of people are going to be in the hot seat over this, once they get going. Foster's widow too, since she's so close to Clark now, and Bill was all his life. My guess is she knows something, but she's not telling.' Alix had the same feeling, but wasn't sure what. The CIA could force Olympia Foster to talk, with the threat of federal prosecution. And if they subpoenaed her, she'd have to tell the truth, like it or not. Alix dreaded the pain of that for her. She was lost in her own world, surrounded by her husband's trophies and mementos, writing books about him, while her husband's best friend was making illegal deals with everyone he could. It was going to be a shock wave felt around the world once it came out. But the CIA had homework to do before it did. It was their problem now, and in some ways, Alix was relieved. She would have loved to break the story if they had found conclusive proof, but she preferred having the CIA stick their necks out, rather than her own. And she said as much to Ben when he got to work.

'I figured they'd catch up with you sooner or later. You did enough digging to wake them up. Someone was bound to tell them. How did it go?'

'Very seriously and not a lot of fun. They weren't happy about our not calling them, but at least it's their problem now, not ours.' She was glancing at her mail as she said it to him, and stopped talking as she read a letter for a second time and frowned. It had come in a plain white envelope, printed by a computer, and the person who had written the letter didn't mince words.

'Stay away from Washington and stop digging or you'll wind up dead.' The letter wasn't signed, and there was no way to trace it. It had been mailed in New York. Alix handed it to Ben without comment, and she called Felix and asked him to come in. Ben handed the letter to him when he did, and Felix let out a sigh, and sat down across from her.

'I'll call Pelham. He should know.' And then he had an idea. 'I think we've stirred up a hornet's nest here, and I'd like to give it some time to calm down.

There's a big story in Paris, it's a puff piece. The French President has just been outed having a hot affair with a French stripper. She's twenty-three years old, he has her set up in an apartment he bought for her, and they had a baby last year. His current girlfriend went berserk and made a public scene and attacked the girl. It's all French histrionics and no one cares, but it's making lots of noise and the girl is gorgeous. There's a rumor he might even marry the stripper, although he's never married anyone before. While the CIA shakes the trees, I don't want you getting hit with any coconuts, and if we're down to death threats now, let's get you out of town. A week in Paris might do you good. How does that sound to you?' He assumed that the CIA would have checked out their information in a week, and maybe even be ready to move forward with an official investigation of Tony Clark.

'It sounds like a great idea.' She smiled, looking relieved. She'd had death threats before, they were always upsetting, even if the threats were never acted on. 'I'd like security for my daughter at Duke while I'm gone. Right away, in fact.'

'And we'll ask the FBI to cover you when you get back,' Felix said seriously.

'If you don't mind, I'd like a few days off while I'm there, to see my mother in Provence.'

'Done,' Felix said solemnly, and looked at Ben. 'You can be her security in the meantime. I'll put you on a flight tomorrow, the stripper story is all yours,' he said, and Alix laughed.

'My mother will be pissed if I make the French President look bad. She loves him.'

'He makes himself look bad.' He had a weakness for very young women and sex scandals, which had tripped him up before. This wasn't new. 'Can you stay somewhere other than your apartment tonight? Let's not tempt fate here. And I'll let the CIA boys know you're leaving town and where you're going.'

'Thank you,' she said, Felix left to organize the assignment, as Alix looked at Ben bleakly. 'Faye is going to be pissed when I tell her she's going to need a bodyguard.' It had happened before, but she wouldn't like it. 'But at least I'll get to see my mother. I haven't been over to see her in eight months. Just don't tell her about the death threat.'

'Why don't you stay with me tonight?' he suggested, she thought about it for a minute and nodded reluctantly.

'I hate to put you out, and I have to go home and pack first. I can sleep on your couch,' she volunteered.

'You don't have to. I have a guest room I never use. I use it as an office, but it has a bed in it.'

'Thank you,' she said, trying to figure out who had sent the death threat. It could have been anyone, but someone sounded seriously pissed. Maybe even Tony Clark, although that was hard to believe. He couldn't have sunk to that. Maybe one of the lobbyists. 'I'll call Faye,' she said, and he went back to his office. He didn't mind Alix staying with him, and he felt sorry the heat was on her now, and might be for a while. She was messing with some big players in the major leagues. And they had a lot at stake.

Alix left a message for Faye, who called her back ten minutes later and sounded busy.

'What? I'm on the way to class.'

'I'm leaving for Paris tomorrow on the French President's stripper scandal. I'll see Mamie while I'm there.' She tried to sound casual about it, and Faye was annoyed.

'Why didn't you just send me a text?'

'Because there's something else.' Alix sounded apologetic. 'I've been working on a big political story, and I got a death threat this morning at the network. It's probably nothing, and I'll be in France for a week, but I requested security for you at school.' She waited for the explosion that came immediately.

'Oh, Mom, for God's sake, I'll look like an idiot with some goon following me around. How am I supposed to explain that?' It hadn't happened in a while, not since she'd been at Duke.

'Tell them your mother is neurotic and checking on you, or he's your boyfriend, or whatever you want, but I want you protected until things settle down. It's probably just a crackpot, but why take a chance?'

'I hate you,' Faye said fervently but didn't mean it. 'That's why I hate what you do. You're risking your own life, and now mine. Why are you always in some kind of trouble?' Faye sounded exasperated and Alix's nerves were raw. It hadn't been an easy day so far, and she had a lot on her mind.

'Because this is what I do,' she snapped at her. 'Just be nice about it and stop complaining. They'll be sending you someone from the FBI,' Alix explained and Faye sounded shocked.

'The FBI? What are you doing, chasing spies or threatening the President?' No, the Vice President, Alix was tempted to say but didn't.

'No, it's one of those jurisdictional issues, where it's either the FBI or the CIA or local police. And in this case, the FBI got involved since threats via the U.S. mail are a federal offense.' Faye knew that her mother's life had been threatened over the years, but she never got used to it. 'I'll call you from Paris,' Alix promised.

'Okay, love you. Warn me before the goon shows up,' Faye blurted at her and they hung up.

Alix and Ben went to her apartment after work and she packed her bag for Paris, and then they went to Brooklyn. He made dinner for them, and Alix camped out in his spare bedroom. She felt stupid being there, and was sure she would have been safe in her own apartment, but she had promised to be careful and sensible. She fell asleep in Ben's guest room almost as soon as her head hit the pillow. It had been a long day of the CIA, a death threat, and now she was going to Paris to interview a President and a stripper. Sometimes her life felt completely nuts. She wondered if her daughter was right and she should be doing something more ordinary, like covering local news, or dog stories, or celebrities in L.A. for *Entertainment Tonight*. There had to be an easier way to make a living than walking through minefields, or trying to prove illegal oil deals, or bringing down a Vice President. But how did you rewind the film and start over? And she had the distinct impression that with what lay ahead with Tony Clark, things were going to get worse before they got better. And now that the CIA had been informed, there was no turning back. She had started something major, and even Faye was being affected.

'The Goon' had arrived at Faye's dorm at ten o'clock that night, and she had sent her mother a text when he did. He was posted outside her room. There would be three shifts a day to follow her everywhere. 'He weighs 300 lbs and he's 200 years old. Am I supposed to be protecting him? I hate you. F.' Alix laughed when she read it and showed it to Ben. At least she knew her daughter would be safe. And Alix had her very own Navy SEAL to protect her. Alix just hoped it would be over soon. Paris would be fun. And a few days with her mother in Provence would be the icing on the cake, or the cherry on top, as the French said.

CHAPTER 6

Olympia had just finished another chapter in her book, about the importance of reinstating old-fashioned values, and she sat looking out at the moonlight. Sometimes she wondered if the book was really important. She had covered all of Bill's major political policies in the first book, but she had wanted to share his more personal principles and values in the second. There was so much to say about him, although the media interest in him had begun to wane in recent years. He was old news now, and no longer current, except to her. She was having trouble finding a publisher for the second book, and was disappointed. She didn't want anyone to forget him. He had loved the country and the American people so much, and had had so many hopes for what he would do to help them, all ended in an instant. And sometimes now she felt as though she was carrying the torch alone.

Even her children were opposed to her doing another book, and had lives and plans of their own now. And Tony, his lifelong friend, was Vice President and had his own view of the world, which was more practical than Bill's, and his own goals and ambitions, which no longer included Bill.

Tony was a businessman above all, and Bill had been a visionary. His dreams for the country had been so vast, and he had wanted to implement them all. Olympia wanted to let people know now what they'd missed. She didn't want her husband to be forgotten. She felt as though she had been spared to carry his message forward into the future, to remind lawmakers and politicians of the shining example he had been, and how they could emulate him. She was sure that Tony would do that if he became President, but in the meantime he had to follow the President he worked with, and bide his time until he won a presidential election himself. She had no regrets about refusing the opportunity to become First Lady at his side. She loved Tony best as a friend, and after all this time, she was still deeply in love with Bill, and writing about him and sharing his ideas kept him alive for her. She had no other life now except her memories of him, rare visits with her children, and dinner with Tony when he came to New York to see her. He said he was in love with her, and she believed him, but she was faithful to her husband, even beyond the grave. She was a beautiful woman, but her life had a grayness to it now, and an ongoing sadness she could not escape. And if she tried to, she felt as though she'd be abandoning Bill. Olympia had remained frozen in time, from the moment he died. It was as though she had died with him. And she felt guilty that she had escaped the unknown assassin's bullets and he hadn't. She had suffered from survivor guilt since it happened.

The phone on her desk rang just as she was putting the manuscript in a locked drawer. It was after midnight, which was when he usually called her. She knew it was Tony without looking at caller ID, and before she picked it up. His deep, mellifluous voice sounded in her ear like a familiar melody. It was comforting to hear him late at night, when her memories engulfed her.

'Am I disturbing you?' he always asked politely.

'Of course not. I love hearing from you. How was your day?'

'Busy. Long. Vice presidential. I had too many meetings or I would have called earlier.' He always relaxed when he talked to her. She was like coming home for him. And she felt the same way about him now. He was the place where she felt safe. She could tell him anything. 'How's the book coming?' He was kind to ask her.

'I don't know. I've hit a dead spot, and sometimes I wonder if anyone still cares. The world has moved on,' she said wistfully. But she hadn't, and was determined not to. If she moved on, it would mean that Bill was really dead, and never coming back. Writing about him kept him part of her daily life.

'Bill is going to be a hero in the public eye for a long, long time,' Tony reassured her. Bill had been an icon to those who knew him. Tony

113

had been more of a man behind the scenes, and still was. He wanted more than that now. He was ready for it.

'I hope so,' she said about Bill. 'How are the kids?'

'I don't know. I didn't see them today. I didn't have time,' he admitted. The older child, a little boy, was three years old. The younger, a girl, was eighteen months old and still a toddler. She had just learned to walk and had a head full of blond curls like his wife. She was a beautiful child.

'And how's Megan?' Olympia inquired about his wife, and Tony sighed. He could be honest with Olympia. She was a breath of fresh air for him. He always said they were soul mates, although Olympia had refused to marry him.

'Megan is young. Sometimes I feel like I should have adopted her instead of marrying her. Twenty-two years makes a big difference. She thinks political life is fun as long as it doesn't inconvenience her. I don't know how she's going to make it through a presidential campaign.'

He knew that Olympia would have done it flaw-lessly, but Megan had tennis, Pilates classes, her trainer, her horses, friends, assorted charities she cared about, and their babies. And now she was pregnant with another one. The thought of a third child exhausted him, and he had much to plan for his future. Olympia was the only one who knew for certain that he was planning to run for President. He wasn't ready to announce it. Megan would love the idea of being First Lady, but seemed to have no idea that it would mean work for her too. 'She wanted another baby. She had been hounding me about it. Two seemed like the right number to me. She doesn't care, she'll just hire more nannies, we already have three, one for each child and a relief. That doesn't look good in the media,' he said, sounding concerned. He always thought of that, about everything he did or said.

'Two was the right number of kids for me too. Bill wanted four, which seemed like too many to me. I wanted to take care of them myself. I never had time to take care of anything but Bill and the kids for the first ten years.' It was precisely the image he would have preferred, although having small children and a beautiful wife in her twenties made him seem young, and he liked that too. It was all about public perception, and what the voters wanted to see in the White House. He would have liked the maturity, elegance, grace, political expertise, and brains of Olympia, but being married to a spectacular-looking young woman hadn't done him any harm either. And she looked fabulous when they went out. In some ways, he thought of Megan and their children as an accessory to him. In his mind, that's what political spouses were all about. And Olympia personified perfection to him.

'Any news from the kids?' he asked her.

'I'm going to call Darcy tonight. We haven't spoken in two weeks. She's having some sort of romance with a young doctor there. He's French, with Doctors Without Borders. She sounds very taken with him, and Josh is still with the same girl on the farm where he works.'

'Oh God, a milkmaid,' Tony teased her and she laughed, but it was actually true. Her father owned one of the largest dairy farms in California, and she was doing an internship at the organic farm where they'd met.

'Every time you say that, I envision her in braids and a dirndl with wooden shoes. She's actually very pretty. She looks like a model, and she has a master's in agricultural sciences from Stanford. I met her on Skype and she seems very sweet. I just hope he doesn't marry anyone too soon.' Her son Josh was only twenty-four years old, but mature for his age. Losing his father at eighteen had made him grow up quickly. She shared all her most private thoughts with Tony, about her children and everything else. She had no one else to talk to. She had shut herself away since Bill's death, and lived in seclusion. Tony felt it was the right thing to do.

'Give them my love when you talk to them. I'm going to try and see you this week, Tuesday, if that works for you.' He tried to come up at least once every week, or more often when he could. It was the high point of her week, and gave her a chance to talk to him, tell him about the book, and hear about what he was doing, which was fascinating. But she had no regrets about having retired from the political scene. She had done all that with Bill.

116

'Tuesday is perfect for me,' she said gently. She had no other plans. She never did now, except working on the book.

'Have you heard from that reporter again? The Phillips woman?' He sounded stern when he asked her.

'No, why would I?'

'I don't know why she bothered you. I think it was all a pretext to ask about me.'

'She said she was a big fan of Bill's, and she was encouraging about the new book,' Olympia said defensively.

'Well, don't let her come back again. You don't need reporters intruding on you.' She agreed with him there, but hadn't found Alix's visit an intrusion. She had liked her, and found her gentle and intelligent, and interested in what Olympia was doing. Tony was far more skeptical about her. 'I'll call you tomorrow, and see you on Tuesday,' he promised, and she hung up with a smile on her face. He was always a comfort to her, and in spite of his warnings, she wasn't worried about Alix. She could handle her. She had asked about Tony's association with the lobbies. Bill had, in fact, mentioned it to Olympia. But that was no one's business now. No one needed to know that Bill felt that Tony was courting certain lobbies, and didn't like it. She wouldn't betray either of them by saying it now, what difference did it make? She knew that Tony was laying the groundwork for his presidential campaign, and whatever he had to do

117

for that to ensure its success seemed fine to Olympia. She wanted to see him in the White House one day. It was his dream, just as it had been Bill's. And she thought Tony would make a great President.

She was still thinking about Tony when she called Darcy on Skype a few minutes later, after Tony's call. It was 6 A.M. in Zimbabwe, and she was happy when Darcy answered. She was loving her time in Africa and had already been there for almost a year, since she graduated from college. She looked healthy and tan when Olympia saw her on the screen. Her hair was in a long dark braid down her back, she had big blue eyes, and she looked like a younger version of her mother. Josh was fair and looked more like his father.

They talked for a little while about what Darcy was doing. They were working on a water system for the village she was assigned to, and planting crops with farm machinery that had been donated from around the world. Olympia was very proud of her, and of Josh too. Both were determined to improve the world and make it a better place. And neither had any interest in politics. Darcy had already decided to stay in Zimbabwe for another year, and Olympia had promised to come and visit her, although she didn't know when. It was a big trip for her.

'So what are you up to, Mom?' Darcy asked her, sounding easy and relaxed.

'I'm still working on the book. It's slow going.

I want to do justice to all of Dad's ideas, so it's going to be a much longer book than the last one.'

'Isn't that depressing for you, Mom?' Darcy looked worried on the screen. But Olympia said it was just the opposite. It still made her happy to write about him. No one could interfere or take him away. 'You should get out more, go to some exhibits, go shopping, have some fun, see friends. You should give a dinner party.' Darcy listed all the things her mother used to enjoy and no longer did.

'Tony is coming up to have dinner with me on Tuesday,' she said, trying to mollify Darcy.

'That's nice of him, Mom, but I wish you did other things too.' Darcy had been saying it for years and Josh agreed.

'I'm working on the book, I see Tony every week, I have Jennifer here with me during the week. What more do I need? Except to see you and Josh once in a while.'

'You need a lot more than that, Mom. You need a life of your own.' Darcy was frustrated. They had the same conversation every time they talked, and it was part of why both her children had left New York. They couldn't watch their mother buried alive anymore, living on her memories of their father and nothing else. She only wanted to be the keeper of the flame. 'You've got to get out more, Mom,' Darcy said, sounding desperate. 'You're too young to give up on life. *Do something.* Charity work, or a sport, or get a dog. Why don't you stop working on the book for a while, and

119

have some fun? When are you coming to see me here?' She knew her mother never would. She no longer had a life, nor wanted one.

'I want to get a better handle on the book before I come to Africa. How's your romance with the French doctor?' she asked, and Darcy appeared discouraged when she answered.

'Fine. But I really worry about you.' She knew her mother was depressed, and Darcy had begun to lose hope that it would ever turn around. She had realized years before that Tony was in love with her mother, but she wouldn't open her heart to that either, and Darcy couldn't understand why she had let him slip through her fingers and marry someone else. Whenever Darcy spoke to her, she felt as though her mother had become a ghost, but Olympia was happy in her cave, clinging to her memories of a man who was gone.

Darcy could no longer imagine what would bring her mother back into the world, and whenever she talked to her brother about it, he said the same thing. She was just going through the motions of living. It made Josh cry sometimes after he talked to her, and Darcy always tried to jolt her mother awake, to no avail. Being with her was so upsetting that neither of them liked to come home to visit anymore. Olympia told herself they were just busy. She didn't realize that her bleak outlook on life had driven them away. She had not only lost her husband, but her children, which made life even lonelier for her.

They talked for a while longer on Skype, and then Darcy said she had to go, she had work to do in the village, and she was going away for the weekend with Jean-Louis. She was having fun with him. He was ten years older than she was. She had told him about her mother, and her father's death, and he agreed that her mother sounded seriously depressed, and he applauded Darcy's healthy decision to get away from her, but it upset Darcy nonetheless. All she wanted was her mother back. It seemed like a dim hope now, dimmer with every passing year. She wondered if it was too late, and all she could do now was save herself. At times, she felt as though both her parents were dead.

Olympia sat looking out the window, thinking about Darcy after they hung up. She knew what her daughter wanted from her, but Darcy was young and had no idea how hard it was to lose someone you loved that much. Olympia couldn't imagine letting go of Bill, even now. Her children had their own lives and paths to pursue, and all she had left was the memory of the happy times before he was killed. And when she saw Tony, he helped keep the memories alive. He was part of that time, and she clung to him like a life raft so she didn't drown. He was all she had left, and the book that she never wanted to finish. She was holding on by a thread.

CHAPTER 7

The trip to Paris to cover the French President's scandalous affair felt light-hearted to both Ben and Alix, and like fun. No one had died, no tragedy had occurred, no one would be shooting at them. The President had made a fool of himself with a young stripper, and the country was incensed at his lack of dignity and good judgment, but she was a pretty girl, no state secrets had been divulged, no harm had come to anyone. The trip was more like a holiday to both of them.

They had to attend an official press conference where he was going to try to explain what had happened, which Alix thought would probably make it all worse. It had been suggested that he might get married, which Alix thought unlikely. He would just flimflam around, while the country and the media shamed and criticized him, and then the waters of disgrace would recede and he'd play with her some more, and find another one, and hopefully be more discreet next time. Sooner or later, life would go back to business as usual, and the stripper would be a dim memory, until he slipped again, as he had before. Men in power seemed to have a penchant for that kind of thing, and women found them irresistible, no matter how unattractive they really were. The story was as old as time. Alix had a hard time taking it seriously. This was going to be a walk in the park for them. Ben was looking forward to it too. He said that Paris was his favorite city, and he was going to take a brief driving trip after he dropped her off with her mother in Provence.

They checked in to the hotel the network had booked for them, had dinner and shared a bottle of wine at a bistro nearby. Alix's French origins showed in the things she ate when she was back in France. She loved kidneys and brains, blood sausage and pigs' feet, and all the food that made Ben wince when she ordered it and explained to him what it was.

He ordered a steak and French fries, and felt very daring having mussels to start with, while she settled on kidneys in mustard sauce and looked delighted. The wine was good, and they didn't have to work until the press conference the next day at the Elysée Palace, where the President was going to attempt to justify his actions and acknowledge the child he had had the year before, with the stripper who had posed nude for a French centerfold, and had a porn video distributed worldwide on the Internet. Local reporters claimed it all would only help her career, which had been negligible anyway. His own children, who were older than she was, had denounced him too. He had never married their mother and they were irate at the idea of his marrying the stripper. As they walked back to the hotel, Ben and Alix laughed about it.

Ben had a live and let live attitude. 'At least he's having a good time, and he's not hurting anyone. I don't know why, but Americans always expect their politicians to be virgins or celibate, and are shocked when they turn out to be human. Europeans are a lot more realistic about the vagaries of their elected officials. Their American counterparts are forced to resign, their wives divorce them, the accused cry publicly on TV and apologize. Here, people are just annoyed she was a stripper and a porn star, and think she should have been classier, which is probably true. But by next week, it'll be all over and no one will care. Can you imagine having this happen in the States? He'd be resigning tomorrow. Instead, he's probably in bed with her tonight, and will meet her for a quickie tomorrow afternoon.' His description of it and assessment of the situation made Alix laugh. He wasn't wrong, and listening to him made her feel French again, or half anyway. She said as much to him, and he reminded her that the Brits could be pretty racy, and had their share of scandals too. 'What made you stay in the States instead of coming back to Europe?' She had grown up in London, her mother lived in France now, and Alix spoke perfect French. She could easily have moved to

England or France. Sometimes she wondered about it herself, and why she hadn't.

'I went to college in the States, I had a baby there, I got a good job right out of college, which I couldn't have done as easily here. And it turned into a career I couldn't have had, or not as quickly, in Britain or France. You have to put in a lot of years before they take you seriously in Europe. America has always been wonderful about giving young people a chance, and I got a green card eventually from marrying Faye's father, which was like gold. And I have an American daughter. There seemed to be good reasons for me to stay, so I did. And it was exciting, and I knew my mother wanted to go back to her own roots then, and I didn't want to be alone in Paris, or in Provence with her.'

'So you opted to be alone in New York. I think I'd have gone to Paris instead. I've always loved it here. I think it's the most beautiful city in the world.' He was happy as he looked around him.

'So do I,' she said. It was still light at ten P.M. in April, the sky was slowly filling with stars, the bridges leading across the Seine were brightly lit, and the Eiffel Tower was sparkling on the hour. It looked like a movie set, and always warmed her heart being there. Ben thought she was a lucky woman and liked being in Paris with her. 'Faye says she wants to live here one day, but if she goes to law school in the States, it's unlikely. It's hard to decide where to be and where to live if you have a choice of nationalities. I always felt torn between my father being British and my mother French. I might have stayed in London if my father were still alive when I grew up. I like it there too.'

'It's an exciting city, but Paris is special,' he said, under its spell.

Being in Paris distracted them both from the realities of their jobs and the death threat she had received and would have to face again when she went back to the States. But in the warm night, as they strolled to their hotel, all was well with the world, and there was something beautiful everywhere they looked.

They were staying at a small business hotel, and had decent rooms. They said good night in the hallway and agreed to meet for breakfast in the lobby the next day. Alix lay on her bed thinking about where they'd been and everything they'd been doing in the past few weeks. She wondered when the story about the Vice President would break, when the CIA would give them the green light, after they had conducted their own investigation. She was glad they had some peaceful time in France before that happened. Breaking the story about the Vice President was going to be a major coup for her. She fell asleep thinking about it, and woke up the next morning before her alarm. She was in the lobby reading *Le Figaro* and drinking café au lait when Ben came downstairs and helped himself to two pains au chocolat and a brioche that tasted homemade, but were actually baked in a bakery nearby and delivered to the hotel every morning.

They took a cab to the Elysée Palace on the Faubourg St-Honoré, and filed in with a hundred members of the press who were admitted for the press conference. There was a respectful silence when the President walked in a few minutes later and addressed them. He made a brief statement, which explained, but did not apologize for, his recent indiscretion, and he assured the French and international press that he had every respect for the office of the President. And he did not promise it wouldn't happen again, which an American would have, and then done it anyway the next time an irresistibly pretty young woman crossed his path. It seemed more like an obligatory formality than a sincere confession. He took a few questions from selected members of the group and ignored the others, and Alix suspected he had made a deal in advance for whose questions he would take. And then he thanked them for coming and left the podium, and everyone shuffled out, grumbling at the uselessness of it, and laughing. One of them said to the others, 'See you next time,' and the others chuckled. It had been a formality and nothing more, and no one really cared who he slept with. If the porn video hadn't been circulated, probably nothing would have been said about his affair. Fortunately, he wasn't in the video. She had supposedly made it five years before, in her teens.

'Well, that's that,' Alix said easily as they stood on the most elegant shopping street in Paris, other than the Avenue Montaigne. She wanted to shop for Faye, but not here. They walked for a while, and she suggested a bistro on the Left Bank for lunch, where she ate another startling assortment of food that Ben said he would never touch, blood sausage among them, and tripe, even worse.

'Remind me never to ask you to cook a French dinner for me,' he said solemnly and she laughed, although she had suggested a dish for him made of duck and mashed potatoes called hachis parmentier, and he loved it. But anything else she described on the menu she translated for him sounded alarming. They had reservations at a fish restaurant she had recommended on the Avenue George V for that night. There was already a holiday atmosphere between them, and they were leaving for Provence in the morning. They were the first days off she had taken in months, and Ben too, since they were always assigned together and joined at the hip.

They'd sent in their feed from the presidential press conference, and Felix sent them a funny email about it and wished them a good vacation. He said there was no further news about Tony Clark, or from the CIA, and Alix was relieved. She didn't want to think about it for the next few days. She wanted to enjoy her time off without interruption and frantic calls from Felix. She hoped no crisis would occur in Europe for several days, so they wouldn't be dragged into service to report on it. She was really looking forward to the days in Provence with her mother, and to introducing her to the work partner she had told her so much about for the past four years. They had never met, and Ben was never seen on-screen since he was behind the camera. But her mother knew she liked working with him, and that he was an ex–Navy SEAL, which made Isabelle feel that her daughter was safer when they were in a war zone. At least Ben could protect her.

They walked around Paris all afternoon, much to Ben's delight, and sat on a bench at the Tuileries, looking at the Louvre, and dinner was excellent that night. It had been a perfect day in Paris. They talked on the drive south about their childhoods, which they rarely did. His had been very American and more mundane, in Michigan. Hers seemed more interesting to him, in London, but she said it wasn't. Being a kid seemed pretty similar to her, wherever you were, she commented, and he disagreed.

'Not if you're eating brains and blood sausage instead of a Big Mac,' he said, making a face and she laughed at him.

'Aside from that, it's the same,' she insisted, 'except that I didn't have a father, because he was as crazy as we are, and got himself blown to smith-ereens in Northern Ireland by the IRA.'

'So why did you go into this line of work? You'd think that would have taught you something.' He was puzzled by what she said.

'I wanted to be like him, smart and brave and reporting the news from scary places. It sounded like a hero's life to me, especially for a woman. I couldn't see myself as a writer or a poet, or a teacher or a secretary. That all sounded so boring, and I wanted to see the world, just like him.'

'What did your mother say?' He guessed that she must have objected, but he was surprised when Alix shrugged in a very French way. She seemed more French here.

'My mother just said to do whatever I wanted. She said working is a lot more fun if you love what you're doing, and she was right. She was a pattern maker in a French couture house before she married my father, and she didn't love it. That's complicated work, but she made beautiful clothes for me when I was a little kid, and for Faye. I was the best-dressed child at school, and then we moved and I went to a school where you had to wear a uniform and I hated it. But she always made my party dresses, and my really nice clothes, before I left for college. She worked for Saint Laurent,' she said proudly, and he was impressed.

They stopped for lunch at a roadside restaurant, and reached Provence in the late afternoon. She directed him down a long country road outside of town, and told him which turns to take, and then told him to stop in the driveway of a neat house that was freshly painted yellow with white shutters, and had a colorful garden. Her mother heard a car stop, and came out on the porch smiling and waved to them. She had gray hair pulled back in a ponytail, and other than that she looked like Alix and was wearing jeans and a bright pink sweater and ballerina flats. She looked youthful and still had a good figure. Alix had said she rode her bike everywhere and almost never used her car, except in bad weather.

As soon as Alix stepped out of their rented car, mother and daughter put their arms around each other, and her mother beamed at her with pleasure and then smiled at Ben. She held out a hand to him and introduced herself and invited him into the house. She spoke English with a British accent after living in London for so long and being married to an Englishman, and she spoke it fluently. Ben followed both women inside to a cozy living room with fine old country furniture, a big fireplace, and beyond it a big rustic kitchen, where they sat down and she made them all tea. She put Ben at ease immediately, and said she had made a cassoulet for them, which was a kind of French stew with beans.

'It's okay, there's nothing scary in it,' Alix reassured him and he looked embarrassed. He was planning to spend the night with them, which her mother thought was the least they could do, and leave the next day.

He went outside after their tea, and wandered around the garden and the neighborhood. Isabelle had an herb garden she was very proud of and showed it to him, and a large cage in the back where she kept chickens that she said laid eggs every day.

'My grandmother had chickens when I was a kid,' he said, amused. He felt like a child again, being there, and Alix took him into town to show it to him before the shops closed at seven, and then they came back and had dinner with her mother. He had bought an excellent bottle of wine in town, and Isabelle was very pleased with it. She liked him, and they sat at the table and talked until midnight. Alix was surprised to discover that he was very knowledgeable about French and Italian art, and Isabelle was impressed by him too. She said he was a nice boy when they cleaned the kitchen after dinner, and he went out for a stroll in the warm night air, when Isabelle wouldn't let him help in the kitchen.

They all went upstairs to bed when he came back. The house had four comfortable bedrooms, and Alix's mother had turned one of them into a sewing room. She did beautiful embroidered linens she gave away as gifts, 'just to keep her hand in,' she said. She sent boxes of them to Alix and Faye.

Isabelle was already in the kitchen when Alix came downstairs the next morning, and Ben appeared a few minutes later, showered and freshly shaved, in jeans with a white shirt. She served them warm croissants with homemade jam, which Alix pointed out she had only learned to make recently. But Isabelle loved her home, and doing domestic things there. She had friends in to dinner regularly. She enjoyed a nice life. And there was a man, Gabriel, she spent time with, a local doctor she had known for many years. He had been widowed for as long as she had, and was a few years older. Alix had met him and liked him, and was happy to know her mother wasn't alone, and had friends and a man in her life. She and Gabriel had discussed living together and decided not to, but often spent weekends together, and he kept a sailboat on the coast, an hour or two away.

Isabelle kissed Ben warmly on both cheeks when he left, and told him to call if he had any problem. He was coming back in three days after he went exploring. He was hoping to get down the coast all the way to Nice, and to stop at several châteaux Alix had mentioned to him. He was looking forward to the adventure, as much as she was to being with her mother. It was the most time off they'd had in a year.

'He's a good man,' her mother commented after he drove away in the rented car, and she gazed searchingly at her daughter. 'No romantic interest?' Alix shook her head in answer. She liked him, but she didn't want to have a relationship with him. Who had time? And it would spoil things between them.

'I like him a lot, and we work well together. Why ruin that?' Alix said matter-of-factly.

'Has he ever been married?' Isabelle was curious about him.

'Yes, he's divorced. No kids. Jobs like ours, and

being a Navy SEAL, don't give you time for romance.' Isabelle already knew that, and that Alix had no faith in men sticking around since her father had died when she was a child, and Faye's father three months after they married. She was leery of forming permanent attachments, so had picked a line of work that didn't allow them. Isabelle was afraid she'd regret it one day, and she suspected Alix used her work to fill the void now without Faye.

'Well, I like him, and he's very attractive. It seems a waste to have someone like that so close at hand and not do anything about it.' Isabelle was mischievous as she said it.

'If it didn't work out, it would be a mess at work. This is better, for both of us. He's not interested either,' Alix assured her.

'You young people today don't seem to want relationships. No one gets married, particularly if they have children. It's all a little backward, isn't it? And it must get lonely.'

'It does at times,' Alix admitted, and she smiled at the term 'young people.' She was turning forty in a year, and Ben was three years older than she was. They were no longer kids, and the die had been cast for both of them. She couldn't see herself getting married again and neither could he, from what he'd said. He always said that his marriage had ended badly, and hers had barely existed, except to legitimize Faye's birth. She could hardly remember her husband now, nineteen years later.

'Maybe my generation doesn't have the faith in marriage yours did. We saw too many end badly, our parents' and our own.'

'Your father and I had a very good marriage,' Isabelle said staunchly. She had always said that to Alix, but she had never remarried either, and didn't seem to feel the need.

They had a lunch of bread and cheese and local salami with a bottle of wine at a table in the garden, and then they biked into town together, and Alix looked over at her mother and smiled. She loved being with her, it made her realize how seldom she had fun anymore, since she was always working. That was the difference in France. Quality of life was so important, and in the States, it was all about work and your career. There were merits to both, but it was so nice to be here and savor the moments together.

They talked and read at night, and her mother did her embroidery. Her friends dropped by to say hello to Alix and bring her little gifts, mostly things they had made or grown. Her mother's friend Gabriel came by and invited them to dinner at an excellent restaurant, and she felt as though someone had fast-forwarded the film when she saw Ben drive up to the house on their last night. He looked tanned and relaxed and said he had had a wonderful time, eating at local restaurants and visiting churches and châteaux. Isabelle made a feast for them that night, and invited Gabriel to join them, and Alix loved seeing how well they got

135

along and that they laughed a lot. They were good natured and funny. Gabriel had a great sense of humor and told amusing stories. He was still practicing medicine at sixty-four, and Isabelle said he was an excellent doctor. It was a perfect evening, and after Gabriel left and Ben had gone to bed, Alix told her mother how much she had enjoyed the time with her.

'You should try to come back more often. You always have a home here,' she said tenderly and hugged her daughter before they went upstairs arm in arm and Alix kissed her outside her bedroom. She knew she would remember this visit for a long time. Isabelle didn't mention Ben again as a possible romance for her, if that wasn't what Alix wanted, but Alix could see how much her mother liked him, and why. He was such a kind man, and away from work, he was funny and easygoing too. Isabelle had commented that it was odd that he'd never had children, when she talked to Alix about him, and she said that some people didn't want them, and if not, it was just as well they didn't have them. And if his marriage had ended badly, it was best that they hadn't had kids, this way he didn't have to see his ex-wife again, instead of battling with each other while a child grew up with parents who hated each other. Children weren't for everyone.

It was painful saying goodbye to her mother the next day after they had breakfast in the kitchen. Ben carried their bags down and put them in the car, and came back to thank Isabelle for her hospitality, and she gave him a warm hug and kissed him on both cheeks. 'Keep her out of trouble,' she said, glancing at Alix.

'Don't worry, I do.' And then he went to wait for her in the car so she could be alone with her mother to say goodbye.

Alix found it hard to leave her, she always did. Her mother was just old enough now at sixty-two for Alix to worry about her.

'I'll try to come back soon,' she promised, but they both knew it might not happen, given the demands of her career.

'I'll be here whenever you want to come home. And Faye promised to come over this summer. She can stay as long as she wants,' and then she held Alix in her arms for a long moment, as tears rolled down their cheeks.

'I love you, Maman,' Alix whispered. Her mother nodded, unable to speak for a moment, and then smiled through her tears and looked proudly at her daughter.

'I love you too, be safe,' she whispered as Alix kissed her again, hugged her one more time, and then tore herself away and ran to the car where Ben was waiting. She waved for as long as she could see her mother as they drove away, and tears were still running down her cheeks as they drove up the road, and Ben gently patted her hand.

'What a terrific woman,' he said, happy to have met her. It gave him new insights into the woman he worked with. Despite the insanity of their job, she was a whole person with a solid base, and a mother who loved her and knew her and accepted her, and allowed her to be herself. It seemed like a wonderful way to grow up, and he wished he had a mother like her. Alix was a lucky woman, and he hoped he'd see Isabelle again. 'Thank you for introducing me to her, and letting me stay there. I didn't want to intrude on your time with her.'

'She liked you,' Alix said, wiping her eyes and blowing her nose on a delicately embroidered hand-kerchief her mother had given her, with lily of the valley on it and her initials in fine silver thread. Her needlework was as beautiful as ever. 'She couldn't understand why we're not involved with each other.' He didn't tell her that sometimes he couldn't either, but it was simpler this way, and like Alix, he didn't want to screw up what they had.

'That sounds very French,' he said, smiling at her. 'I liked her friend Gabriel. They're cute together.' Alix nodded, and thought the same thing.

'French people are never too old for love. There's a saying here, "Love has no age," *L'amour n'a pas d'âge*. Maybe they're right. I think I'll save that for when I'm old. I'm too busy now.' What she said was true, and he thought it was too bad that Alix felt that way. She had a lot to offer a man, if she was willing, and she deserved to have a full life. They both did. They just didn't have time to devote to another person full-time.

'You'll be as beautiful as she is at her age. You two look like sisters.'

'Thank you for that,' she said, and smiled at him.

Everything seemed more human here. It made her think she might want to come back to live in France one day, maybe when she retired, but that was light-years away.

They rode along in silence for a while, and when they got back to Paris, she was sorry to see the brief holiday end. It had been everything she had hoped it would be, and she was glad Ben had been there, and met her mother. It made them seem more like real friends now, not just two people assigned to a job as a team.

CHAPTER 8

When Tony came to have dinner with Olympia on Tuesday, her housekeeper stayed to serve them. And his Secret Service men ate in the kitchen. Tony and Olympia had crab salad, which she knew he loved, steak for him afterward, and they drank champagne. It always felt festive when he came to dine with her, and she tried to serve him what he liked to eat. He often complained that Megan wanted to go out every night, and hated staying home with him. If the cook was off, they went to a restaurant in Washington. That was the trouble with being married to a girl her age. Even having babies hadn't slowed her down. So Olympia tried to provide a peaceful private haven for him when he came to New York, just as he tried to make her feel cared for and protected, like Bill used to do. But the two men were very different.

Bill had always encouraged her to overcome her natural shyness and step out into the world. Tony urged her to stay home, out of sight, away from prying eyes, and told her that after the trauma she'd experienced when Bill was shot standing next to her, he would understand if she never left the house again. It gave her permission not to, and after he had said it often enough, she hardly ever did. She was more comfortable at home anyway, with familiar things around her, and she couldn't bear the curiosity of strangers, and sympathetic whispers once they recognized her, so she never went out anymore, even with him. She hadn't even seen her brother in Connecticut and his family in a year. He was too busy to visit her, and she didn't make the effort to see them, since they had never been close.

The result was that she existed in isolation, except for Tony's visits to New York, when he came to dinner and sat by the fire with her afterward, telling her about what he was doing, and asking about her progress on the book. He entered her world like a secret garden, where she was hidden away. It was precisely what her children found so upsetting, and Olympia's brother thought so too, although he never came to see her. Olympia's children felt as though their mother had been kidnapped by aliens, and had no idea that Tony was convincing her to become a shut-in, and wanted her to himself. Even Jennifer was worried about her. Now that she was working on the second book, she never even left the house to take a walk and get some air. She stayed in her study with Bill's photos and memorabilia around her, steeped in their lost world.

They had Grand Marnier soufflé for dessert that

night, another of his favorites. Their evenings together were like a fantasy for him, and he always told her he loved her, and would never let anything bad happen to her again, as though he could protect her from real life. But she no longer had a life, except when she saw him. If he couldn't have her, he didn't want anyone else to either, not even her children. And when they pressed her to come out of her shell again, he assured her he thought she was still too fragile and it would be too traumatic for her, and she believed him.

Jennifer thought there was something sinister about his influence over her in total isolation, but she knew how fiercely Olympia trusted and respected him, and she was afraid to challenge what he'd said. She thought the worst possible thing for Olympia was staying shut away like an invalid, and what she needed was to get back in the world again, just as Darcy insisted. But Tony's voice was stronger, closer, and more frequent, he saw Olympia more often than her children, who were too far away. Olympia believed every word he uttered, and accepted it as gospel.

'I'll try to come back, maybe this weekend,' he promised when he left her. 'Megan's in a tennis tournament, and she's having dinner with some of her women friends afterward. She won't care if I come up here for dinner. I'll let you know what works.' Not that it mattered, since she didn't go out anyway. All she needed to do was ask the cook to stay to prepare dinner for them, and pick the menu. He kissed her gently on the forehead, put his arms around her, and held her before he left. Those were the moments she lived for now, knowing that someone cared about her, as she existed in an eternal winter, without human touch or even conversation for days on end, except with him on the phone or with Jennifer about the book. It made Tony even more important to her, and made her even more dependent on him than she might have been otherwise. And her children still thought him a godsend and their mother's only savior and friend.

Darcy often said to Josh that she didn't know what they'd do without him, since she refused to see any of her old friends. If they had been older, and closer to home, Jennifer would have talked to them about it, but she didn't think they were mature enough to understand that their mother was being systematically isolated and controlled, and it was destroying her. She was becoming more disconnected from the world every day. And the key words Tony used when he talked to her were 'fragile,' 'frail,' and 'traumatized' to reinforce the idea that she was. Hearing Olympia repeat it afterward about herself made her assistant want to scream. She didn't know what Tony's game was, or his purpose, but whatever it was, it was a dangerous one for Olympia. It reminded Jennifer of the old movie *Gaslight* with Ingrid Bergman, where her husband had convinced her she was insane. In this case, Tony had convinced Olympia that she was too damaged by her husband's shocking death to face the world again, and it had worked. She believed every word he said, and there was no one to counter it. Jennifer didn't dare say anything against him, and she knew her employer wouldn't have tolerated it.

When he left her house that night, Olympia went back to her desk, to work on the book. She often sat there reminiscing about Bill and looking at old photographs until three or four A.M., and then slept the next day until noon. Jennifer felt helpless to influence her or change it. It was Tony who subtly ruled her life now. She hadn't married him, but instead he owned her. And not only had she lost Bill so shockingly, she'd lost herself as well, and didn't even know it.

The day that Ben and Alix flew back from Paris after their brief vacation, another threat letter arrived for her at the network. Her assistant delivered it to Felix, and he called the CIA to inform them. It was similar to the first one, but slightly more vehement. The letter blamed her for inquiries about the lobbyists, which had continued. The CIA had been doing some digging to follow up on Felix's tip, and someone had attributed the investigation to Alix. The National Clandestine Service officer asked to speak to her, and Felix explained again that she wouldn't be back until the next day, and she had been out of the country for a week. They advised that she not stay at her apartment, and that she would need bodyguards. Felix sent both her and Ben a text, which they received when they landed, urging her to stay with Ben or someone else until further notice. He said the officers were coming to see her again the next day at work. And the FBI had been told to provide protection for her, starting the next day as well.

'Welcome home,' she said, looking unhappy as soon as she read Felix's text. They hadn't even gone through baggage claim yet, and she was already being faced with another threat letter, and couldn't go back to her own apartment. 'I'm really sorry,' she said to Ben. 'I'll talk to them tomorrow. They've got to let me go home.' He had offered to let her stay with him again.

'Not if it's not safe for you,' he said sensibly. 'What's the big deal? I'm happy to have you. It's company for me.' But she wanted to sleep in her own bed, surrounded by her own things, not camp out with him.

'If they give me a bodyguard tomorrow, I don't see why I can't go home,' she complained as they got their bags and went through customs. Neither of them had anything to declare so five minutes later they were on the sidewalk, and then in a cab. She was going to Brooklyn with him. She had just texted Faye to say she had landed and would be staying with Ben again. And Felix had assured her that Faye still had security with her at school, until they knew who the threats were coming from, or they stopped.

'I'm better trained than the FBI guys,' Ben said calmly about bodyguards for Alix.

'Well, I can't move in with you. And besides, I want to go home.'

'You don't like my guest room?' he asked, pretending to be insulted, and she laughed. It was fine, but it wasn't home.

'Thank you for being a good sport for another night,' she said in the cab.

'I like having you there,' he said easily. They stopped to pick up a few groceries, enough to make breakfast, and she was hoping they'd let her go home the next day. She couldn't even unpack at Ben's since she didn't know how long she was staying. She wondered if they had made any discoveries they were going to share with her. More often than not, federal agencies did not share full information with victims, and sometimes none at all.

Typically, the next morning when Officer Pelham came to see her, with two of his colleagues, they had nothing to tell her, or didn't want to. What they wanted was for her to contact Olympia Foster again.

'Why don't you go to see her?' she asked them bluntly, and Pelham pointed out that Alix had already established a rapport with her, and they had a difficult project to suggest. They had been informed that Olympia had dinner regularly with the Vice President at her home, and they wanted her to question him on some delicate subjects, and wear a wire so they could listen from an unmarked van outside.

'Oh God,' Alix said, looking at Ben, who was with them. 'She'll never do it. He's her whole support system now. She trusts him completely. She won't set him up or betray him, and she'll never believe that he's done something wrong. I touched on it lightly and she sprang to his defense immediately. I don't think there's a chance in hell that she'll do it, and why do I have to be the one to convince her?'

'She may think we're trying to frame him.'

'And if she won't do it?'

'Her husband may get blamed for malfeasance along with Clark. This has been going on for a long time. People may think that Foster was part of the plan, even if no one can prove it now. A cloud could hang over him forever, they'll think he's just as much to blame and just as guilty as Clark. They wanted to run on the ticket together.' Alix was silent while she thought about it, and realized it was the only card they had to play with her. As much as Olympia wanted to protect Tony, she wanted to protect her husband's spotless reputation even more. But it was going to be a hard sell to get her to set Tony up with a hidden wire. Alix cringed at the thought, and asking her to do it was going to be difficult at best.

'You want me to ask her this on my own?' Alix asked, hoping that at least one of them would come with her.

'Yes, I do,' Pelham said, looking grim. 'She knows you, you have a better chance with her than we do. We want her to ask him casually about the lobbyists he spends time with, and the Saudis.' It didn't sound casual to Alix, and it wouldn't to Tony either. It seemed like a crazy idea to her, and Olympia was likely to throw her out, and she wouldn't blame her.

'I've only met her once,' she reminded them. 'That's not a lot to trade on.'

'All you can do is ask her, but I was serious about her husband. This could tarnish his reputation forever, by association.' Alix knew that was true. The question was if Olympia would believe her and agree to set Tony up over dinner. The CIA left half an hour later, and she sat in her office with Ben and Felix.

'Why do I get to do all the dirty work here?' she said. The vacation was definitely over, and they had told her she couldn't go home, unless she had a bodyguard. They were willing to have the FBI provide security for her or she could hire her own, but she had to have protection because of the threats she was getting. And Faye still had an FBI agent with her at Duke. And now Alix had to set up a perfectly nice woman, and coerce her into cooperating with the CIA against the man she had considered to be her best friend, her only friend, for the past six years. It was a miserable situation.

Alix called Olympia after Felix and Ben went

back to their offices. She didn't want an audience when she called. Jennifer answered, and Alix asked to speak to Olympia, and was relieved when the senator's widow came on the line. Jennifer sounded suspicious of her and was fiercely protective.

'I'm sorry to disturb you,' Alix said to Olympia in an apologetic tone. 'I was wondering if I could come and talk to you for a few minutes.'

'Now?' Olympia was startled. She couldn't imagine what Alix wanted and she remembered Tony's warnings.

'Whenever it's convenient for you, but soon.' There was a sense of urgency in Alix's voice that telegraphed to Olympia that it was important.

'Is something wrong?' She was worried.

'There could be,' Alix said honestly. 'I think we should talk. I have some information I think you'll want.' Alix's stomach turned over as she said it, and she knew Olympia's would too when she heard. She hated to put her through it, but now she had no choice. Olympia could hear it from Alix or the CIA, and Alix would be gentler.

'You can come now, if you want,' Olympia said thoughtfully. She was wondering if she should warn Tony that Alix was coming back, but something told her not to. She could always tell him later, if it had anything to do with him. After she hung up, she told Jennifer that Alix was coming by.

'Do you think that's a good idea?' Jennifer asked her, concerned.

'Yes, I do,' Olympia answered in a firm voice.

149

Twenty minutes later, Alix was there. Felix had sent one of the security guards from the network with her, and he waited outside.

Jennifer let her in and escorted her up the stairs to Olympia's office. She was sitting in one of the big comfortable chairs and stood up when Alix walked in. The two women exchanged a long, serious look and said very little until Jennifer left the room. Olympia didn't offer her coffee, and waited to hear why she'd come. They sat down facing each other, and Alix took a breath before she explained.

'I'm not sure where to start. The last time I came to see you, I asked you about the Vice President and his relationship with lobbyists. The question had been raised by some of our sources, but now it's a lot more than that. The CIA have gotten involved and conducted their own investigation, and I'm fairly certain he's going to be accused of taking large sums of money from at least one of the most important lobbies, and two or three lobbyists, possibly to start building his campaign fund, in exchange for favors and bills he could get passed if he wins. Now there are at least two people willing to testify against him in exchange for immunity. Apparently he's been doing it for a long time, even before Senator Foster died. He stopped for a while, but now there are large amounts involved, and he's doing it again.' Alix looked serious as she explained it to her, and Olympia was visibly upset by what she heard. 'I wanted to tell you myself.'

'I appreciate that. But are you sure? That doesn't sound like him.' Olympia was paler than usual, and Alix's palms were sweating. She hated to have to tell her all of it. 'Could it be someone trying to set him up?'

'Anything is possible, but the CIA Clandestine Service is involved. I don't think they make mistakes, or not very often. And there's more. He's involved with the Saudis, and has been for years, he's taking bribes on oil deals he can help place for them. And he's done that for a long time as well. He's involved with four very important Saudis, he's met with them in Tehran and Dubai. This is going to be a very big deal when it comes out.' Olympia looked sick as she listened, and averted her eyes. Alix couldn't tell if this was news to her or not, but she was obviously distressed.

'Why are you telling me now? And why you and not the CIA?' She was frightened and suspicious. She no longer knew who to trust.

'The CIA operations officer in charge asked me to talk to you. Did Senator Foster know? Did he suspect? Did he ever say anything to Vice President Clark about it? I'm not here for a story, I'm here because I don't want to see your husband's reputation tarnished. I think he was an incredible man. The CIA will want to talk to you, but they wanted me to talk to you first, informally. I think we're all hoping that Senator Foster knew nothing about it. No one wants to see your husband implicated or accused of the Vice President's crimes.' Olympia sat silent for a long time, staring into the fireplace, as though listening to her husband talking to her, and then she met Alix's eyes. She was clearly agonized and afraid. She had just made a conscious decision to be honest with Alix, for Bill's sake. Alix had done her job well and gotten the point across, that Bill Foster's flawless reputation was at stake.

'Yes, he knew,' she said in a barely audible voice. 'Not everything you just told me, but some of it. We talked about it. He was furious with Tony for making friends with the lobbyists. Tony said it was just social, but Bill didn't like the way it looked, or would look if it came out. He told him to back away from them. They had a terrible argument about it, and then Bill heard he was making trips to meet the Saudis. Tony said he wasn't taking money from them, he was just facilitating things for them, in exchange for favors later on.' It was precisely the kind of arrangement Bill hated. Bill never sold out to anyone, and didn't make deals like that. And he didn't want Tony to either. He said Tony didn't realize how dangerous it was and could cost them the election if it came out.

'Tony Clark is a dealmaker and he's brilliant at it. Bill thought too much so for his own good. He didn't want any secrets in their past when they ran as their party's nominees for President and Vice President.'

'Reliable sources say that Tony Clark was paid huge amounts of money that were deposited in a Swiss bank for him, in a numbered account,' Alix added. 'The CIA is looking into it, and I have no idea what they've found out. But if it's true, and he did that, he's going to take Bill down with him, or maybe even sell him out and blame him to save his own hide. He's involved with at least one lobbyist who has admitted buying him, and a group of Saudis who are paying him a fortune. Your husband's reputation is on the line. Only you can protect him now by exposing what you know about Tony Clark.' Alix hadn't minced words, and Olympia was shocked. The full force of what Alix had said had hit her. And she decided she would tell her what no one had ever suspected or known about Clark.

Olympia spoke in a hoarse voice, filled with emotion. 'Two weeks before he died, Bill knew enough about it, but not all of it, to tell Tony he wouldn't run with him. They were best friends, but he said Tony was dirty and he wanted no part of it. It would have destroyed their campaign. He was going to announce his separation from him. Tony said he'd run against him for the nomination, but he didn't have the political clout to do that. Bill did, but Tony didn't. He needed Bill to run. Bill was sick over it, but he told him there was no way he wanted to run with him as Vice President if Bill got the nomination. Bill was convinced Tony had sold out. Tony denied it. But Bill finally had evidence, I don't know what it was. Tony tried to convince him to let him run with him anyway, but he was tainted. It was a terrible decision for Bill to have to make. If any of this had come out, Bill would have gone down with him.

'Bill never had a chance to announce the separation. Tony had asked Bill to reconsider. Bill didn't change his mind, but he was killed before he could announce it. He was going to say they were separating due to different personal opinions, not expose him. I didn't want to tell you when you asked me because Tony has been wonderful to me, and my children, since Bill died. I wouldn't have survived it without him. And I didn't think lobbyists were still an issue. It was in the past, and I assumed he was clean now since he's the Vice President, and wants to run for President next time. I didn't think he'd take the chance to continue those activities. And maybe he hasn't, maybe the CIA and the informants are wrong and they've unearthed his mistakes from the past. But if they're not wrong, I can't let him take Bill down, not now, when Bill isn't here to defend himself.

'Bill loved him, in spite of his bad decisions. He didn't want to run with him, but he cared about him deeply, and so do I. He's a wonderful man, but he can't destroy Bill's reputation now, after everything my husband worked so hard to build. This is exactly what he was afraid of happening, before he died, and why he told Tony he wouldn't run with him. But Bill was loyal to him till the end, and Tony is the best friend I have. What will happen to him if all of this, or even some of it, is true?' she asked with a look of deep concern for Tony Clark. But her deepest loyalty and allegiance were to the man she had been married to. She would let nothing touch him now.

'I'm only guessing, but I assume he'll be removed from office, and he could go to prison. These are serious crimes,' Alix answered her. 'How did your husband find out?'

'I don't know. I think he found out by accident. An informant, a rumor. He had no legal proof, but enough evidence to convince him it was true. He had no doubt. But Tony has no idea that Bill told me any of it. I still find it hard to believe. Tony is such a decent man.' And convincing too, Alix thought but didn't say.

'They were almost like brothers, they had been best friends since they were kids. But Bill couldn't take the chance that Tony was taking bribes, and he was sure he was. Money is very important to Tony, much more than it was to Bill. And Bill had nothing to do with what Tony did. My husband was a very principled man.'

'I know,' Alix said quietly.

'I never said anything because I didn't see the point of damaging Tony's career now. I had no idea that he actually has taken bribes and made deals with the Saudis and is even more deeply involved. What is the CIA going to do?'

'You'll have to ask them, I honestly don't know,' Alix answered, and then took a breath and went on. 'But they want your help now.'

'How?' Olympia looked panicked. 'What do they want?' The thought of betraying Tony made her feel sick, but allowing him to tarnish Bill's reputation by association broke her heart. She couldn't let that happen.

'They know he comes to see you frequently for dinner. They want you to have him here, and wear a wire, ask him pertinent questions, and see what he says. They'll be outside listening, in a truck.' Alix didn't envy her that task, and she felt sorry for her, having to betray a friend who meant as much to her as Tony did. Olympia's eyes filled with tears and her whole body seemed to sag. There were tears rolling down her cheeks when she looked at Alix again. She wasn't afraid, she was crushed.

'They want me to set him up,' Olympia said and Alix nodded confirmation. There was no other way to put it. 'But Tony doesn't know that I knew. Bill didn't want to drag me into it. He never told Tony, but Bill used to tell me everything. I knew he had told Tony it was over, but since Bill never got a chance to announce it publicly, I think he assumes Bill kept it to himself.'

'What if you told him you came across some papers of your husband's, while doing research for the book? You could hint at the lobbies and the Arabs, or even the senator's decision not to run with him, and see what the Vice President says. You don't have to accuse him or be blunt, don't put yourself in any kind of danger, but you could act confused about what you found and see how he responds. He'll probably deny it and try to minimize it. I doubt that he'll confess to you, but the Clandestine Service wants to see what he says. In the world as it is today, they think he's a threat to national security, and they want your help. I hate to say it, but if I were you, I would do it to help Bill.' She took the liberty of calling the late senator by his first name, but Olympia didn't seem to mind.

'I have no other choice,' Olympia said with a look of despair. She had to sacrifice her best friend out of loyalty to her husband, but there was no question in her mind of where her loyalties lay. They had always been with Bill and still were. She was heartbroken to hear what Tony had been foolish enough to do. Bill had told his wife at the time that Tony had become the kind of friend that he could no longer afford, and it nearly broke his heart. And now it was breaking hers, again. His betrayal was unforgivable. But there was no other way, and she knew that Bill would have expected it of her, and done it himself with proof of the bribes. Tony had played a very dangerous game, and was about to lose big-time. His political career would be over, and his dreams of the presidency. It had all been within reach and he had thrown it away and would probably go to jail. Olympia was devastated for him. 'How much money do you think is involved?' she asked Alix.

'I have no idea. Billions? Or certainly millions. They're not small amounts.'

'Bill always worried about where Tony's money

came from. He made a lot in a short time and always said he did well with his investments.' But they hadn't been investments, they were bribes, on a massive scale.

'I'm sorry I had to tell you all this, Mrs Foster. I know it's got to be incredibly hard.' Olympia nodded silently for a minute and then looked at her again.

'Thank you for coming to see me. I'd rather have heard it from you than from the CIA. I know you respected my husband.' She could sense it, and she was right. And Alix admired her too, as a loyal and honorable woman.

'I think the CIA will contact you now,' Alix said quietly. 'They'll want to know if you're willing to wear the wire the next time you see Tony Clark. It's up to you.'

'I have to think about it,' she said in a ragged voice. 'I don't know if I can pull it off. He knows me too well. Why can't they get someone else to do it?'

'Because he knows you and trusts you. He'll be more honest with you. I'm sure he won't tell you everything, he can't afford to. But he might betray himself if you tell him you found papers among your husband's things that mention the lobbyists and some Arab deals. And he won't know what you've found, so he'll have to bluff his way through, but he might tip his hand, or implicate himself. I think that's what they're hoping.'

'I wish I didn't have to do it.' Alix's heart went

out to her. 'He's coming here for dinner, probably on Saturday,' she said mournfully, and after what she knew now, it would be the last time. He should never have continued to put Bill's reputation at risk. She had incorrectly assumed that whatever deals he had made were a thing of the past, not that he was continuing. He had sworn to Bill there was no money involved, and he was trading favors, which was bad enough. This was infinitely worse.

'Are you going to wear the wire?' Alix asked her again, and Olympia looked shaken and unsure.

'I have to think about it,' she repeated. 'Tell them I'll let them know.' Alix handed her Pelham's card, and told her to get in touch with them directly. She had delivered their message. It was all she could do. The rest was up to Olympia and the CIA. Alix was off the hook, and Olympia Foster was on it, but so was Bill. And Olympia had lost her only friend. Alix felt desperately sorry for her.

CHAPTER 9

The following day, Alix got another threat in the mail at the network. It was the same theme as the first two. If she didn't stop meddling in politics and stay away, someone would kill her. It was simple and clear. But she had made no inquiries about Clark and the lobbyists in weeks. Why were they still threatening? She talked to John Pelham about it, and he assured her they had gone underground with their investigation. But the threats were continuing. What else were they hiding or afraid she would expose? And who was writing the letters?

Faye had three shifts of bodyguards per day at Duke, and Alix had at least one shift now too, and was still staying at Ben's, and longing to go back to her apartment. She could only go there with the bodyguard to pick up clothes and take them to Ben's. And she had insisted that she didn't need security when she was with Ben. As an ex–Navy SEAL, Ben had a license to carry a concealed weapon and he knew how to use it. He carried a gun now when he went out alone with her, or brought her to work in the morning. It made her uneasy just knowing he had it on him, especially at night in his apartment. She used the bodyguard at work in case someone showed up at the network.

By then, Olympia had contacted Pelham, and agreed to wear the wire when Tony came to dinner on Saturday night, as she had thought he would. Alix had been sure that she would do it, for Bill's sake. Olympia had met with the Clandestine team to brief her on what she needed to say and ask him. She was going to play heavily on her innocence, and follow their script to the letter. She felt like a monster, but if Tony were guilty it would hurt Bill. She wondered if he'd really go to prison. It seemed hard to believe, and she knew her children would be devastated too. He was their idol, and he had a young wife who was pregnant again. Everyone was going to get hurt because of what he'd done, even innocent children, like his two very young ones, and even his unborn baby. Instead of being there for them and Megan, he would be in prison, probably for a long time.

Felix decided he wanted Alix and Ben out of town again by the end of the week. With the threats against her, it was too stressful for her and everyone else to keep her in New York. Ben never let her out of his sight now, except in the bathroom. He was her own private bodyguard. And an agent of the FBI was at her disposal whenever she needed him.

There had been a massive flood in New Orleans when a levee broke again. The damage wasn't as bad as after Hurricane Katrina, but the city had been declared a federal disaster area in a state of emergency, and Felix decided he'd rather have Alix there than in New York. Things were getting too tense over Tony Clark.

After talking to Felix, the CIA agreed to let her leave town, as long as they could reach her, and they suggested that Ben remain armed. Olympia Foster was being cooperative with them, although she was terrified of the dinner with Tony, and wearing the wire. The CIA had promised her that nothing dramatic would happen at dinner. She would make a few casual comments and see what they elicited from him. Probably a few vague responses and lies. The panic would come later, after he left her, when he tried to figure out where the leak was and how bad. He would never suspect Olympia of cooperating with the CIA to ensnare him. And by the time he knew, they would arrest him and he'd be in jail. They were already poised with a secret grand jury waiting to hear evidence to indict him, and a judge to sign a warrant at any hour. All the pieces of the machinery of justice were in place, depending on what he said on Saturday night, and did after he left. Clark had no idea what was coming, the National Clandestine Service was sure of that. And the Director of National Intelligence was aware of the situation too. Nothing like it had ever happened with a Vice President before.

★ ★ ★

Ben and Alix got on a plane to New Orleans on Thursday morning. She was relieved to get out of town, and so was he. The tension had become unbearable, waiting for the dinner to happen, Olympia to play her role, see how Clark would respond, and what he would do after that. And the death threats against Alix were the last straw. She was delighted to get away and be on assignment, even to a flood. They checked in to a motel at the airport, rented a car, then got as close to the flooded area of the city as they could and got into a police boat wearing their press badges. Ben had the videocam rolling the entire time to show the damaged areas, and they stopped to pick up people wading through the water or swimming, and several large dogs, along the way. It was a long, grueling night, and they were both exhausted and wet, despite their high boots and rain gear, when they got back to the motel at four A.M.

They were up again at seven and dressed by eight the next day. Alix turned on the TV, while Ben went to get coffee at a nearby Starbucks, and he returned with cappuccino and cinnamon rolls for both of them, which they ate while watching the news on TV, when it was suddenly interrupted by a news bulletin from North Carolina. The scene on the screen was one of chaos, with students running and screaming, the sound of gunshots ringing out as the cellphone video they were watching danced crazily, while the person holding it ducked behind some form of obstruction with

163

their arm still held out and the video rolling. It only took a second to realize what was happening. It was a campus shooting, and the announcer and a band of text across the screen said that fourteen students had been killed in the first few minutes and twenty-two injured, three more students and one teacher had died on the way to hospitals, and the shooter had committed suicide. There were a total of nineteen dead so far, and it had happened half an hour earlier at Duke University.

News teams were on the scene by then, as students and professors hugged each other and cried. They ran the video again as Ben and Alix watched in silent horror. What if Faye had been at the scene? Alix set her cup down on the table and stared at the screen with a sense of panic, as the announcer said that all that was known of the shooter was that he had left the university for reasons of psychiatric disability six months before, had been hospitalized briefly, released, and returned to the school to work as a maintenance man on the grounds. It was a classic scenario of a young person who had exhibited mental problems for a long time, been identified, and then slipped through everyone's fingers. A former fellow classmate said he had talked about building a bomb in his apartment from instructions he got on the Internet, and the classmate had thought he was kidding, so he never reported it to anyone. His parents had not been reached yet for comment, and among those he had shot was his former girlfriend, who was in critical condition at a local hospital. Alix started calling Faye immediately on her cellphone. It kept ringing and no one answered. What if she was dead?

Alix's terror was palpable as she rambled to Ben. 'It's always so goddamn obvious. Everyone knows how crazy they are, and they don't do anything about it, and then suddenly nineteen people are dead and twenty-two injured and . . .' She stopped talking as she watched a young girl being carried on a stretcher with paramedics running beside her. She was crying and screaming and her face was covered with blood, and it took Alix only an instant to realize that the face covered with blood was her daughter's. She saw them put the stretcher in the ambulance, which took off at high speed with siren screaming as they switched to another scene of students hugging each other and crying. Alix was on her feet instantly, looking terrified. 'Oh my God! . . . Oh my God, Ben . . . that was Faye!' Suddenly the campus tragedy they'd been watching had a whole new meaning. She looked at Ben with wild eyes, not sure what to do next. 'I've gotta go . . . oh God, Ben, that was Faye!' Ben grabbed her by the shoulders to try to slow her down and calm her.

'She's alive. You just saw her. She's okay.' He tried to get through the haze that had engulfed Alix when she saw her child's face on the screen. Only a mother would have recognized her, her face was so covered in blood. And where was the FBI bodyguard? 'We'll call the hospitals right now,' he reassured her, as Alix pushed him away to grab her purse and rush for the door.

'I have to go to her!'

Ben held her arm in a firm grip and forced her to sit down on the bed.

'Let's call the hospital first. She's alive, Alix,' he repeated sternly to fight her obvious panic. She nodded dumbly and started sobbing, as he looked up local hospitals in the area of the university, but no one had her registered yet and the scene at the hospitals was pandemonium, as reporters continued to broadcast from the campus with updates. Ben called Felix in New York then and explained what had happened, and that Alix had to leave immediately to get to her daughter.

'The earliest I can get someone there to replace you is tonight,' Felix said, apologetically. 'Is Alix's daughter okay?'

'She's among the injured. It looked pretty bad on-screen, we just saw her,' Ben said in a low voice. 'Alix is very upset.'

'You can leave tonight,' Felix said, trying to figure out who to send to replace them. As always happened in a crisis, he was short-staffed that day and had all his best people out on stories in the field and he couldn't recall them fast enough to relieve Alix. A five-alarm fire had killed six fire-fighters in Brooklyn, and the chief of police had just quit after a fight with the mayor. It never failed.

Ben hung up and told her that Felix had promised to get someone there by that night, and Alix looked at him in a fury and leapt to her feet again. 'Fuck Felix! I'm not waiting till tonight. My kid is hurt, and she could be dead by now. I'm leaving here on the next plane and I don't give a damn about the flood.' Ben could see that, he was caught in the middle, and he wasn't going to let her leave alone. She was in no condition to be reasonable or even face what might happen when she got to her daughter. The television droned on behind them as Alix yelled at him in rising panic.

'We can't just walk out of here, Alix,' he said in a soothing tone, which got him nowhere. She was beyond negotiating about it, and he didn't blame her.

'Watch me!' she said in an irate tone. 'I'm not staying here for another minute.' She called the airline herself then and discovered that there was no flight to Raleigh-Durham until six o'clock that evening. She was even more desperate after that, and Ben made a rapid decision. They both knew that Felix could use local feed for the day if he had to. It wasn't a stellar solution and didn't look good for the network, but the flood wasn't top of the news now anyway. It had been preempted by the shooting at Duke.

'I'll call Felix. He can use the local broadcasts here,' Ben said calmly. It was more important for them to be at Duke now anyway. For Faye, and the network.

'How am I going to get out of here?' Alix said, crying harder. 'And where the hell was the FBI guy?'

Ben wondered if he had been injured too.

'I'll drive you. Pack your stuff,' he told Alix, having made the decision. His phone told him it was a thirteen-hour drive, which was the best they could do for now. He had a tense conversation with Felix, and told him there was no other choice. Alix wouldn't stay, and he was going with her. Felix knew when he was beaten and gave up trying to convince Ben to wait until that night. He was pissed, but he couldn't force them to stay there in the circumstances. Ten minutes later, their bags were in the car, and the TV was still on when they left the room and drove away after paying for the room, as Alix looked at him gratefully.

'Thank you,' she said, as he headed toward the highway. 'Are we both getting fired?' she asked Ben as they drove, he was driving fast, and she was a little calmer.

'Do we care?' He glanced over at her, and she smiled a wintry smile.

'No, we don't. Or at least I don't. I'm sorry if I got you in trouble,' she said sincerely. He was a good friend as well as a great work partner.

'Fuck that. I'm sorry your daughter is hurt.' They were on the highway twenty minutes later, going just over the speed limit, as Alix called the hospitals again, and an hour later, they found her, but Alix couldn't talk to her. All the trauma unit nurse would say was that she had a head wound and was in serious condition.

'Oh my God, she must have been shot in the

head,' Alix said, as panic washed over her again, and she wished she could call her mother, but she didn't want to terrify her, with too little information to balance what she did know. She would call her when she got there and had seen Faye. And she was hoping the shooting wouldn't be reported in France, or at least not yet, which gave her time to learn the facts before contacting her mother.

'She was conscious when we saw her,' Ben reminded Alix, as he kept a foot steadily on the gas and wished they had rented a better car. He was pushing the one they had nearly to its limits. Alix continued to call the hospital every half hour as he drove, but there was no news. They just kept giving her the same information, and the hospital was in chaos, with the injured that had been brought in. Ben had set the radio on a news channel, and the death toll had risen to twenty-one, but thank God they knew that Faye wasn't among them for the moment. The chancellor of the university had given an interview, and Alix was staring grimly straight ahead. 'Are you doing okay?' Ben asked her, and she nodded. He had a look of deep empathy in his eyes and she thanked him again. He was a good man to have in a crisis, he had a cool head and acted quickly, without panic. After a while, he spoke again. 'I know what you're going through,' he said softly. 'I had a son who would be a year younger than Faye now.' It was the first time in four years that he had ever mentioned it to her and she was stunned. He was a man of many facets and secrets, none of which he shared easily.

'What happened to him?' She was afraid to ask, but she had to after what he had just said.

'He drowned when he was three. I was away, as usual, on a mission in Libya, it was a hostage situation at the embassy. His name was Christopher. My wife took him to a friend's house, there were lots of little kids and a pool, he fell in, or jumped in, he was a brave little guy, and they didn't see him until too late. He'd been dead for two weeks by the time she reached me. I didn't even get to his funeral. I was pretty harsh with her. She loved hanging out with her friends, and I guess they were all talking and it must have happened very fast. The paramedics tried to revive him, but they couldn't, and by the time they got there, they said he would have been brain-dead anyway. Our marriage was over after that. She blamed me for being away and never being there with them, and I blamed her for not watching him properly. She was pregnant and lost the baby from the shock, and we never got over it. We got divorced a year later. She has two more kids now. I never wanted more after Chris. He was the cutest little guy you've ever seen. I figured I couldn't go through it again, to have a kid you love that much, and lose him. Chris was it for me. No more kids.' He knew exactly what Alix was feeling or thought he did, and she didn't know what to say to him. She put a hand on his arm as he drove, and tears rolled down his cheeks after what he'd told her. Neither of them spoke for a few minutes, too moved by what he'd said.

'It wasn't your fault, Ben. You were doing your job. And maybe it wasn't hers either.'

'Probably not. He wasn't afraid of anything, and he loved the water. I had taught him to swim, but he jumped into the deep end and I guess it was too much for him. But why the hell wasn't she watching him instead of talking to her girlfriends? I've asked myself that for fifteen years. I was angry for a long time, and I took the worst assignments they'd give me, hoping I'd get killed in the line of duty. And then I just ran out of gas, and stopped hating her and feeling sorry for myself. It's just destiny, I guess, or the way things are written somewhere, like what happened to Faye today. She'll be okay. She looked alert when we saw her on the screen. And head wounds bleed like crazy, even superficial ones.' Alix nodded, and kept her hand on his arm as he stopped crying.

'Thank you for telling me about Christopher.' She was deeply touched and her heart ached for him. She could see how painful it still was. And there was no way to make it better. Even time hadn't healed it, and never would.

'I never talk about him. It still hurts too much. I was always terrified something would happen to him because I loved him so much. And then it did.'

'That's how I feel about Faye. And I always feel so guilty for not being there for her for the first five years, and I'm away all the time and always have been. My marriage was kind of a non-event. We got married so that the baby would be born in wedlock, we wouldn't have gotten married otherwise. We hardly knew each other. His parents wanted us to get divorced right away. And then he died in the accident. But I fell in love with Faye eventually. It's a terrible thing sometimes to love someone that much. I wouldn't want to do it again either. I worry about her all the time, and she hates me for the work I do. She's always afraid I'll get killed. And instead, we spend our life in war zones and she's the one who gets shot on a college campus. How does that make sense? And she had a bodyguard near her somewhere.'

'It doesn't make sense,' Ben confirmed. 'I did some pretty nasty missions with the SEALs. I was the only survivor once, in the Sudan. And my three-year-old drowns in a swimming pool, with his mother ten feet away from him. It never made sense to me either. You read about that stuff, but you think it will never happen to you. And once you know it can and does, life is never the same again.' Alix nodded, she felt that way too.

'I used to have nightmares that she'd get meningitis and die, or have an accident, while I was away. But by now, I figured she was home free, or almost, at her age. I guess you're never home free, no matter how old they are. It's all a matter of luck or chance, think of how all those parents must feel, or those awful kindergarten shootings. You

172

drop them off at school with a Tinker Bell lunchbox, or in their Spider-Man sneakers, and then someone kills them while you're at work and think they're safe. They're never safe, and we aren't either. Look at my father.'

'Do you think we're crazy to do what we do?' he asked her honestly. 'Sometimes I wonder. It doesn't matter so much for me. My brothers will show up at my funeral, if they have time, and that'll be it. There will be no one sobbing over me, no wife, no girlfriend, no kids.'

'Felix and I will come,' she said to lighten the moment, and he smiled at her.

'Thank you. Maybe you should switch to something a little tamer one of these days, for Faye's sake,' he said seriously. The shooting that morning had brought the point home to both of them.

'Maybe one day. But for now I'd rather be dead than bored to death for the next thirty years, and we can't just live our lives in fear. And nothing's happened to me yet.' She justified the kind of work she did. She loved it, and it would be hard to give up now.

'You take a lot of chances, Alix,' he reminded her, and she felt guilty when he said it. She knew she did.

'You keep an eye on me,' she said, and they were both aware that it was true.

'You're a hard woman to keep track of once we're out there.' She nodded in acknowledgment.

'At least they don't send us to the hot spots all the

time,' he said somberly. They talked about the Vice President then to pass the time, and the stupidity of the risks he'd taken and what he'd been doing. It was all about greed for him.

'I swear, he's a classic sociopath,' Ben commented. 'He'd screw anyone over, his wife, his country, his President, his best friend, his kids. It's all about what he wants, and whatever he has to do to get it. I hope they nail him, he deserves it. And I hope he doesn't pull Bill Foster down with him, if Clark tells a bunch of lies now to save his own ass.'

'I think Olympia Foster will do everything she can to see that doesn't happen.' Her dinner with Tony Clark, wearing the wire, was the next day. 'There's a woman who doesn't do enough with her life. She might as well have died when Bill did. Maybe this will shake her up and wake her up again. Sometimes you can love someone too much, the way she did him. That's a dangerous thing too,' Alix said, feeling sorry for her again.

'It sounds like survivor guilt to me. She was with him when he got shot. Maybe she wishes it had been her, or doesn't understand why it was him, and not her, who got killed. We don't get to make those decisions. I used to wish that I had died, and not Chris. But it's not up to us, is it?'

They alternately talked and were silent on the way to Durham. He kept up a good speed, and it was almost ten o'clock when he pulled into the hospital parking lot, after a thirteen-hour drive. Ben and Alix hadn't stopped for food or coffee on the way. They immediately noticed a helipad for the trauma unit when they got there. It was the best hospital in the area, and the parking lot was jammed with cars, police vehicles, and ambulances. Most of the critically and seriously injured victims had been brought there. She jumped out of the car as soon as he pulled over, and ran into the building, and he followed her two minutes later. She asked for Faye at the nurse's desk, and a harassed attendant looked her up and sent Alix to the treatment room where they had kept her. Alix whispered a silent prayer of thanks that she was still alive, and she found her easily after she made her way through the gurneys in the hall, with nurses and paramedics standing near them. Most of the faces were young, and parents everywhere looked panicked and were crying. There were little clusters of people talking to doctors and it was obvious that some had gotten bad news and were sobbing, and then Alix found Faye in a large treatment room with a dozen beds separated by curtains. Her head was heavily bandaged and she looked dazed, and she started crying the minute she saw her mother. Alix put her arms around her and held her tight, crying too, and neither of them noticed Ben standing a few feet behind Alix, with tears rolling down his cheeks as well.

'I got shot, Mommy,' Faye said, sounding like a little girl again.

'I know, baby, I know . . . I'm here . . . You're okay . . .' She was trying to reassure herself as much as her daughter, and a doctor joined them a few minutes later and said that Faye had been incredibly lucky. A bullet had grazed the side of her head, and only done superficial damage. It had never entered her skull as it whizzed past her.

'Another half inch and it would have been a different story,' he said, looking at both of them. He had seen several tragedies that day, and miraculously Faye wasn't one of them. 'She's staying tonight for observation, but you can take her home in the morning.' He said she had a mild fever, most likely from the trauma of the injury, and they wanted to be sure the wound didn't get infected. Faye said she could still remember the sound of the bullet flying past her, as she saw other students fall all around her, and two of her classmates and her roommate had been killed. She said that the FBI agent with her had tried to protect her as soon as the shooting started. He had taken two steps toward her, been shot in the leg, and dropped like a rock next to her. She had turned to look at him when the bullet whizzed past her. Faye still couldn't believe all that had happened. She said the FBI agent had been flown to Washington, and she had been told he was in stable condition. His replacement was in the hospital corridor when Alix and Ben arrived, and introduced himself to them when they left Faye for a few minutes. One of the nurses told Alix that local residents had been arriving by the score to lay wreaths and bunches of flowers at the shooting sites, which seemed like all they could do now.

The doctor left them a few minutes later to tend to other patients, and when they went back to Faye, Ben approached her bed cautiously.

'You gave us a hell of a scare, Faye,' he said to her in a deeply moved tone, which touched Alix, especially after what he'd told her earlier about his only son.

'Me too,' she said, and winced as she lay back against the pillows. The wound still smarted, and they didn't want to sedate her too heavily to be sure she was alert.

'Do you two want something to eat?' he asked mother and daughter. Both of them declined and Faye smiled up at him, grateful that her mother was with her.

'How did you get here?'

'We drove up from New Orleans as soon as we heard, we were on a story there,' Ben answered.

'I want to go home, Mom,' Faye said in a tired voice. The university had announced that they would be closed for two weeks, to honor the dead, tighten security measures, put new systems in place, and give everyone a chance to calm down. Alix didn't want to tell her that with the threats against her because of the investigations into the Vice President's involvement with the lobbies, they couldn't stay at their apartment, and she was still staying at Ben's. There was time enough to tell her on the way home. And Alix didn't ask her if she wanted to return to Duke after what had happened. But it could have happened anywhere, and was all too normal an occurrence these days. Campus shootings had become almost commonplace.

Three of Faye's friends had come to see her earlier and she told Alix that they talked about her roommate who had died. Her funeral was going to be in Atlanta, where she was from. The nurse came to give Faye a mild tranquilizer to help her sleep finally, and Alix and Ben went to the cafeteria to get something to eat, while Faye dozed off. She'd had an incredibly traumatic day. They walked past the FBI guard again and he nodded and remained discreetly at his post. In the chaos of the hospital, he didn't stand out at all. In the cafeteria, Alix looked relieved and exhausted and so did Ben. His heart had been with hers as they drove as fast as they could to reach Faye and see how badly she was injured. She had been incredibly lucky compared to some of the others. The death toll was still at twenty-one. And it had been announced on the news that Alix's daughter had been among the injured at Duke. She was startled to get a call from Olympia on her cell-phone when she was leaving the cafeteria.

'I don't want to bother you, but I just wanted to tell you how sorry I am about your daughter,' she said in her soft smoky voice, which Alix recognized immediately despite the blocked number she'd called from. 'How is she?'

'She's okay, a bullet grazed her head and she has a superficial wound. It could have been so much worse.' As she said it, a family walked past her, with their arms around each other, in deep mourning. Their son had just died from his wounds, which brought the death toll to twenty-two.

'I'm so glad to hear that she's all right. These things are so terrible.' Alix knew that it struck close to home for her, a crazed gunman shooting someone she loved. 'We need a better warning system and treatment plans for these untreated mental patients that slip through the cracks in our society. We need better gun laws, to keep firearms out of the hands of unstable people. They let them out of mental hospitals and then they do something like this.' Countless lives had been destroyed that day, parents, children, friends. No one would ever be the same, just as she wasn't after Bill's death. 'I'm so glad she's going to be okay. I thought about you the minute I heard it on the news.'

'Thank you for calling me,' Alix said, genuinely touched. Olympia was such a nice woman, she hated to see her lead such a sad life now, and with her children so far away. 'And good luck tomorrow,' she said and meant it. She knew how hard it was going to be for her to be used as a decoy to try to trap Tony, if they could.

'I'm not looking forward to it.' She felt sick as she said it. She had ordered his favorite dinner and felt like Judas.

'You'll do fine,' Alix said and hoped it was true. 'We'll be back in the city by tomorrow night, if Faye feels up to going home tomorrow. They're keeping her for observation tonight.'

'I hope she'll do well,' Olympia said warmly and a moment later they hung up. The two women had a definite affinity for each other, and a deep respect. Alix really liked her, and was sure she would have liked the senator too, and she said as much to Ben.

'He was a great man,' Ben agreed. 'Do you know her brother, the senator from Connecticut?'

'I know who he is. He's kind of a colorless sort, very straight, very serious. He has a dull wife, six kids, and there's nothing remarkable about him. Just good, solid people. There's something special about her,' Alix said.

'Yes, there is.' Ben nodded. 'I would have loved to see the Fosters in the White House, not what we've got there now, or Tony Clark and his child bride, God forbid. He's in it for the money, and she for the thrill of power. Not exactly what I'd call true love.' He sounded cynical as he said it, but Alix thought so too.

'He's a real politician, in the worst sense of the word.'

'I'm surprised he didn't try to marry Foster's widow. It would have been a perfect political and PR move for him, and just the kind of thing he'd do to win the election,' Ben said in a tone of disgust.

'I don't think she would have. She's too loyal to her husband's memory. Too loyal for her own good, in fact. I think she's planning to mourn him forever.' The book she had written about him was testimony to that, and the fact that she had vanished from public view and retired from the world. She hadn't even appeared when her brother won his last senatorial campaign, and she always had before. Marrying Tony Clark and going to the White House with him did not fit that picture.

They went back to Faye's cubicle then, and found her asleep. And as Alix looked at her, she was grateful again that she was alive. The plan was to leave the next day, if Faye was up to it, and Alix was going to sleep in a chair next to her that night. She wanted to keep an eye on her.

The next morning, after they started the paper-work for her release, Faye looked at her mother with worried eyes.

'I don't know if I want to come back, Mom,' Faye said softly. Her head hurt and the wound burned. 'Maybe I want to go stay with Mamie for a while in France.' She would feel safe there, far from the traumatic events that had just happened, and her friends who had died. And she'd been planning to spend time in France that summer anyway. Maybe she'd just stay.

'You can take a term off, if you want to, or transfer to another school,' Alix said quietly. 'Whatever you want to do, you don't need to make the decision now.' They called Isabelle a little while later to tell her what had happened, and say that Faye was all right and Alix was with her. Isabelle said that she had seen something about it on the news, but didn't hear which university it was and make the connection with Duke, or she would have panicked and called Alix immediately. She was upset to hear about Faye's injury, but grateful it wasn't worse. Gabriel was with her, and she told him while she was still on the phone with Alix.

'I want to come and stay with you, Mamie,' Faye said when she talked to her.

'Of course, whenever you want to. After you finish the semester,' she said matter-of-factly, 'you can spend the whole summer here.' Faye was a little startled. Her grandmother was old school, and believed in getting back on the horse, and finishing the term, even if you'd been shot. Alix laughed when Faye told her after the call.

'That's my mother. You don't screw around with school with her.' Ben laughed and then went to get breakfast from the cafeteria for the three of them. The food service had been disrupted and was late, and the hospital food was awful, but none of them cared. The cafeteria food was slightly better, and Alix was pleased to see Faye eat something after the trauma of the day before. Ben and Alix left her then to talk to her FBI agent on duty and tell him they were leaving that morning. He would accompany them to the airport and leave them there. New York–based agents would be assigned to her in New York, and he was going to notify the New York field office of their plans. After they spoke to him, Ben and Alix walked around the parking lot for a few minutes. Alix looked exhausted, and had hardly slept all night. She kept waking up to check on Faye.

'What a day yesterday was,' Alix said with a long, tired sigh, as Ben put an arm around her.

'You were very brave, Alix,' he complimented her and she smiled up at him.

'So were you. Thank you for dealing with Felix and getting us here so quickly. There's no way I would have stayed in New Orleans until last night.'

'Neither would I,' he assured her. Their replacements had already been on the air the night before from New Orleans on the ten o'clock news, so Felix had it covered. He had wanted them to cover the story at Duke, and Ben had refused that too. He said that Alix was in no condition to do it, and they had sent another team to the campus. You had to draw the line somewhere and they had. They went back to Faye then. A doctor was checking her, and said they would discharge her if she felt up to it. Faye said she did. She was anxious to go home. All she wanted was to get away from Duke now, and the scenes of carnage she knew she would never forget. The memory of it was forever engraved on her mind. Alix could see all of it in her daughter's eyes as she helped her dress to go home. Her hands shook every time she thought of how close Faye had come, and her bandaged head was a reminder to them all. Alix had never felt as lucky in her life, as she put her arms around Faye and held her tight.

'Let's go home,' she said to her daughter in a choked voice, and Faye nodded, as tears ran down her cheeks again.

CHAPTER 10

On the flight back to New York on Saturday, Alix explained to Faye that they had to stay at Ben's, because of the threats she'd been getting. The FBI would assign Faye three shifts a day of agents in New York. She groaned but wasn't surprised.

'I wanted to sleep in my own bed,' Faye said plaintively, but Alix didn't want to take any risks. Three death threats were enough to convince her they might not be safe at home, and Ben could protect them at his apartment in Brooklyn. The threats went with the territory of investigating and reporting on crime. And an exposé of the Vice President, and his accepting bribes from the Saudis and possibly from key lobbyists, was serious business, although she couldn't discuss the story with her daughter. Faye didn't argue with her about it, she could guess that it was an important story, but she was disappointed to still need security and not be able to go home. The two women had to share the bed in Ben's guest room and it was cramped. His room was no bigger or he would have let them sleep in his. Alix was grateful they could stay there, even if Faye wasn't pleased. The FBI agent hadn't arrived yet so she had to wait to go out. Faye had called several friends when they got to Ben's, and two of them promised to come out to see her in Brooklyn, they were so happy to know she was all right. By the time she finished her calls, the FBI bodyguard was standing outside Ben's apartment.

'Thank you for letting us invade your space,' Alix said to Ben, looking embarrassed. 'If you want, we can stay at a hotel.'

'I love having you here,' he said, and sounded as though he meant it. He tidied up as best he could, and he and Alix went to buy groceries, while Faye stayed in bed, texted her friends, and watched movies on her laptop, which she'd brought home with her.

Alix felt closer to Ben after what they'd just been through. They hadn't mentioned his son, Chris, again, but Alix was touched that he had confided in her, and she noticed a framed photograph of a little boy on his bookshelf that she hadn't paid attention to before, and she felt certain it was him but didn't ask. She didn't want to reopen the painful subject. Isabelle had called them earlier from France, to see how they were.

The doctor had told Faye to take it easy for a few days, and after that she could do whatever she wanted, and get the wound checked in a week. Alix was changing the dressings for her, and it was very clean and already healing. But the coverage on TV of the aftermath of the shooting was heart-breaking. They ran photographs of the victims and their families again and again, and the funerals in various cities where they had lived would begin on Tuesday. Alix and Ben were off till Monday, with the blessing of their boss.

They had dinner at his kitchen table that night, a big salad Alix had prepared, some Chinese food Faye had requested, and a roast chicken from a nearby deli, and her friends arrived to visit her just as they finished. The girls retired to the guest room with Faye, to lie on her bed and talk, while Ben and Alix had a glass of wine in the kitchen. The atmosphere was festive, but subdued, and it felt like home, even to Alix. Ben was warm and hospitable to both of them.

'Thank you again for having us,' she said as he poured her another glass of the wine he'd found in a cupboard. It was Spanish and inexpensive, but surprisingly good, and the impromptu meal had been too.

'You make my apartment a happy place,' he said, smiling at her. 'It's too quiet most of the time, but I'm hardly ever here, except to sleep.' Her presence and her daughter's changed it all.

'I feel like that about my place too when Faye isn't home. That's what makes the difference, although her friends coming and going at all hours drives me crazy at times. But it's too depressing now that she's at school, I hate going home.' He nodded agreement but didn't comment for a minute.

'At first, when I left the SEALs, I loved the peace and solitude. Now it's a little too quiet at times. I've been thinking about moving into the city. But we're gone so much, I'm not sure it matters. I never have the time to go anywhere anyway. I keep thinking I'd go to museums and the theater if I move to Manhattan, but maybe I wouldn't.'

She smiled, thinking the same thing. 'It's hard to plan anything when you work as much as we do, and travel all the time.'

'I had a great time when we took those few days off in France,' he said, remembering the châteaux he'd visited and the time in Provence with her and her mother. 'I should do more of that here.' She nodded agreement, but it seemed like all she ever had time to do was laundry and pack, and read the research on her next story, which made her think of Olympia having dinner with the Vice President that night, and wonder how it was going.

As he always did, Tony had arrived precisely on time, and Olympia was waiting for him in the library, wearing a simple black dress and a string of pearls, with high heels, and her dark hair neatly done. She had a hairdresser who came to the house now and had been there that afternoon, in anticipation of his visit. She was always impeccable when he came to see her, she was a beautiful woman, with style and grace.

'You look terrific,' he complimented her, and opened the bottle of champagne waiting for him in a silver ice bucket on the coffee table, with two flutes. She was nervous with the wire taped under her dress, but he didn't notice how tense she was. A female CIA agent had come two hours earlier and attached the wire while she dressed. It was barely more than a thread on her skin, and a very efficient device. And three of the officers from the National Clandestine Service were in a van outside, parked halfway down the block, listening to every word from the moment he walked in.

Tony asked what she'd been doing that day, and she said working on the book. They sipped the champagne, and she asked politely about Megan and the kids, as she always did, and he said the little one had the flu, and Megan was excited to be pregnant again.

'Three kids will probably look better than two during the campaign,' he said with a grin. 'Family man.' It was one thing Megan had been able to offer him that Olympia wouldn't have, children of their own, and her father's money to pour into his campaign. But other than that, he still thought Olympia would have been the better choice by far. She had a mystique that a girl Megan's age couldn't match, political history, and the whole country loved her. He never pretended to Olympia to be madly in love with his wife. Olympia always wondered if it would last. He had been unfaithful to his first wife repeatedly, and she had tired of it and divorced him shortly before Bill died. He hadn't been devastated by it, and had admitted to them for a long time, in order to justify his infidelities, that the marriage had been dead for years and hadn't been the right fit for either of them since the beginning, and she couldn't have children, and he didn't want to adopt. Politically, for his image, Megan was a better choice than his first wife. She was intelligent and educated, good looking, and had given him kids. But Olympia would have made him a legend, like Bill. He said as much over dinner, and made it very clear to the three CIA agents in the van that whatever he did had a political motive behind it, even who he married. It told them instantly who he was, and they made no comment as they listened, but one of them raised an eyebrow. Tony couldn't have heard what they were saying, but they didn't want to miss a word. All three of them had earphones on, so as to hear him more clearly.

They were halfway through the excellent dinner she'd had prepared for him, when she brought up the subject that interested the CIA. Until then, they had commented on the campus shooting at Duke, a conversation she'd had the day before with Darcy about her doctor boyfriend, and some of Tony's activities in Washington that week, all of which sounded relatively banal to the agents in the van.

Finally, they heard Olympia mention offhandedly that she'd gone through some more of Bill's papers that week, trying to beef up several of the chapters in her new book with his own words to bring him to life again for her readers. He'd been gone for a long time, and she was afraid that some people might not remember how vital he had been and how deeply committed to a variety of causes.

'I came across some notes I don't think I've ever seen before, in his own handwriting, and a journal. None of it was very exciting. He talked about how well liked you are, and how popular, and that you have lobbyist friends, and people you know in every sector,' she said blandly, and glanced at Tony with innocent eyes. She would have seemed almost stupid and naïve to anyone who didn't know her. Tony frowned at what she said.

'I didn't get involved with the lobbies. I never did,' he said, sounding curt and dismissive. 'I played golf with a few of them once, and Bill got hot under the collar about it. He was a little too sensitive on the subject, and a purist, as we both know. Anything else you unearthed in his notes? Where did you come across all this?'

'In a bunch of boxes they sent over from his office afterward. They never looked very important to me, so I didn't go through them for the first book.' None of what she was saying was true. She had read every scrap of paper he'd written on, and there were no boxes she hadn't gone through in the last six years, but she made it sound entirely plausible and the agents were impressed. She had done it with just the right light touch. 'But I'm a little short of material for this book, so I'm having to dig deeper.' It would have sounded ominous to

190

anyone who was concealing something, and inane to someone who wasn't, and standard procedure for a book, especially six years after her husband's death, when the material she had for it had begun to seem a little dry.

'Was there anything else of interest in his notes?' You could hear the faintest increase of tension in his voice if you listened carefully, and the agents thought it would have been interesting to see the expression on his face that went with it.

'Not really,' she said, sounding vague, and smiled at him. 'Something about a trip you made to Saudi Arabia, which didn't make any sense either. Did you ever go? I thought Bill must have been confused. It was more in the form of notes, with some dates, than a proper journal entry. It sounded like a couple of trips, maybe three of them, and a mention of one to Iran. Maybe you wanted him to go with you, and he wrote down possible dates. I don't think you ever went, and I know Bill didn't.' Her eyes opened wide again, and she smiled at him. 'Bill was always talking about trips he never went on. He was too busy at home, and the Middle East was never a high priority to him, or to you. I think I'm down to some pretty meaningless stuff in the boxes now. I still have a few to go through, but it looks like they sent me everything including what was in his wastebasket. A lot of it makes no sense,' she said again, 'like the dates for trips to Jedda and Riyadh. Have you ever been there?' she asked politely and as though she didn't really care.

'No, of course not,' he flat-out lied to her. 'I went on a senatorial junket to Tehran once. I didn't like it. I'd never go back. The Arab world is not for me, except in the context of a presidency, of course. But in civilian life, I'd avoid it. I don't like countries or people who treat women badly,' he said, to impress her. 'And the Saudis were nomads in the desert a generation ago. There's nothing there.'

'Except oil,' she said, smiling. 'I saw a group of Saudi women at Bergdorf's a long time ago. They were each buying about ten alligator bags, they must have left the store with a hundred of them between them. It's hard to imagine that kind of money.' She tried to sound naïve and easily fooled. It was everything he wanted to believe about her, and she realized now that that must be how he saw her, and it was far from the truth. 'I didn't think you'd ever been there,' she concluded. 'Maybe you could look at this last batch of papers sometime, and tell me if there's anything relevant to his policies and ideologies that I'm missing. That's really what this book is about, what he believed in and lived for. I know he was much more interested in using our own natural resources and not importing oil, so Arab oil tycoons were of no interest to him.'

'Or to me,' Tony said firmly, lying to her again. 'We were in complete agreement on that score, and I think his policies, promoting our own resources, were the right ones.' She couldn't believe he was lying to her through the entire conversation. She wondered how many times he had done that before. He clearly thought she was an innocent and a fool. It was a blow to realize it now.

She changed the subject then, and he came back to it a few minutes later. 'Where are you keeping all these boxes of Bill's notes that you haven't gone through yet? Maybe I should just have them sent to my office and go through them for you. I could do it some weekend when I'm not busy.'

'I'd hate to bore you with it,' she said gently. 'It looked like mostly junk to me, and it takes time to sift through it. I have about a dozen boxes left, but I think I used all the good stuff in the first book. I don't think there's much there I want to use. And it's so tedious reading it. I found some sweet photographs of the children I want to frame, a nice one of him, and the two of you, but so far that's about it. I'll probably archive the rest. I haven't thrown any of his papers away.' Tony was quiet for a minute after she said it, and he sounded irritated when he spoke again.

'God knows I loved the man, almost as much as you did, but he was such a purist, and such an extremist in his own way. Everything was black or white to him, you were right or wrong, good or bad. There were no gray areas with Bill, no shadings, no compromises, no understanding of the nuances of politics and the adjustments you make in order to have something work. I tried to explain that to him, but he was stubborn as a mule about it.' Tony continued, sounding fierce for a minute. 'Something was right or wrong because he believed that. The world just doesn't work that way.'

'His world did,' Olympia said, almost in a whisper. 'He would never do something he thought was wrong, or let us do that. He was such a good person.' Her voice drifted off. 'I think that's why people loved him so much, because he had so much integrity,' she added a moment later. 'You have to admire someone like that. He didn't compromise what he believed in, and he had so much compassion for everyone. That's why you loved him too,' she reminded his closest friend, who didn't look as though he loved him at that instant. He was remembering the arguments they had had when he couldn't sway Bill to his point of view. And now he was worried about the boxes Olympia had mentioned. God only knew what was in them. And he was relieved that she didn't seem to know what was in them either. 'He was everyone's hero,' Olympia reminded him and Tony nodded.

'Certainly . . . yes, he was . . . In a way, it's not surprising that someone killed him. Throughout history, men of high ideals and inflexible standards have been martyred, like Jesus and countless others, right down to modern times. The man who killed him didn't know him, but men like Bill, who are lit from within, almost draw tragedy to them.' It was an odd thing to say, and the first time he had said it to her. It almost sounded as though he thought that her husband had been destined to be assassinated, and the thought of it made her shudder.

Her housekeeper cleared away the plates then, and brought in a tarte tatin for dessert. It was a fancy apple tart made at home, with whipped cream to go with it. She knew it was one of Tony's favorites. As the housekeeper served it, Olympia thought of everything Tony had said about his friend. Some of it was very startling, and it struck her that it was almost as though he accepted Bill's death as inevitable. To Tony, she saw now, the end justified the means, even if that meant lying to her, which she realized now he had, probably many times.

She looked tired by the end of the meal. It had been a strain for her to appear casual and light-hearted, and guide him into the subjects that interested the CIA. But she could also see now how easily he would have sold Bill out, portraying him as unreasonable and rigid, and pretending that Bill had agreed with him when he hadn't. It was frightening thinking about what he might say to save his own skin. She thought him capable of anything now, any lie that was useful to him. He was completely self-serving. And the CIA agents in the van understood it too. Olympia saw now, all too clearly, that Tony was not the man she had thought him, and she knew more than ever that Bill had been right in the decision to separate himself from his old friend. And six years later, he was dirtier than ever, just as Bill had feared.

Tony sat with her for a few more minutes after dinner, over coffee, and then left early to catch his flight to Washington. He had a plane waiting at the airport. And he reminded her again before he left to send him Bill's last boxes so he could go through them and spare her the trouble.

'I hate to do that to you,' she said, sounding embarrassed. 'You've got more important things to do.'

'I'd love to, it will be like a visit with him to read his notes.' It was how she felt about going through her husband's papers, but Tony had other motives, and didn't realize she knew it. The boxes she had spoken of were mythical anyway, they didn't exist, and she had invented them in order to introduce the pertinent subjects, and the ruse had worked well. She would have been proud of herself, if what she had discovered hadn't been so disappointing. Suddenly everything he had said to her in the six years since Bill died sounded hollow and false. She wanted to cry when she closed the door behind him, after he kissed her on the forehead and told her again that he loved her. She saw now that he didn't love anyone but himself.

The agents from the van rang her doorbell fifteen minutes later, to be sure that he didn't return for some reason. They relieved her of the wire and were pleased with what they'd heard. He had lied to her again and again, about the lobbyists he knew, his involvement with them, his trips to Saudi Arabia and Iran and the men he knew there, even his beliefs about buying foreign oil. And he was clearly worried about his late friend's notes and had done everything to convince her to send them to him.

Olympia knew when the agents left that she had seen Tony in her home for the last time. Even if he wanted to come back, she couldn't let him. She had the same black-and-white perception of the truth as her late husband. And Tony Clark was a liar. It was only a matter of time before the CIA would close in on him and he'd go to jail. She hoped they wouldn't ask her to be a decoy for him again.

She went upstairs to her bedroom with a heavy heart, and all she could think now was that she wanted to get away from her house and get some air. She wanted to see people, her children and old friends. She was tired of the book, and carrying Bill's message into the world. She needed a break from it, and she wanted to get as far away as she could from Tony Clark. She realized that what she wanted to do now was see her children. Her son was close by in Iowa, but he never came to New York anymore, she hadn't seen him in months. Darcy lived so much farther away, in Zimbabwe, and would have to wait.

She sent an email to Jennifer before she went to bed, asking her to book her on a flight to Chicago the next day, and she sent Josh a text asking him if she could come to visit him for a few days, if he had time. She wanted to put her arms around him and give him a hug. She was tired of mourning as a way of life. And somewhere amidst all of Tony's lies that night, the spell had been broken, along with her heart. She had lost a friend, if he had ever truly been one to either of them, which she now doubted. But she had finally started on the long journey back from Bill's death. It was time. Discovering the truth about Tony had freed her.

CHAPTER 11

Jennifer managed to get Olympia on a flight to Chicago the next morning. She wanted to spend a day visiting old haunts. It was where she and Bill had spent the early years of their marriage, while he laid the groundwork for his political career. In time, they had moved to Washington, but kept an apartment in Chicago on the lake for several years, and Bill's father still lived there. He was ninety-two years old, and Olympia hadn't seen him in a year, since he last visited her in New York, although they spoke on the phone from time to time. She was extremely fond of him and had missed seeing him more frequently. She was excited to see him now. She called him before she left New York, and she was having dinner with him in Chicago that night.

She checked in to the Four Seasons, and walked around the city she had once loved so much, admiring the recent changes and smiling at familiar sights. She felt her heart catch when she walked past their old address, and stood quietly looking at the lake. It was a trip back in time for her, as memories of Bill and the happy years they'd spent there came rushing back. She had always been happy there, and both their children had been born in Chicago. It was a sophisticated city, but smaller and gentler than New York, where she had grown up. Bill had brought her to the city when they were first married, and she had loved living there with him.

She was planning to visit Josh in the small town where he lived in Iowa the next day. He had been startled by her text and call that morning, and happy that she was coming, and had arranged to have some time off. He couldn't believe that his mother had finally left the house and was traveling again. And she said she was having dinner with his grandfather in Chicago that night. Josh called Darcy to tell her, and she was as stunned as he was.

'Maybe she's on drugs,' Darcy suggested. 'Is Uncle Tony coming with her? Maybe he got her out.'

'I don't think so. She didn't mention him.' The reason for her visit was a mystery to both of them, but it seemed like good news. And their grandfather was equally relieved and surprised by the change. They'd all given up hope of seeing Olympia out in the world again. She'd offered no explanation and just said she was coming, on the spur of the moment.

When Olympia went to meet her father-in-law that night, he was delighted to see her. Charles Foster was a strong, intelligent man, originally an attorney, who had become involved in the behind-the-scenes world of Washington politics fifty years earlier, and had been influential ever since. He was energetic and vital and an extraordinary person. It was he who had convinced Bill to run for the Senate, and set his sights on the presidency one day, and he had a profound affection and admiration for his daughter-in-law. Like her, he had been devastated when Bill died, but he had recovered from it in healthier ways than she had, had gone back to work, which kept him busy, and engaged in life every day. Even at his age, he was on numerous boards around the country, and in England. He was a power broker, and still had considerable influence in Washington. He was revered by all who knew him, much like his son. They were both charismatic people with powerful ideals, big dreams, and solid values.

He took Olympia to Les Nomades for dinner, which was fashionable and elegant, and he was current on recent books and world events, knowledgeable about music and art, knew all the key players in Washington, and even many of the young ones. He was a living legend and looked more like a man of sixty-five than his actual age. All of his faculties were in order, and he continued to play tennis and golf, go to social events, and see friends, of which he had many of all ages around the world. And he looked like a much older version of his late son. He visited his grandson in Iowa at least once a month, and had been deeply saddened to see his daughter-in-law turn her back on the world.

'I'm so happy to see you here,' he told Olympia with obvious pleasure after they were seated. He had been widowed for twenty-five years but had gone on with his life with determination. He had worried about Olympia since Bill's death and her inability to move forward without him. But he also knew that the decision to recover had to come from her. No one else could do it for her, or force her to embrace life again. He was well aware that her trip to Chicago was an important first step for her, and the hopeful sign they'd all been waiting for.

'I thought it was time to get going again,' she said shyly, as he nodded agreement. It was long overdue. 'I'm going to see Josh tomorrow. And I want to visit Darcy sometime soon. She has a new beau, a French doctor.' Listening to her, and seeing a new light in her eyes, Charles was thrilled. He cared about her a great deal.

'So I hear.' He was up on family news and stayed in touch with both his grandchildren. 'What about you, Olympia?' he asked her seriously after they ordered dinner. 'What are you going to do now?'

'I don't know. I'm working on another book, about Bill.'

Charles looked unhappy to hear it. 'Is that a good idea?' He didn't think so. 'It keeps you looking backward instead of forward. I don't think that's what Bill would have wanted for you. The first book was terrific, and a wonderful tribute to him. I'm not sure a second one is necessary. He's not going to be running for office again,' he said with a nostalgic smile. He had adjusted to the reality of the loss far better than she had.

'I know. I've started to have my doubts about the book too,' she said honestly, and was relieved to hear him say it. 'I don't know what else to do. The kids are gone . . . Bill . . .' She looked at him with momentary panic, but he could see that she was trying to find her way back. It was what they all wanted for her, and writing another book about her husband seemed counterproductive to him. He wished she would find some other activity to keep her busy.

'You've got a law degree,' Charles reminded her. 'Why don't you use it? Take some classes to get up to speed, and get a job.' She looked shocked by what he said, but she liked the idea. He had always been a source of good advice for her. He was all about living and being engaged in life, and passionate about everything he did, which his son had learned from him.

'I haven't practiced law since the kids were little and we moved to Washington,' she said quietly. She couldn't see herself practicing law again after so long.

'You can get everything you need in six months or a year. And even if you don't practice again, you can get a job that uses your skills. I think working is important, for all of us.' He had never rested on his laurels, nor had Bill. And Olympia no longer had the excuse of young children who needed her. 'You have a lot to offer and there's so much you could do.' It was a new idea to her, and he could see that she had lost faith in herself and the world. She looked unsure, which wasn't like her, and life without Bill had proved to be even harder than she feared. Losing his wife hadn't stopped Charles, but the shocking circumstances of Bill's death, murdered while standing next to her, had paralyzed her. It embarrassed her now, listening to everything Charles was doing, he was so excited about life, engaged in so many projects, and doing so much good.

'Maybe I will go back to school,' she said thoughtfully, and he hoped she would. And after that, get into the workforce, or take on a philanthropic project. He had the connections to help her, and would have gladly. He had offered to before, but she'd been buried in the book. He hated to see her lose time all over again with a second one.

'You can travel, do pro bono legal work, get a job, work for a foundation. There are a lot of things you can do. You're free now.' He made it sound like an opportunity instead of a death sentence, which was how she had viewed it for six years, and Tony had reinforced that. She didn't mention Tony to her father-in-law because she knew Bill's father had never liked him, and more than once had called him sleazy, and an opportunist trying to prey on Bill, which was turning out to be true.

He had never trusted him, and if Tony was indicted for illegal activities, Charles would know soon enough, and so would everyone else, including her kids. She didn't want to say anything to anyone yet. She knew her children would be crushed, and were deeply fond of him, but Charles had regarded him with suspicion for thirty years.

They chatted animatedly all through dinner, and Olympia was excited about Charles's ideas when he dropped her off at her hotel. His vitality and enthusiasm were contagious. She was glad she had come to Chicago to see him. Her instincts had been right to do so, and she wished she'd seen more of him in recent years. It felt wonderful to be in Chicago again and out in the world. And she could hardly wait to see Josh the next day. When Charles left her, he made her promise not to lose her momentum, start exploring new activities, and put the second book on hold. And she said she would.

Olympia drove the three hours to Iowa in a rented car the next day, which gave her time to think about Charles's suggestions the night before. The farm where Josh worked was just outside Davenport, she met him at his home and was excited to see him. He looked tanned and healthy, his blond hair almost white from the sun, and he was thrilled to see his mother. The girl standing shyly beside him looked almost like his twin. She was his girlfriend, Joanna, Olympia hadn't met her although they'd chatted on Skype for two years. Joanna was a bright, cheerful girl, with a positive attitude about life, they were living together and worked at the same farm. She had a master's from Stanford and had grown up in California, and Josh had told his mother since the beginning that he was serious about her. He didn't want to marry her yet, but he hoped to one day, so Olympia paid close attention to her. She was in awe of meeting Olympia. Josh's mother was impressive, and a legend. But Olympia was so natural and normal in the flesh, and so unassuming that Joanna felt at ease with her, and the two women took to each other quickly.

They had dinner at a simple hamburger place in town and Olympia told Josh all about dinner with his grandfather the night before, and how much fun it had been, Olympia's eyes lit up when she said it.

'He invited us to visit him in Europe this summer,' Josh told her. 'He's renting a house in the south of France,' he said with a smile that was identical to his father's, and tore at his mother's heart. 'We're planning to go, and we're going to spend some time with Joanna's family in Santa Barbara too.' It made Olympia realize even more that the rest of the world had gone on living after Bill, and she hadn't. 'What are you doing this summer, Mom?' It seemed a safe question to ask her now that she was out at last, and not hiding at home. He still had no idea what had changed, and didn't want to press her about it. But whatever it was had to be a good thing.

'I don't know.' She looked blank at the question about her summer. She hadn't thought about summer in years. There were no seasons in her secluded world. She had a lot of catching up to do. 'Maybe I should rent a house at the beach somewhere?' It suddenly sounded like a great idea. 'Would you come to visit?' she asked them both, and they nodded with broad smiles. It saddened her to come face-to-face with the fact that she had even isolated herself from her children, except for visits on Skype. She had been leading a virtual life, and not a real one. She had become their virtual mother for six years, with the excuse of the trauma she'd been through, and Tony reminding her of it constantly, as though to separate her from them too. Everything he did was about controlling her, and she hadn't seen it, but she was beginning to now.

'How's your book coming, Mom?' Josh asked her politely during dinner, since it was usually all she talked about. A fleeting sadness passed through his mother's eyes like a cloud obscuring the sun, and she sighed.

'I've been thinking about putting it aside for a while. Your grandfather thinks I should go back to school, and get a job practicing law again. He suggested it last night, and I kind of like the idea. I'm pretty rusty, but it would be fun to get up and running again. I wouldn't mind working for a nonprofit involved in women's rights.'

'Way to go, Mom!' Her son cheered her on,

beaming, and Joanna smiled at them. Josh couldn't wait to tell his sister. Their mother was alive again. He just hoped it would last. They had missed her for too long. And Joanna knew only too well how sad he'd been about it and how helpless he felt. He talked to her about it a lot.

Olympia dropped them off at home after dinner and went back to her hotel. It was a small bed and breakfast and they were going to spend the next day together. She liked Joanna very much, and she thought Josh seemed happy. He liked his job, his way of life, and he was satisfied with his choice of partner and career. He wanted the simple life, and a career in agriculture suited him perfectly. He loved the outdoors, was knowledgeable about livestock and new breeding techniques, and had learned a lot at the organic farm where they worked. And Joanna shared his goals and interests. They seemed like a perfect match. He said he wanted to have his own farm one day, but he still had a lot to learn first. Joanna was very know-ledgeable from working at her father's dairy. Olympia was smiling, thinking about Josh as she got ready for bed, when her cellphone rang. She saw that it was Jennifer, and she was happy to hear from her. She started to tell her about her visits with her father-in-law and Josh, and Jennifer interrupted her, sounding tense.

'The house was ransacked last night,' Jennifer said, and was obviously shaken.

'What house? My house? What do you mean?'

It made no sense. 'Why would anyone ransack my house? Was anything stolen?' She had some valuable art she had inherited from her parents, and things of sentimental value, but ransacking the place seemed crazy to her.

'Nothing of value was taken,' Jennifer answered her question. 'But your papers were all over the place when I came in, and I think some of them are missing. Whoever did it just randomly took boxes of papers.'

'My papers? Why?' And then she instantly remembered what she'd told Tony . . . all the imaginary boxes of papers she had invented for him, to elicit a reaction and see what he said.

'They took a lot of them, and your stereo system for good measure. And there's a small painting missing in the front hall. I think they tried to make it look like a robbery, but it wasn't about that. The silver was untouched, none of the other paintings are gone. You left a pearl necklace on your dresser and it's still there.' Jennifer was aware that she had had several meetings with the CIA, but Olympia hadn't explained them to her, and Jennifer knew nothing about the wire she had worn at dinner on Saturday night, nor the reasons for it. 'I called the insurance company and the police to report it. Is there anyone else you want me to call?'

Olympia thought before she answered, and realized that she needed to call John Pelham. What if her dinner with Tony and the mention of Bill's papers had caused this to happen?

209

'I'll take care of it. When did it happen?' Olympia said, sounding calmer than she felt.

'It must have been Sunday sometime after you left. They disarmed the burglar alarm very professionally, according to the police, but they made a hell of a mess in your study, and they left a trail of papers going down the stairs. I came in and called the police this morning and they've been here all day. This is the first chance I've had to call you. Let me know if there's anything else you want me to do.'

Olympia thanked her and called Officer Pelham immediately and told him what had happened.

'I listened to the recording of your dinner with the Vice President on Saturday night. He's obviously frightened of what you've got in those papers you told him about. You did a good job,' he praised her, and there was no doubt in either of their minds by then who had orchestrated the break-in. Tony wanted any incriminating evidence he thought she had, before she read it herself. But there was nothing to read. It didn't exist, and the papers he'd taken were worthless, as he would discover when he read through them. She wondered if he'd come back for more, looking for the rest.

Before she could ask for it, Pelham told her he would assign two agents to protect her and the house. She explained that she was in Iowa visiting her son, but planned to return on Wednesday. 'I'll get two agents to your house tonight,' he promised. 'I have your assistant's number, we'll work it out with her. It sounds like Clark is starting to panic. And taking one painting and a stereo isn't going to fool anyone. He's looking for something. He's trying to cover his tracks. He has a lot to lose here. I don't want to go into it in detail, but we have his Swiss accounts. We have all the records of his transactions and deposits from the Saudis during those years. And we have two witnesses who are willing to testify to the grand jury about bribes he's taken recently. We're getting close here. I want you to be careful, Mrs Foster. Don't discuss this with anyone. I want you to call him and tell him about the break-in. If he's who you would have turned to for help before, you need to call him now. If you don't, he'll know you suspect him. I'm afraid we're going to have to rely on your talents as an actress again. You did a good job on Saturday at dinner, that's why he ransacked the house, or rather had it done.'

Olympia's heart sank at the thought of calling Tony. She didn't want to, and she didn't want to spoil her time with Josh. She felt as though she'd flown the coop with her trip to Chicago and Iowa, and she didn't want to go back into seclusion, or start telling Tony her every move again.

'When do you want me to call him?' she asked in a dead voice.

'Now. You just found out, so you need to do it now, just as you would have before you began suspecting him or spoke to us. We'll stay in close touch, and I'll get the two agents to your place right now, in case they come back for more. Let me know what happened when you've spoken to him.'

Olympia reached Tony on his private cellphone number as soon as she hung up with Pelham, and told him about the break-in. She managed to seem distressed and almost hysterical and was very convincing.

'I just don't understand it, they made a mess of my office, and took all my notes for the book I'm working on. It's as though someone is trying to stop me from writing the book about him. Why would anyone do that? And they took a beautiful painting of my mother's, and my stereo, which is worth nothing. But I'm upset about the painting and Bill's papers.'

'Of course you are,' he said sympathetically, expressing deep concern. 'It sounds like vandals, probably young drug addicts who took the stereo to sell for a fix, and the painting just for the hell of it. And what miserable luck that they took Bill's papers. Were any of them important?' He sounded hopeful, and pathetically transparent.

'Not really, except for the book. It was just a wanton act. None of that has any value except to me. And there were no fingerprints anywhere, so they knew what they were doing.' She didn't know if that was true or not, she just threw it in for good measure. 'Poor Jennifer is a nervous wreck. She hired guards to watch the house, so they don't get in again. I'm out of town and I won't be back till Wednesday.'

'I'm glad you did that. Where are you, by the way?' She hadn't told him, and he tried to sound casual when he asked. She hadn't been out of town in six years, so it was an unusual occurrence, to say the least.

'In Iowa, with Josh. I haven't been here in ages.'

'I'll try to come up and see you this week. I don't have my schedule yet, but I'll let you know as soon as I do. Try not to worry about this, you probably have enough for the book already.' He sounded as protective as always.

'Yes, I do, but it's an eerie feeling and so violating. Who would do such a thing?' He agreed with her about her sense of violation, and after they hung up she called Pelham back and reported the conversation to him.

'We're almost there, Mrs Foster. It won't be long now,' he reassured her. She just wanted it to be over, and she didn't want to see Tony again. Their dinner on Saturday had been hard enough. 'We'll be in touch,' Officer Pelham promised, and Olympia hung up thinking about what a snake Tony was. He was a frightened man, fighting for his life now and covering his tracks as fast as he could. Her father-in-law had been right about him all along. He was sleazy and an opportunist. And now he had turned out to be a criminal. It was everything Bill had begun to fear before he died. All she wanted now was for Tony to be out of her life forever. And she realized he would probably go to prison, which was shocking. He had lied to

Bill, and to her, and jeopardized Bill's reputation. And now she had begun to realize that Tony guarding her so closely hadn't been to protect and support her, but to control her and what she discovered and said about him. He had convinced her that she was weak and frightened and permanently damaged by what she'd been through. And now, just distancing herself a little, she had begun to find her wings again. She was as strong as ever. She just didn't know it for the past six years. But now her eyes were open. Tony Clark could not control her, nor coerce her into silence, and make her doubt herself and what she knew. Tony's game was over, and the truth about him had set her free. As much as she had loved him and valued his friendship, she knew she would never forgive him for being willing to risk Bill's reputation and take him down with him. It was time for Tony to pay for his dishonesty and his crimes, and for her to return to sanity and freedom from him.

Olympia lay awake for a long time that night, thinking about the break-in. What would they have done if she'd been there? Tie her up? Blindfold her? How desperate was he? The only thing she knew for sure now was that Tony was not the man she'd believed him to be. He had convinced her of his innocence and good intentions, none of which were true. She had even begun to believe that Bill was wrong about him and had judged him too harshly.

She dreamt of Bill that night, at dinner with her

and his father, and she could see that he was pleased. It reassured her that she was doing the right thing. She had no doubt about it now. Tony was everything Bill had discovered about him, a dishonest man, serving only his own purposes and no one else's. He was motivated by a thirst for power, and greed, willing to do whatever he had to, to get what he wanted. Tony Clark was no one's friend, not Bill's, or hers, and never had been.

CHAPTER 12

When Olympia woke up the morning after she heard about the break-in, the day she spent with Josh and Joanna was particularly sweet. They drove to some of his favorite places and had lunch at a farm that had a wonderful restaurant, using everything they raised and grew. He drove her through the countryside he loved so much, and she got to know Joanna better, and had great respect for her. Their relationship was all based on kindness and mutual admiration and they were mature for young people their age. At twenty-four, he was surprisingly grown-up and centered, and so was she. She was the oldest of five children and an impressively responsible young woman. Olympia could easily see them getting married one day and almost hoped they would. Their values and goals appeared to be the same, much like she and Bill. And Josh said openly that he wanted to spend the rest of his life on a farm, and bring his children up in a healthy, simple rural atmosphere. The more sophisticated life he'd grown up with, with a father in politics, as a senator, held no appeal to him. New York,

Washington, and Chicago were all big cities he didn't care if he ever saw again. Even his uncle's quieter life as a senator in Connecticut seemed much too public and worldly to him. He wanted the opposite extreme of what he'd always known, and Joanna was content to share that with him, and had all the same goals.

Olympia wondered sometimes how their children had turned out to be so different from their parents. Bill had had his sights set on the White House, after all, but given how his life had ended, murdered on the campaign trail, it was not so surprising that her children were disillusioned and had an aversion to politics, any kind of public life, and even city living. And Darcy was even more extreme, living in an African village, and helping desperately poor people get basic food and clean water, although Olympia couldn't imagine her staying there forever. But clearly, Josh was at home where he was. He had rejected everything he'd grown up with, they both had, which was their reaction to their father's death and the price he'd paid for his dreams.

The three of them cooked dinner in the tiny house he lived in. Olympia drove from Iowa to the Chicago airport the next day, to fly back to New York. Unlike her son, she preferred big cities, and she and Bill had been comfortable as public people. But she felt relaxed and peaceful after spending two days with him and Joanna in their rural life. She sat looking out the window of the plane, thinking about them, as she flew home to New York that night, and she was happy for them, and thrilled she'd gone to visit. It had strengthened the bond with her son again. She was grateful he hadn't given up on her. After two days together, they were closer than ever.

And now she had to face the realities of her life and the case that the CIA was building against Tony, the lies he had told her and Bill, and the friendship he had pretended was so important to him while he manipulated her and even had someone break in to her home and steal what he thought were incriminating papers about his illegal deals. She also had to face the prison she had built for herself in the past six years at his urging. Now she saw clearly the negative influence he'd had on her, every bit of it with an ulterior motive, which served him, to her detriment. It all had to change. She had to rebuild her life again.

She was sad to see the spot of the missing painting when she walked into her house that night. Two CIA agents were waiting for her, as a reminder of the break-in her supposed best friend had orchestrated, and when Tony called her at midnight on her cell, she didn't have the heart to talk to him, and let it go to voicemail. She didn't want to be lied to again, or be false with him and pretend that nothing had changed. What she knew now had tainted and erased all their years of friendship. She didn't even know who he was anymore. She went to bed that night and tried not to think of any of it, except the happy days she had just spent with her son. But the echo of Tony's words and the memory of his lies haunted her. All she wanted now was for the nightmare to end. John Pelham promised it would soon.

Alix had gone back to work on Monday, after they brought Faye home from Durham, and the first thing she did was tell Felix that she couldn't leave town on an assignment for at least the next two weeks until Faye went back to school. *If* she did, which wasn't sure either. For the moment, she wanted to stay home, and be in the same town and under the same roof as her mother.

'How is she?' Felix asked her in a hushed tone.

'Very shaken up,' Alix said with a serious expression. 'It was an incredibly horrifying experience.' The kids had seen the fallen bodies of their slain classmates lying on the ground with blood in pools around them. Faye had described it to her in minute detail, and it made Alix cry just listening to it. And another of her injured friends had died since then. Alix wasn't sure it would be wise for her to go back to Duke after the experience. She wanted to see how Faye did in the next couple of weeks, and the university had already offered counseling to those who planned to return. There was no question in anyone's mind, it was going to mark them forever. You didn't live through something like that and remain the same.

Felix agreed not to send Alix or Ben on

assignment for the next several weeks, and to keep them in the city. And the death threats against Alix hadn't been resolved yet either. The threats hadn't been traced. Although it was clear that they had resulted from the digging she'd done into Tony Clark's secret life and the bribes he had taken, there was no proof to link the threats to him. It was possible that someone in the lobbies was threatening her, but the CIA hadn't been able to discover who. There hadn't been one now in a week, and Officer Pelham had assured her that they were investigating the case and the suspicions against Tony in depth at full speed. He hoped they were days away from a grand jury hearing.

Pelham came to see Alix on Tuesday morning, and she met with him in her office. He told her that they were investigating all of Tony's accounts, in the States and elsewhere offshore, which he was unaware of, and any payments he had received in the last fifteen to twenty years would be carefully traced, and many already had been. He didn't tell her that they had nearly all the evidence they needed. They were waiting for a few final pieces of information about the payments he'd received from the Saudis. His Swiss bank accounts alone, given the amounts, were enough to put him away for a long time on tax evasion. Their two star witnesses, important lobbyists themselves, were waiting to testify in front of the grand jury, with hardcore evidence against him. They were almost ready to issue a warrant, which he didn't tell Alix.

And she was shocked when Pelham told her that Olympia's home had been ransacked on Sunday, after what she had told Tony over dinner the night before. He had gone for the bait, hook, line, and sinker, and cartons of what he assumed were incriminating papers had been removed from her home. They were meaningless, and he was too late to save himself now, but he didn't know it. He had believed Olympia's innocent patter, and the false information she'd dropped, while he lied to her throughout the meal.

Alix felt very sorry for her when she heard about the break-in, but more than that she knew how much Olympia had believed in Tony, how she had valued their friendship and been loyal to him. She was a decent, honest woman, and Alix knew it must have been a terrible blow to her to realize that he was a liar and a fraud. Alix was sure Tony would have blamed Bill if he had to. Anything and anyone was fair game to him, and he had played Olympia for a fool. Their friendship had been reduced to ashes, there was nothing left. And Alix could easily guess how disillusioned Olympia must feel.

She told Ben about the break-in after Pelham left, and explained how it had happened.

'What a scumbag,' Ben said without hesitation. 'Poor woman. You said he was her best friend.'

'Her *only* friend since her husband's death. That's what she thought anyway. It must have taken a lot for her to cooperate with the CIA against him. She only did it to save her husband's reputation. We convinced her that Clark was going to take him down. I really think he would have, and he might still try, unless there is flawless evidence against him that he can't deny.'

'And is there?' Ben asked with a concerned look.

'I think they're getting there, according to Pelham. They want to build an airtight case. They don't want to make a move until they have all their ducks in order. I don't know all of it, but what I do know sounds like almost enough to bury him, particularly if some of the lobbyists who bribed him testify against him to save themselves. They don't want to take the hit for him either and are willing to talk in exchange for immunity. If not, they're going to take a fall too, for paying bribes to the Vice President. It's all so sick and twisted and convoluted.' 'Scumbag' was too kind a term.

'They're not going to get any Saudis to testify against him,' Ben said skeptically.

'No, but if they can prove he was doing business with them over a long period of time, and took money from them, that's enough. The evidence may be circumstantial, but the paper trail behind him goes back years.' He nodded in agreement. And she had given the names of the four Saudis Tony met with, thanks to her contact in Tehran. Her information had proven to be solid.

'What did Pelham say about the threats against you?'

'He said to wait a couple of weeks before I go

home. Bad news for you.' She smiled at him. 'But seriously, I can move to a hotel with Faye any time you want. He said they'd keep the agents to cover Faye, and assign additional ones to me. We'll be fine.'

'To be honest, I'd rather have you at my place, if the two of you don't mind. I feel safer guarding you myself. I haven't lost my touch.' His training from the SEALs was instinctive, and he wouldn't hesitate to use it to protect her and Faye.

'No, but you've lost your privacy and your guest room. Having a teenager in the house can't be ideal for you,' Alix said apologetically.

They had dropped her off at a friend's that morning on their way to work, and she wasn't going to move all day. Her head still hurt a little, and a group of girls were going to sit in bed and watch movies in a highly secure Fifth Avenue apartment building. Alix felt sure she was safe, and they were going to pick her up on the way home, unless she decided to spend the night with her friend, which Alix thought was fine too. And just before she and Ben were ready to leave work, Faye called and said that was what she wanted to do. They were having Thai food sent in and there were four of them watching movies and their favorite shows on TV. Her dressing didn't need to be changed that night, Alix had done it in the morning, before they left. Faye said she could stay at her friend's. Alix and Ben stopped and bought groceries on the way home. But Alix wasn't hungry, she was exhausted. She kept wondering when they were going to arrest Tony Clark, and she was sure that Olympia was wondering that too. Waiting for the other shoe to drop was like a cloud hanging over their heads. Olympia's, even more than Alix's. Alix had no personal stake in it, Olympia did.

Alix had work to do that night, reading research on a story Felix had assigned to her that was in its early stages, and Ben was trying to catch up on his expense account at his desk. He went to bed before she did, and it was after midnight when she finally walked into the guest room, put on her nightgown, got into bed, and tried to fall asleep. But she kept thinking about Olympia and Tony Clark. They were like pieces of a puzzle that still didn't fit. What had he wanted from her and from Bill? What he really wanted was the presidency, but before that he had been content to ride Bill's coattails and hope for a vice presidential nomination, an alliance which might still get him into the White House as President eight years later. All of that made sense, there was his dream, his fallback position, and his long-term goal. And Olympia had no real role in it, until a madman killed her husband. Once he was gone, Clark had a clear shot at both the vice presidency and the White House again, and without Foster, he even had a shot at Bill's 'secret weapon,' his beautiful wife, an icon whom everyone loved. Bill had threatened to disassociate himself from Clark before he died, which would have ended all his dreams. But without Bill, after he died, Tony was back in the running again, on all fronts. It was perfect. He controlled Olympia with claims of love and friendship, became her mentor and best friend, which appeared noble and tacitly implied Foster's posthumous approval, if they were so close, and he married a rich, pretty young girl whose father would bankroll his campaign so his daughter would wind up as First Lady. And she even had babies with him to make him look like a respectable, lovable guy. So what was the fly in the ointment? Alix kept looking but couldn't find the piece that didn't fit, except that in some ways, Bill Foster's death had been fortuitous for him.

Alix went over the details in her head again, like counting sheep. The misfortune for Tony Clark was that Alix started snooping around, and blind luck turned up more nasty information from Alix's source in Tehran. Then the CIA got involved after Tehran, putting it all together. And suddenly the Vice President was screwed. The lobbyists who had paid him handsomely didn't want to take a fall for him. The informant in Iran led Alix to the Saudis, and she even had their names and evidence of years of meetings. There were Swiss bank accounts for the money they paid him, and the house of cards started tumbling down. And now he was desperately trying to destroy the evidence he had been told about, notes that Bill Foster had allegedly made of his illegal activities . . . which led Alix back to Bill, who had discovered that

225

Clark was a liar and a cheat and a dangerous man. And he was going to part company with him, which would have left Tony disgraced and out in the cold. Overnight Bill had become a major threat to Tony's dreams. Despite their longtime friendship, Clark knew that one day it would come out, or it could, as long as Bill Foster was alive . . . Bill knew everything. Alix sat bolt upright in bed as she thought about it. It was one in the morning by then, and she leapt out of bed and ran to Ben's room. She knocked on his bedroom door and before he could answer, she walked into the dark room. She heard a rapid stirring from the bed, and a click, and a second later, he flipped on the light and had a gun pointed at her head. She gave a gasp and took a step back. The sound she had heard was Ben cocking the gun. He had his finger on the trigger and was standing six feet away from her, with rage in his eyes, his entire body tense, as he stood in his boxers. He let out a groan when he saw her, and pointed the gun at the floor, and then sat down on the bed with a shaken look.

'For chrissake, Alix, don't do that!' He put the gun on his nightstand and stood up again. 'I could have shot you. Don't walk in here in the middle of the night and scare the shit out of me like that.' He was seriously upset. Old habits died hard.

'I didn't know you sleep with a gun,' she said, looking nervous. He had scared her too. The gun pointed at her head had frightened her, and the look on his face. She knew that he had hair-trigger

226

instincts and the training to go with them. He could easily have shot her and he wouldn't have missed.

'You're here so I can protect you, remember?' he told her.

'Just don't shoot me, if you don't mind. I thought of something,' she said, staring at him intensely, and remembering why she had come running to his room at that hour.

'It couldn't wait till morning?' He was still upset that he had pointed a gun at her and might have shot her by mistake. He couldn't bear thinking of what that could have been like. He was an expert marksman, trained to shoot to kill.

'I don't think so. This can't wait,' she said fervently. 'Bill Foster is the key here. He knew what Clark was doing. He was going to announce his separation from him as a possible future running mate. That's a hell of a message to deliver, and sooner or later the reasons why would have come out. Bill Foster was the greatest threat to Tony's future. He could have destroyed him with what he knew, and Tony was fully aware of it. Foster's wife said they argued about it. He was an honest guy, there's no way he could have stayed allied with a man like Clark once he knew what he was doing. And what if the reasons for it got out? Where would Tony be then? Finished. Forever. The whole country loved and trusted Foster. I don't think even Tony Clark could have discredited him, even if he tried, and he knew that too. He needed the alliance with Foster and his blessing, and he was about to lose it. He had to get rid of him, Ben. He *had* to, there was no way to keep it quiet forever otherwise. Bill Foster could have destroyed Clark's whole political future. Clark couldn't let that happen.' Her eyes were blazing as she said it.

Ben was staring at her, and he looked as unnerved as he had when he turned on the light and realized he was pointing a gun at her. 'What are you saying to me?'

'I think Tony Clark had Foster killed to shut him up forever. He had to silence Bill Foster. And there was only one way to do that, kill him. I think Tony did it. Not himself, but I think he paid for the hit that killed Bill Foster.'

'They never proved it was a hit,' Ben reminded her. 'I think you watch too much TV, or have too many friends in the FBI or something,' he said, groaned, and sat down on his bed again. She had woken him out of a sound sleep and scared the shit out of him, and now this, her crazy theory. He looked at Alix with dismay. 'Senators don't go around having each other killed, Alix. Clark is a bad guy, there's no denying that, but he's a crook and he's after money, big money, and I think he's willing to lie, cheat, and steal for it, take bribes, and even marry it, but I don't think he'd have his best friend assassinated so he could shut him up. That's a little too out there for me.'

'It makes perfect sense,' she said, looking annoyed

at him. 'And why wouldn't he have him killed? As long as Foster was alive there was always the risk that it would come out. He *had* to get rid of Foster. There was no other way. He was killed by an unknown gunman, allegedly a Syrian with an illegal passport and no traceable trail. They killed him before they could interrogate him. The Saudis Clark was dealing with could have arranged it for him, or hooked him up with someone to do it. Clark moves in a dangerous world. And the shooter's real identity was never clear. I don't think it was terrorism. I think it was a hit, bought and paid for by Tony Clark.' Ben stared at her after she said it, hoping it wasn't true. But Alix was convinced, and the puzzle pieces all fit, alarmingly so.

'You really think he'd have Foster killed?' Ben didn't want it to be true. It was too ugly to believe.

'He's a sociopath, or haven't you figured that out yet?' There was an edge to her tone, and Ben could see that she believed it. It was too far-fetched for him. He didn't trust Tony Clark and was willing to believe him capable of all kinds of crooked deals, but murdering his closest ally and best friend seemed beyond the pale even for Tony Clark.

'I don't buy it,' Ben said cautiously. 'Maybe someone did put a hit on him. But it wasn't Clark. That's just too evil, Alix, even for him.'

'And what if he did?' She was trying to get him to see the possibilities and not project his own values onto Clark.

'If he did, the guy is a monster, but I don't think

Clark is capable of something like that, to kill the man, destroy his children's lives, and rob them of their father, all so Foster wouldn't talk? No way.'

'It makes sense to me,' she said quietly, 'but maybe I'm crazy. I want to talk to Pelham about it tomorrow and see what he thinks.'

'Maybe you're not crazy,' Ben said thoughtfully, rolling it around in his mind again, 'but honestly, Alix, I hope you are. That whole family is going to be destroyed all over again if you're right. How do you even recover from that . . . his kids . . . his wife . . . God, it'll be awful if it's true.' They stared at each other for a long moment, and Alix nodded.

'Yes, it would be. Maybe I'm wrong.' But she didn't think so. 'I'm sorry I scared you when I ran in,' she said.

'Why don't you try and get some sleep, and not run in here and risk getting shot again, and try not to think up scenarios of senators paying for hits on each other. Could you dream of something happy?' he asked her, looking at her like a naughty child. 'We can talk about it again in the morning. Maybe you'll convince me.'

She went back to her room then, and lay on the bed again, but her theory kept swirling around in her head, and by morning she was more certain than ever. Ben still didn't believe Clark had had Bill Foster killed. It was too crazy and unlikely and sounded like a bad movie to him.

She didn't mention it again on the way to the

office, but when she got to her desk, she called John Pelham at the CIA office and asked him to come and see her. She wasn't going to tell him something like that on the phone, and she didn't mention it to Felix. She already knew Ben thought she was crazy. He had scolded her again for nearly scaring him to death the night before when she knew he was armed, and she told him she didn't know he slept with a gun in his boxers.

'Something wrong?' Pelham asked her, concerned. 'Another threat?'

'No, it's more complicated than that.'

'Did Clark call you?' They were hours away from arresting him, or days at the most, and the senior officer had his hands full. He didn't want to waste time if he didn't have to, but she sounded as though it was important.

'No, he didn't.'

'Is this serious?' Pelham asked her in a somber voice. He'd had an early morning meeting with the head of the CIA and the Director of National Intelligence, who had flown to New York to see him, about the incredible mess it was going to make when the Vice President was indicted. They weren't looking forward to it, and the meeting had been intense.

'It is serious if I'm right,' she said calmly. He didn't like the sound of it, and all of her theories had panned out so far. He trusted her instincts and sources.

'I'll be there in half an hour,' he promised. And

twenty-five minutes later he walked into her office. She invited him to sit down, and told him her theory. She was dead serious as she explained it to him, and he didn't say a word as he listened. She couldn't tell if he thought she was crazy or not. The expression on his face was blank. It had taken him years to perfect that.

'I think Bill Foster's death was a hit, not just a random act of violence or terrorism, as previously thought. I think Clark set it up. I would swear to it. He had to shut Foster up. He was a walking time bomb in Clark's career, which is all Tony Clark cares about. It would have been all over for him if Foster ever talked. Clark had to kill him, or have it done. He couldn't shoot him himself. And he had everything to gain from Foster's death.' Pelham didn't make a single comment, and when she was through he stood up with an inscrutable expression. 'What do you think?' She couldn't tell if he believed her.

'I'll get back to you on that,' was all he said, and strode out of her office as she stared after him, and Ben walked in a moment later.

'So what did he think?' Ben asked her.

'Probably that I'm nuts. He didn't say much. In fact, he didn't say anything. He just listened to me mouth off, stood up, and walked out.' She still looked stunned by Pelham's reaction.

'Just like that?' Ben questioned her with a serious expression.

'Just like that. No reaction at all.'

'Then he believes you.' Ben was impressed.

'How do you know?'

'Because that means he's going to check it out, which he isn't going to tell you. If he thought you were nuts, he would have said so and blown you off. My CO in the SEALs was like that. When we were right on the money, he never said a word. He just moved into action.'

'Now what?' She was puzzled.

'We go back to work, and he does his job. You gave him a whole new can of worms to deal with.' Ben went back to his own office then, and Alix went back to her computer to answer emails. She hated being in the office, it was so boring, and all she could think about now was Tony Clark.

Alix didn't know it, but a team of ten men were sitting in Pelham's office at that moment. They had their work cut out for them, and each of them had been given part of the assignment. They scurried off like mice afterward, and Pelham sat staring out the window of his office. The case against Tony Clark was getting more complicated by the hour.

And at her house, Olympia had just asked Jennifer to look into several law schools, among them NYU and Columbia. She wanted to check out a master's class for a year.

'You're going back to school?' Her assistant looked at her in surprise. She'd been dealing with the alarm company all morning. The men who had broken into the house over the weekend had destroyed the system they had, which was a fairly sophisticated one. The burglars knew what they were doing.

'I'm thinking about it.' Olympia smiled at her. Jennifer considered it a major step forward, and hoped she was finally healing. Jennifer thought going back to school was a great idea. She had some printouts from the Internet for her by that afternoon, until the catalogs she'd requested arrived.

Olympia was looking at the printouts when Officer Pelham called her. 'I'm sorry to ask, but I'd like you to have the Vice President over to see you again, just one last time. We need some more information from him.' Her eyes filled with tears as he said it.

'I'd rather not,' she said honestly. She didn't want to see Tony again. She knew too much about him now, and trying to draw information out of him was so stressful. She still hadn't recovered from the last time, and felt sick every time she thought about it.

'I'll do everything possible to avoid it, if I can,' he promised, and as soon as he hung up, Tony called her, almost as though he sensed they'd been talking about him. He said he was in town unexpectedly, and couldn't stay for dinner with her, but he wanted to come by for a cup of tea to at least see her. She didn't know what to say, and she didn't want him to be suspicious if she refused to see him. She agreed to let him come, and dialed the emergency number she had for Pelham immediately. He wanted to know now anytime she heard from Tony or planned to see him.

'What do I do now?' She sounded panicked when she asked.

'Let him come. The timing is good for us. I'll have an agent at your house in ten minutes. I want you wired.' She didn't argue with him, and the same female agent she met before was there ten minutes later and taped the wire to her again. The van with the listening devices was due on her block in five minutes. And the agent left before Tony arrived. He was late, had gotten caught in traffic, and he looked happy to see her.

Jennifer brought in tea for them, and Tony asked Olympia if there was any news from the police on the break-in, and she said there wasn't. He was sympathetic and concerned, as always.

'I hope I get my mother's painting back,' she said sadly. 'I loved it.' He gazed at her and nodded, and she noticed that he seemed stressed. When she asked him about it, he said it had been a busy week, and he had Senate hearings to attend the next day and for the rest of the week after that. He was curious about why she had gone to Chicago. Listening to him, Olympia was surprised by how little she felt as she looked at him. She was numb. He had suddenly become a stranger to her. She didn't even feel guilty for wearing the wire this time, but their conversation was innocuous. She realized that he must have gone through Bill's papers that they'd taken and discovered there was nothing incriminating in them, and he didn't ask her about them again. He seemed to have other things on his mind of greater importance, and he was the Vice President after all.

'How was your visit with Josh?' he inquired as he got up to leave, and she smiled at the memory of it.

'It was wonderful. It was nice to see him in his element. He's a real farm boy now.' Her face relaxed as she said it and Tony smiled, and looked like the man she remembered but no longer knew.

'I'm impressed that you went to see him. That must have been hard for you,' he said, sounding protective. 'I worry about you doing things like that. You're safer here at home.'

'Why would it be safer here?' She looked at him wide-eyed, particularly with her house getting broken into. But she didn't mention it and continued before he answered. 'And I had dinner with Bill's father in Chicago the night before I went to see Josh.' Tony looked annoyed. He knew Charles didn't like him. He made no bones about it and never had.

'How is he?'

'Still going strong. He's terrific.' Tony nodded and didn't comment, and she followed him to the front hall. He turned to look at her then, hesitated for a minute, and startled her with what he said next.

'You should have married me, Olympia,' he said in a serious tone. 'It's what Bill would have wanted, for both of us. He wouldn't want you alone in this house, at the mercy of people who break in, who want to hurt you or take advantage of you. I could have protected you from all that. He was always at risk for what happened to him. He was never afraid to stick his neck out too far, for what he believed in. Men like Bill are an invitation to terrorism and attacks of all kinds. He would rather stand and fall, and die for his beliefs, than back down and be flexible. I would never have done that to you.' It was a vicious thing for him to say about his best friend. Olympia knew it wasn't true, and she hated Tony for it.

'What are you saying to me? That he knew he was going to die? Had someone warned him?' She stared Tony directly in the eyes as she asked him, and he met her gaze squarely.

'I'm saying that men like Bill care more about their principles than they do about the people who love them.'

'I don't think so,' she said in a voice that sounded unusually harsh in answer to what he said. 'He loved me, and I loved him.' She was shocked by what Tony was saying.

'So did I,' Tony said sadly. 'But our love didn't save him. His destiny caught up with him in the end. Take care of yourself, Olympia, I'll see you next week.' He brushed the top of her head with his lips, looked at her for a last time, and then left, and she was shaking when she closed the door behind him. She didn't like anything he had said to her, and it didn't make sense. Tony sounded bitter and angry at Bill, and even at her, as though they had let him down, and she didn't know what he meant. She almost felt as though he had just said goodbye to her.

One of the agents came in to take the wire from her twenty minutes later, and she was having breakfast the next morning when Officer Pelham called her and apologized for the intrusion, but asked if he could come by. He had heard the recording of Clark's visit to her the day before and understood it better than she did.

There were two agents with him when he came to see her this time, and he looked serious when he walked in. Jennifer escorted them into the sitting room, and she had the sense that something bad was about to happen, but she left the room discreetly when the three men sat down, since Olympia didn't ask her to stay.

'Mrs Foster,' he began quietly, hating what he was about to say to her. 'I have something very difficult to tell you. A new element has come up in the government's case against the Vice President.'

'Did he do something else? Will it affect my husband?' She was frightened as she asked. There seemed to be no limit to Tony's perfidy and his betrayal of him.

'It already has. The damage is done,' he said cryptically, and then he jumped in. She had a right to know before it became public. And there was no time to prepare her. 'We have reason to believe that the Vice President was instrumental in your husband's assassination. Your husband's murder appeared to be a random act of terrorism, striking at all that is good and principled about this country.

'But we've just begun to explore another theory, that the Vice President had the most to gain from your husband's death, to silence him. His whole political future was at stake from your husband learning that he was taking bribes and making illegal oil deals.

'We've looked closely into the Vice President's offshore accounts. There is no conclusive evidence, but he paid five thousand dollars to a man in Dubai two days before your husband's death. We've been unable to trace the recipient of the money, and I doubt the person's identity is real, but the amount is standard for a hit of that kind, and the date is too coincidental. We now believe that Tony Clark paid for the hit that killed your husband. Motive and opportunity are there, and circumstantial evidence.' Olympia stared at him in horror as he said it. Her mouth opened and closed and she didn't make a sound. She couldn't. She wanted to scream but nothing came out, and as she stared at Pelham, the room spun around her, her eyes rolled back in her head, and she fainted. What she had heard from Officer Pelham was the last straw. It had been hard enough surviving Bill's murder, but knowing or believing that Tony had probably paid for it to happen was more than

Olympia could bear. He had paid five thousand dollars to end the life of the man she loved so much, her children's father, a hero in his country. It was unthinkable, and as the room swirled around her, all Olympia wanted was for Tony to die too.

CHAPTER 13

When Olympia regained consciousness, the CIA agents had left the room and were waiting in the hall, and Jennifer was with her. She gave her a glass of water while Olympia struggled for composure, and then John Pelham came back in to talk to her again, leaving the others outside in the hall. He apologized for the shocking information he had shared with her, but there was no doubt in his mind, after Alix's suggestion to him. And it checked out through Clark's offshore accounts and their underworld informants. It was almost certain that Alix was right, and they were going to do everything they could to add murder to the indictment, and get all the evidence they could to prove it. And Olympia had a right to know.

'Are you sure?' she asked him in a weak voice when Jennifer left the room again.

'Yes, I am. It will take us time to prove it, but we have a record of the transaction through one of his offshore accounts we found in addition to his Swiss accounts. And one of our reliable informants in the Middle East has confirmed it. It was not political. It was a personal hit, which is why the amount paid was so small. This is going to alter the case against him drastically. We're talking about a murder trial now, as well as money laundering, tax evasion, and taking bribes. We're going to hold the grand jury hearing tomorrow, with the two lobbyists who are going to testify against him.'

'And then you'll arrest him?' she asked wanly, still feeling dizzy, almost as though Pelham had hit her. In fact, Tony Clark had. He had done the worst thing she could imagine. She felt sick.

'As soon as the grand jury gives us their verdict for an indictment, we'll arrest him, I'd say by the next day. He won't be aware of the proceedings until we do. And given what we know now, or believe, I don't think you should see him again.' She realized now that he had all but admitted it to her when he left the house the last time. He had tried to make it sound as though Bill had abandoned her and betrayed her, but Tony had. He had betrayed them both, and paid to have Bill killed. He was a monster. She was still in a state of shock over what Pelham had told her, and she was deathly pale when he left a few minutes later.

When Jennifer came back into the room, Olympia told her, and the two women sat holding each other and crying. It was so unthinkable that Tony had wantonly destroyed the life of a good man who had so many people who loved him. And he justified it in his own mind and blamed Bill for what had happened and not himself.

Pelham called Alix at the network right before she left for the day. He told her in a subdued voice that her hunch had been right about Bill Foster's death.

'We don't have all the details yet, but we're fairly certain it was a paid hit, and that Clark paid for the hit from an offshore account.' Alix felt sick as she listened.

'Does Mrs Foster know yet?' Alix sounded horrified and couldn't imagine how she would take it, or live with it after she knew. Losing him at all had been hard enough.

'We told her today.'

'How was she?'

'It was a shock. We're moving ahead with the grand jury. I know you won't say anything.' She had been totally honorable about it so far, and he respected her for it. 'I'll let you know when you can break the story.' It was the least he could do for her, since she had given him all her leads and information, including her final theory, which had proved to be accurate. Now they could all see the whole picture. Tony Clark had been willing to do anything to protect his future, including killing his future running mate and best friend. It was beyond sordid, even to a pro like John Pelham. And it was tragic considering all the people Clark had hurt.

Alix sat staring into space at her desk for a few minutes after she hung up, trying to absorb it, but it was almost too big and too ugly to understand, that anyone could be that evil and that heartless, and she couldn't even imagine how Olympia must have felt when she heard it, or how she and her children would survive knowing what Clark had done. How did you recover from something like that? But at least Bill was already gone and had been for a long time. Somehow, it would have been even worse if he had just died.

Alix was still looking dazed when Ben came to find her. They had to pick Faye up at a friend's. He had become their chauffeur, bodyguard, chef, host, and best friend, and Faye had stopped complaining about staying at his apartment. He was so kind to them that she wasn't grousing about not being able to go home, and after what she'd been through, she liked sharing a bed with her mother. It made her feel like a little girl again. The wound on her head was healing nicely, and she had nightmares about the shooting, but she felt better than she had at first. It was going to take time, and she hadn't made a decision yet about going back to school for the short time left, or whether she wanted to stay in New York. And she didn't know about the fall.

'Are you okay?' Ben asked Alix, looking worried. 'Something wrong? Is Faye okay?' She nodded and stared at him with a shocked expression.

'I was right.'

'About what?'

'Bill Foster. It was a hit. They think Clark paid for it from an offshore account. He obviously figured he wouldn't get caught, and he didn't till now.'

'Oh my God. Who told you?' Ben sounded stunned.

'Pelham. He just called.'

'How is that possible? And no one knew or suspected it?'

'Apparently not. They assumed it was random terrorism. They had no reason to suspect Clark, until now.'

'Jesus. He really is a sociopath. Does Foster's wife know?'

'They just told her.'

'It must be like having him die all over again. Murdered by their closest friend. Whoa, this is going to be ugly when it comes out. Bribes, illegal oil deals, one senator murdering another. It doesn't get much worse. The President is going to love this.'

'It's going to a secret grand jury hearing tomorrow. They'll get a warrant after that.' She stood up then. They had to pick up Faye, and they were late.

Alix didn't say anything in the car. She couldn't, she was too upset and shocked. She had come up with the theory, but she had hoped it wasn't true. She wished it weren't, for Olympia's sake. She had been through enough.

Faye noticed how quiet her mother was on the way to Ben's house. 'Are you okay, Mom?'

'Yeah, I'm fine.'

'Bad day at work?' She worried about her.

'Sort of.' She couldn't talk, or fake it. She was lost in thought.

Ben tried to fill in the gaps in the conversation, but he was shocked too. They fumbled around his kitchen when they got home, and finally decided to order pizza, and when it came Alix couldn't eat. All she could think about was Olympia and how she must feel. She hoped she wasn't alone and had someone with her. She would have liked to call her, to offer her some support, but didn't know her well enough to do so, about something this huge. This was a private moment that no one else could share, except her children, who had been robbed of the father they loved by someone they knew and loved too.

Alix went to their room after dinner and lay down on the bed, and Faye came in a little while later to check on her.

'Are you feeling sick?' Faye asked gently.

'Kind of.' She didn't want to explain it. 'We covered a bad story today, or at least I found out about it. I know the people involved, slightly, and I feel terrible about it.'

'What kind of story? Like at Duke?' Faye's eyes were sad when she said it. 'A shooting?'

'Actually it was a murder, six years ago. They only found out today who did it. The victim had a nice wife and two kids your age at the time. Their best friend paid for the hit. Sometimes the human race really lets you down,' Alix said sadly, and Faye nodded.

'I kind of feel that way after what happened at school. I just don't understand it.' And then a

246

minute later she sighed and looked at her mother. 'I've decided to go back, Mom. It'll be hard. But there's only a little time left anyway. I can figure out what I want to do after that. Maybe I'll do a semester abroad next year, in France. I'll see how I feel, after I go back.' Alix's heart fluttered a little when she heard her daughter say she might do a semester abroad, but it might be good for her. And she thought it was right that she wanted to return to school now. They were opening again the following week, and it was almost summer break.

'I'll go with you and settle you in,' Alix promised. She wanted to make sure that Faye was up to it and that it wouldn't be too traumatic for her, but Alix thought she could handle it, she was a strong girl. They had discussed it a lot, and she would have counseling at school.

They talked quietly for a little while, lying on the bed, and then Alix went to the kitchen for a cup of tea, and ran into Ben putting dishes in the dishwasher. It almost felt like a family being there, even though they were only friends. She told him that Faye had decided to go back to school.

'I think it's the right decision,' he said seriously.

'So do I, but it will be hard while she's there.' He nodded.

'The kids can console each other. You have to get through the tough times in life, you can't go around them or run away. I think she's smart to make the decision, and be brave.' He smiled at Faye when she walked in, helped herself to a bottle of water, and went back to their room, which now seemed comfortable and familiar.

They had all been through their tough times, Alix when she had Faye as barely more than a child herself, and her husband's accidental death right after, Ben when he lost his son, and now Faye after the shooting. No one was exempt at any age. And Alix couldn't help thinking that now Olympia Foster and her children would be facing tough times again, reliving the death of their father, and the betrayal by their most trusted friend. Alix felt deeply sorry for them.

She and Ben sat at the kitchen table for a while and talked about it, before they went to bed.

'When are you taking Faye to Duke?' he asked her.

'Not this weekend, the one after. The semester's almost over.'

'I'll come with you if you want, if Faye won't consider it an intrusion.' He wanted to be respectful of them both, and give them space if they needed it, and time alone, but he wanted to be there to offer support too, to the degree that he could.

'She likes you, I'm sure she'd be happy if you came.' And this time, they could fly, which would be a lot easier than the drive from New Orleans had been.

Ben followed Alix to her room and said good night to her in the hall. It reminded him of the night she had been convinced that Clark had killed Foster and he thought she was crazy. As it turned out, she wasn't crazy at all. Clark was. And a terrible man, beyond anyone's wildest imagination.

When Alix walked into the guest room, Faye was asleep, and looked like a little girl in her pink pajamas with her hair in a braid. She still had a bandage on the wound, although it was closed now. Alix slid into bed and put her arms around her daughter, and was grateful again that she was alive. It was all she needed. Nothing else mattered.

After Pelham's visit to her, Olympia spent a quiet evening when Jennifer left for the day. She had offered to stay, but Olympia wanted to be alone. She wanted to think about what had happened, and how she was going to tell her children. It was going to be a huge shock to them, but they had a right to know. She didn't know whether to tell them now, or after Tony was arrested. And in the end, she decided to wait. She didn't feel up to talking to them tonight and giving them the support they needed. She wanted to feel stronger when she called them. It had been a terrible blow.

She hardly slept that night, and she was glad that Tony didn't call her late, as he often did. She knew he was busy preparing for the Senate hearings the next day, and she was relieved not to hear his voice. There was nothing left to say. She never wanted to speak to him again. Now that she knew the truth, she just couldn't.

Jennifer saw that she looked exhausted the next day but didn't comment. The catalogs had come in from NYU and Columbia, and Olympia flipped through them, trying not to think of the grand jury hearing that was happening that day and what the verdict was going to be. She saw that there were several classes she might be interested in. She couldn't wait to tell Darcy about them the next time they spoke, when things calmed down again. But before that, she knew that she'd have to tell them about Tony, and what he had done. She dreaded sharing it with them, and their reaction. They would be devastated, and so would Bill's father.

And much to her horror, Tony called her that night. He was the last person she wanted to talk to. But she forced herself to take the call so he didn't suspect anything. It was agony talking to him and made her feel even sicker. He told her the Senate hearing had gone well that day, and he'd had dinner at the White House with the President in the private quarters. The First Lady was away on an official trip, and they'd had some business to attend to. He sounded very self-important when he said it, and Olympia felt dizzy.

'And what did you do today?' he asked, in a condescending tone. 'Are you working on the book again?'

'Not really. I've been looking into law school classes, as a kind of refresher. It was Charles's idea when I saw him, and I think I'll do it.' It was something to say, and Tony sounded shocked.

'Why would you bother? You're not going to practice law again, are you? Why would you?'

'I might,' she said vaguely, desperate to get off the phone. 'How's Megan feeling?' she asked, to change the subject.

'She's starting to have morning sickness,' he said, in an unsympathetic tone, 'but she wanted another baby, so she'll have to put up with it.' Olympia couldn't help thinking that she was going to feel a lot sicker when she heard that her husband would be going to prison for all that he had done, including murder. She wanted to feel sorry for her, but she didn't. He had fooled Megan too, but Olympia wasn't convinced she loved him either, and thought she had ulterior motives of her own.

'I was going to try to come up and see you this weekend,' he said breezily, 'but I don't think I can. I've got too much homework to do. The President has a new project he wants my help with. I'll come up next week.' She was noncommittal, and hoped he wouldn't be going anywhere the following week except jail.

And then they hung up after he told her he loved her, and she felt nauseous as she sat staring at the phone in her hand. She wondered if the grand jury had reached a decision, what the two lobbyists had said in their testimony, and if they had convinced the grand jury of his guilt sufficiently so he would be indicted and stand trial. John Pelham had said he didn't think it would come to that yet. Tony would have to resign, and probably plead guilty to a deal. And with murder added, it would be a huge scandal. The CIA was going to be presenting evidence at the hearing, with the caveat that there would be more later, and they were adding what they knew of Bill Foster's murder, and Tony's presumed involvement in it.

She lay awake most of the night, thinking about him, and waiting to hear from Pelham in the morning, but he didn't call, and she didn't want to call him. She was well aware that she had to be patient and wait for news. The wheels of justice turned slowly, but she also knew they would get him in the end. Tony's life, as he knew it, was over.

CHAPTER 14

John Pelham waited to call Olympia until they had the indictment. The grand jury had taken their time and made a careful decision. He was being indicted for taking bribes, receiving illegal payments from the Saudis on oil deals for at least a dozen years, tax evasion, money laundering for his offshore accounts, and being responsible for the murder of Senator William Foster. There were so many charges against him that it took them two full days to hear all the evidence, and a third to pronounce their verdict. Tony was to be given the opportunity to resign, and if he didn't, then he would be impeached by the House of Representatives, and the impeachment itself would be conducted by the Senate. It was a complicated procedure, and the President had to be advised before they arrested him. There were rules about it that had never been implemented before, and then the President would have to appoint a new Vice President. The ripple effect around the whole situation was huge.

Officer Pelham had the signed warrant on his desk from a federal judge, when he called Olympia

Foster and told her they were going to arrest him that night. The Director of National Intelligence had been advised as well. He had followed the case every step of the way.

'Has he called you?' Pelham asked her about Tony.

'Every day,' she said unhappily, 'but he was too busy to come up. He's been in Senate hearings all week.'

'I would prefer it if you didn't take his call, if he calls you tonight. He might hear something in your voice. We want this to go as smoothly and quietly as possible,' although he knew the entire country would be in an uproar by the next day once the news was out. And he had promised to advise Alix immediately after they made the arrest. He wanted to give her a jump-start on the story. She deserved it. She had done everything she could to help them, without leaking any part of it on the news.

Olympia thanked him for the call and wished him luck, and waited to hear that the deed was done. And then she would have to call her children, at whatever hour, so they didn't hear it first on the morning news. She was worried about them. And it was a long night, another one. There was no news from John Pelham until seven o'clock the next morning, and when he called her, he was tired and tense, and she could hear it. His night had been even longer and harder than hers, and she was sure that arresting Tony had been unpleasant.

'Is he in custody?' she asked him, guessing how shocked Tony must have been when they arrested him.

'No, he's not,' Pelham admitted to her in an exhausted voice. He'd been up all night for several days. 'He had an early warning system better than ours. When we got to his home, he was gone.' It took a minute for what he said to sink in.

'You mean out?' she asked in a choked voice. She sounded breathless.

'No, I mean gone. There are federal agents looking for him in all the locations he could be. We think he flew to Canada on a private plane last night. An informant has told us that two of his longtime Saudi friends were waiting for him in Montreal, we believe that he's with them with a new identity. There was a leak somewhere,' he said bleakly. 'He managed to slip out of his home and shake his Secret Service detail, who assumed he'd gone to bed. He must have gotten out through a window or disguised somehow. We missed him, and he won't be back. By sometime today, he'll be in Saudi Arabia, either Jedda or Riyadh. He's gone, Mrs Foster, for good.' And he wouldn't stand trial. Pelham had just told the President the same thing, and in the next hour, it would be on every network and all over the Internet. 'I'm sorry. We want him brought to justice as badly as you do. It's been a massive and intense operation, but he skipped. He's a clever, very dangerous man. Even more so than we thought, and his ties in the Arab world are very strong. They'll protect him. We won't be hearing from him again, and I doubt you will. If you do, let us know.'

They had pieced it all together in the past several hours and he didn't tell her that the President was livid. What Tony Clark had done was outrageous, but no more so than the rest, and his eleventh-hour escape was a national disgrace. John Pelham wasn't sure he'd have a job after this, but more than anything, it infuriated him to have a criminal like Clark outsmart them and go free. He had been too well prepared, and knew his life depended on it. Clark's exit plan had been flawless.

Olympia sat staring out the window after the call, thinking of Tony and how much she hated him. The only comfort she had had in the past few days was knowing that he would pay for his crimes and go to prison. It wasn't enough, but it was something. And now he was free. And she had to tell her children. She picked up her phone and called Darcy on Skype in Zimbabwe, before she could hear it on the news.

She looked happy to see her mother on the screen when she answered, and devastated after her mother told her. Olympia spent half an hour on the phone with her and sounded strong, and then she got off the call and called Josh. He cried like a baby. They had loved Tony all their lives. So had Olympia and Bill. They all had. And Tony had loved no one except himself. And now he was gone. After the children, Olympia called Charles in Chicago and told him the whole story. He was silent as he listened and then cried along with her.

The plane lifted off from Dulles International Airport just after 10 P.M., with one passenger with a British passport, and it landed in Montreal at 1 A.M. A 747 owned by the Saudi royal family was waiting to leave Montreal shortly after. The flight plan had been filed. Members of the family and their employees were on board and continued to arrive for the next hour. The passports had been checked and stamped, and there were a variety of nationals in the entourage. French, British, German, Filipino, Italian. There were no Americans. Their visas were all in order. Their flight plan was approved, and the plane lifted off at 2:10 A.M., with Riyadh as their destination. They had diplomatic immunity but hadn't exercised it, and it hadn't been necessary, there had been nothing out of the ordinary about the departure, the crew, or the passengers on board.

But on closer scrutiny at the request of the CIA in the early hours of the morning, they discovered there was a German national aboard who matched Tony Clark's description, but not the name. And there was one additional Saudi passport, for a male subject, which no one could explain. All they could figure out was that it was Tony and he was traveling with three passports, and none of them issued by the United States or in his own name. It was

257

impossible to determine from the ground which was his, or all, or any. Tony Clark as a U.S. citizen had dissolved and vanished into thin air, and had become German or Saudi, and no one in Riyadh was going to check or question the royal family and who they had with them, if he was even on board. He could have been hiding out anywhere, even in the States, but an escape with the Saudis was the most likely scenario, and he could go anywhere from there, as long as he didn't enter a country that had an extradition agreement and would return him to the States to face criminal charges, and there were many countries, even in Europe, that wouldn't. He had made it impossible to bring him to justice, even find him, or identify him. He had created a dilemma for the President, and every federal law enforcement agency that existed. His exit plan had been brilliant.

Alix got the call shortly after seven A.M., and Pelham told her what had happened. He had just spoken to Olympia right before her. Alix leapt out of bed as soon as he ended the call, and pounded on Ben's door.

'Don't shoot me!' she said through the door, afraid to walk in on him naked coming out of the shower, and he yanked the door open when he heard her.

'What's wrong?'

'Tony Clark skipped town last night. Actually, he fled the country. They think he's on his way to Saudi Arabia, via Canada, with a new identity.

258

They're going to announce it in an hour, with the indictment. The President called a press conference. I've got to get to the office.'

'Shit, are you serious?'

'Totally.' She ran back to her room and pulled on jeans and ballet flats, and put on a red jacket in case she was on camera, which she assumed she would be, and explained to Faye what had happened. She grabbed her purse, didn't bother to comb her hair or put on makeup, and called an Uber taxi from her cellphone, and she was out the door three minutes later as Ben and Faye stared at each other. Alix had no bodyguard with her, but the threats had stopped as suddenly as they started.

Ben flipped to the news on the TV, but there was no mention of it yet. The President was speaking at 8 A.M., and Alix had less than an hour to get to the studio and be ready to comment on the broadcast in hair and makeup. Felix was already at work when she got there and gobbling antacids. She had called him on the way in from Brooklyn.

'Holy shit, what happened?' he asked as he followed her into hair and makeup and she filled him in. 'And they're going to tell the American public that? It's going to be the biggest scandal in the history of U.S. politics, the President is going to look like an idiot, and so will the CIA and every other federal agency. There will be so much egg on everyone's face, it'll look like Easter.'

'No,' she said sensibly. 'The President will look

like a hero, because they've been tracking him. And if he's smart he will appoint someone who'll step up to the plate fast and clean this up with him.'

'And who would that be?'

'That I don't know. But Tony Clark is one smart sonofabitch to have gotten himself out of this one,' Alix said tersely.

'Yeah? Into what? Life on a camel for the rest of his life? Have you been to Saudi Arabia? A hundred and forty degrees in the summer, no White House dinners, and he won't be going to the White House as President in this lifetime. How smart was that? And he *murdered* Bill Foster and paid for the hit with offshore money. If you ask me, he's insane.' But not too crazy to get himself out of it. It was incredible. Her hair was picture perfect by then and her makeup flawless, and she had just enough time to get to her desk and write on her iPad what she wanted to say. Felix was having her do the intro before the press conference and the editorial after, since she knew more about it than anyone else at the network, and she knew what not to say too, and how not to piss off the CIA forever by making them look incompetent for losing him. She felt sorry for John Pelham, who had done a remarkable job pursuing all the leads and tying them together, but Tony Clark was smarter. And there was no way to tell who had warned Tony Clark of what was coming. Maybe even someone in the CIA. It was unlikely they'd ever find out.

The assistant producer came to get Alix for the countdown. She looked serious and calm when she came on the air, and dignified but pretty in her plain red jacket and somber face. She said that there had been a national crisis in recent days, involving the Vice President. She gave a brief, shocking summary of all that he was accused of, and then they switched to the President at the White House, looking solemn. They had cleaned it up as best they could, but the story wasn't pretty. A Vice President who had allegedly engaged in every imaginable form of illegal activity, including murder for hire, and had been indicted by a grand jury, had fled the country before he could be arrested. It was a national shame. The entire nation was shocked into silence as they watched over breakfast. The President's final part of his message stunned Alix. The Vice President had left a letter at his home, resigning the vice presidency. The letter had been found and delivered to the President moments before the broadcast. Alix was amazed. Tony Clark had thought of everything to the last detail.

After the press conference, the shot went back to Alix, who analyzed the situation as rationally as one could and explained the workings of a grand jury and how they functioned. And what would have to happen to appoint a new Vice President. Everyone was guessing who the President would choose to replace Clark as Vice President. It was all anyone was talking about on the air on every channel, as Ben and Faye watched Alix on the screen from his living room in Brooklyn.

'Your mom is brilliant,' he muttered as they listened to her editorial afterward, and Olympia and Jennifer were watching Alix at Olympia's home too.

'I feel like I'm dreaming,' Jennifer said, but it was more like a nightmare, and Olympia thought of Megan, who was left with two babies and another one on the way, by a man who had disgraced her and would go down in history as one of the worst criminals of our time. Her father's money couldn't change that. It might have helped Clark win the presidency, but it couldn't change the fact that he was being charged with twenty-two federal crimes, including murder. There was a shot of Megan later on, hiding behind dark glasses, boarding a private plane to go to her parents' home in California with her children and a nanny, and the Secret Service with her. She had been tainted by association and there was little pity for her on the news. She had instantly become a spoiled rich girl who was married to a criminal. The rest was irrelevant. But sympathy was running high for the Fosters again, and the news that the Vice President had been instrumental in Bill's death touched everyone's heart. Along with every-thing else, he was a father, a husband, and a good man. Armies of press were camped outside Olympia's house and jammed her street, but they had been unable to reach her for comment. And compassionate New Yorkers had begun leaving flowers at her door. Local police were trying to control the crowds and traffic on her street, but no one had seen her. She was deep inside her home, mourning her husband's senseless death again, and obliged to live with the fact that her husband's best friend had paid to have him murdered, and had successfully escaped.

There was pandemonium at the network for the rest of the day, and a list of possible vice presidential nominees was being discussed on air and in the press. The next day the President appointed the Speaker of the House as the new Vice President, which was the wisest and most conservative choice to present to a shocked nation, and one that would ensure immediate confirmation by Congress. There were comments from the media around the world, and heads of state, about what had happened. Saudi leaders had denied any responsibility for the disgraced Vice President and his escape, and weren't pleased about it either. They wanted no part of the American scandal or the crimes of Tony Clark.

Olympia was reading *The New York Times* the day after when her cellphone rang with a number she didn't recognize. She picked it up absentmindedly and was shocked to hear his voice. It was Tony. She sat frozen in silence.

'I didn't get a chance to say goodbye,' was the first thing Tony said to her. She was too startled to speak, she just listened. 'I want you to know that the one thing that was true in all of it is that I loved you. I always did, from the first minute I saw you. Bill didn't deserve you. I needed you more.' It was always about Tony and no one else.

'You killed my husband,' she accused him openly now.

'He was always a marked man,' Tony justified it. 'You can't live by those rigid rules in today's world. It doesn't work that way. Someone was bound to kill him. I had no choice. And he would have destroyed everything I spent years building. That wasn't right, Olympia, we were friends. When he disavowed me, he would have had to explain why, and it would have been all over for me. He knew that and didn't care. What kind of friend is that?' He sounded like a madman with his twisted values.

'So that made it all right to hire a hit man to kill him? He was loyal to his country and wouldn't cover for you. It's over for you now anyway. Look what you did, and to Megan, and your children. They'll never know you,' although she thought they'd be better off without him.

'They'll be fine,' he said, dismissing them. 'You're the only one I'll miss. Maybe you'll come to see me one day,' he said, sounding wistful for a moment, with no sense of reality about how she felt about him, and what he had done to them. He was deranged, with a totally distorted view of what he'd done and the gravity of it. His narcissism blinded him to all else.

'What are you going to do? Hide forever?' Her voice was shaking and cold.

'Well, I'm certainly not coming back to go to prison. It's a different life here. It suits me.' He would be a fugitive on the run forever, and live in hiding, and he knew it, but he didn't seem to care.

'You weren't in on it, Olympia, were you? It would kill me if you were. It was that bitch of a reporter who started all this. She's lucky nothing happened to her. But I don't care now.' Olympia noticed that he didn't wait for her to answer about her own involvement, and she didn't answer his question. He had no right to know. 'I'm going to miss you terribly.' He sounded sad as he said it.

'I'll never forgive you for what you did to Bill,' she said clearly. 'I loved you as a friend, and so did he. You betrayed us. You robbed my children of their father. You killed the man I loved. You've got a lot to live with and a long time to think about it,' but it didn't seem to matter to him. There was nothing and no one he cared about, not even his own children. 'Don't call me again. You're dead to me. You should have died instead of him.'

'You should have married me when I asked you to. It would all be different now, and you'd be happy instead of alone.'

'I'd rather be alone forever than with you,' she said and meant it.

'Take care of yourself, Olympia, I'll be thinking of you. I love you.' He had no sense of how wrong it was to say that to her. And then the line went dead and she sat staring at her phone, wondering where he was. Somewhere in Saudi Arabia probably. Or in hell, where he belonged.

Olympia called John Pelham about the call from Tony afterward, and then she called her children again. They sounded better, as it began to sink in. Olympia kept reminding them that they had never really known Tony, and who he truly was. None of them did. Bill had seen him for what he was years before, but he was the only one who had, and it had cost him his life. She knew Josh and Darcy were going to be all right now. They were young and strong and healthy, leading good lives with good people around them. Losing their father had been a terrible blow, for all of them, but he had given them a shining example to follow and be proud of, and the memories they had of him would last forever, longer than the memories of the man who had killed him. The friend Tony had appeared to be to all of them had never existed. Tony Clark had been nothing more than an illusion, a mask with nothing behind it, and a heartless killer.

CHAPTER 15

The country had begun to calm down and return to some kind of normalcy by the time Ben and Alix took Faye back to Duke. Their bodyguards were gone, and life was back to their regular routine, although they had continued to stay at Ben's until Faye left. It was easier not to move back home yet. Faye was understandably silent on the flight down. She wore her headphones and listened to music on her iPod with her eyes closed, as Alix glanced at Ben over her head from time to time. They could too easily visualize the images going through Faye's mind of the day she had left when she was shot, and her friends were killed.

When Faye saw the campus, the memories of the shooting were overwhelming. There was a field of flowers at the main entrance when they drove up to it. Twenty-two wreaths were replaced every few days by local florists, to pay tribute to the final number of victims.

The atmosphere was subdued as they drove past the flowers to her dorm, and Faye squeezed her mother's hand. Alix put an arm around her waist as they got out of the car in front of the familiar building. She was going to be alone in her room for a while. She wouldn't be assigned a new roommate until the fall semester, out of respect for the one who had died. Her parents had removed their daughter's belongings while the university was still closed. When she walked into the room, Faye's heart ached knowing she would never see her again, and they'd had such good times and were so well suited to each other. She was from Atlanta, and Faye had gone home with her several times for the weekend. She'd had a beautiful letter from her parents, and called them once from New York. Faye's roommate was their only child and it was a tragedy for them, just like all the others.

On the first day the university reopened, there was an interdenominational memorial service for the fallen students and professors who had lost their lives in the shooting. Alix and Ben went with Faye, and they walked around the campus afterward, and Faye ran into a few people she knew, fellow students and an assistant professor who'd been injured too. They put their arms out and hugged each other, and three girls came to Faye's room to visit her when they went back. They knew she'd be lonely without her roommate, and Alix suggested she request to transfer rooms, which seemed like a healthier solution than staying where she was, even for a short while. But Faye didn't want to, for the brief time she'd be there.

They left Faye with her friends, and Ben and

Alix went back to their hotel. She had a heavy heart, thinking of what Faye was going through, and she didn't want to leave her, but she knew that sooner or later, Faye would have to pick up the threads of her normal life again, and she was trying to.

'She'll be all right,' Ben tried to reassure her, and Alix nodded as he put an arm around her. He had been such a comfort to them both. He was so warm and compassionate that it made her wonder why he had never gotten seriously involved with another woman since his wife. He had so much to offer someone, even as a friend, and he had been so kind to them, letting them stay with him during the threats to Alix, and now coming to Duke with them, and right after the shooting. He was such a kind, gentle person, and it was obvious that he cared about Alix and her daughter.

'I know she'll be all right,' Alix said thoughtfully, 'but this is going to be with her forever.' She would never forget what had happened there that day, nor would Alix forget when she saw her daughter covered with blood on the screen when she was watching TV in New Orleans.

'So will the good things that happen to her. Life is about balance. She'll have both,' he said, and Alix couldn't help thinking about Ben's son. They chatted for a while sitting on a bench outside the hotel. It was a peaceful evening, under a star-filled sky, as Alix thought about how quickly the years had flown by. One minute Faye had been a baby and Alix was terrified, and now she was almost grown up, and on her own at college. Sometimes it made her want to turn back the clock and start all over again. She realized now that at times you didn't know how much fun you were having until you looked back. She said something about it to Ben, and he laughed.

'I felt that way about the SEALs once I got out. I didn't realize at the time how great it was. I was too busy going on missions and staying alive. Some things in life are better with hindsight. I feel that way about our assignments too. I wouldn't necessarily want to do them again, but they make for some incredible memories.' He smiled at her as he said it.

'I didn't understand how fast she would grow up,' Alix said, and he nodded, understanding what she meant. Faye had been only fifteen when he and Alix started working together, and she used to talk about her and complain at times about how difficult it was to have a teenaged daughter, and now Faye seemed like a woman, and Alix was lonely without her at home. 'My mother says the same thing about me.'

They left each other outside their rooms, and met again in the morning to take Faye to breakfast off campus at a coffee shop she liked, and then Alix went back to her room with her to help her unpack the rest of her things. Faye was feeling better than she had the day before, and was happy she had made the decision to return to school.

But she was still considering doing the fall semester of junior year abroad, in France. She could even take classes in French, since she was still fluent.

The afternoon went by too quickly and Ben and her mother had to leave at six o'clock to catch their flight to New York. Faye had some studying to do, and she met up with friends right before they left. There were two good-looking boys in the group. One of them had lost his roommate too, and he and Faye were talking about it. He was shocked to realize she'd been shot, and thought she was very brave to come back after that, but she said she was glad she had. They were able to comfort each other since they'd all lived through it, and Faye felt better with them than she had with her friends at home. Here, they understood. They were all going out for Thai food when Faye held Alix in her arms and kissed her, with tears in her eyes as she said goodbye, and Ben was moved too.

They could hear the boy talking to Faye, asking her if Ben was her father, as they walked away, and she said he was just a friend. Ben and Alix smiled at each other, and Alix was glad he was with her. They drove to the airport, talking about the weekend, as Alix tried to convince herself Faye would be fine without them. They returned the rented car, and had cappuccinos at the airport Starbucks before boarding the plane.

'Thank you for being here with us,' Alix said seriously, with a white foam mustache on her upper lip that made her look like Santa Claus, and Ben smiled.

'What are you smiling at?' She didn't feel it.

'You've got a mustache,' he explained, and she laughed as she wiped her face with a napkin he handed her.

She looked thoughtful for a minute, and then turned to him as they waited for their flight to be called. 'I've been wondering something all weekend, now that we've been staying at your apartment and I know you even better than when we go on assignments. Why aren't you married? You'd be good at it. You're incredibly patient and domestic, and good with kids. I have a lot less patience than you do. I get nervous at times around kids. Faye and I used to fight a lot,' she confessed and took another sip of the froth on her coffee, which was delicious.

'I remember. You used to tell me about it.' But she hadn't in a long time. They got along well now, and had for a few years. 'I guess I don't like labels, to answer your question. I was young when I got married, so I didn't think about it. I was twenty-four, in the navy, and that's what people did. They got married as kids. At this age, it's a lot more complicated, you expect more. You want it to be a perfect fit, you have to like the same books and movies, have the same political opinions, and compatible ideas about how to spend your money. There's a whole checklist people want to be a match by our age. I don't want to be anyone's checklist, and I honestly don't think I could conform that way anymore. I'm too independent after doing what I want for all these years. I don't want anyone telling me what to do.'

'Neither do I,' she admitted. 'It's one thing living with your child, and you make the rules. But I've never met a man I wanted to live with, or even had a roommate, except my daughter. I would drive someone crazy, and I would kill somebody who interfered with my life. I don't have a need to get married,' she said honestly. 'My mother says I'll regret it one day when I'm old. She and Gabriel seem to have a lot of fun together, but she doesn't want to get married either. I think he would, and has asked her a few times. And I don't want to take a chance on a relationship not working, and having it affect Faye.'

'She's not home anymore,' he reminded her. It was a poor excuse. And Alix had opened the subject, he hadn't, but she was curious about him, having seen how good he was with Faye, and even with her. It had been different from when they were working, when they were both more rough and ready, climbing in and out of military Jeeps, hanging around with soldiers, and living with a kind of wartime camaraderie. Staying at his apartment had been more like playing house, which neither of them was familiar with anymore, but it had gone well, much to her surprise.

They threw away their coffee cups when the flight was called, picked up their bags, and boarded the plane. She did some work on the way back, and used her computer on the plane since they offered Internet, and Ben read magazines. He looked over at Alix again.

'I wonder when they're going to ship us out again,' he mused out loud. 'Has Felix said anything to you?' She shook her head. There had been too much going on about the Vice President. For once, all the action had been here at home.

'Probably pretty soon. There's no big story for us at the moment, but as soon as something comes up, I'm sure he'll send us on assignment.' And now that Faye was back at school, Alix was willing to travel, and Felix had been true to his word and kept them at home.

They were both wondering where Tony Clark was, and assumed he was somewhere in Saudi Arabia in his new life. She couldn't imagine how he would adjust to it, and there was no escaping the choice he had made, even if he regretted it later. Ben didn't envy him either. There would be no turning back for him. His bank accounts had been confiscated since it was all ill-gotten gains from bribes and tax evasion, so he had no funds of his own, and was completely dependent on the men who had facilitated his escape and taken him to wherever he was. It was a totally different culture, and he was at their mercy now, an unenviable position to be in, and one that wouldn't change, since he couldn't work in Saudi Arabia. He would just be there, doing nothing and relying on his previous business partners for every penny he needed to spend. Pelham had discovered that he had paid them a vast amount of money before his escape to ensure his safety in future, so they didn't kill him. And he had pointed out to them that one day he might be of use to them in some kind of negotiation, or information trade. And on the off chance that he was right, they must have agreed to keep him alive, although he was of no use to them now.

Since they didn't have checked bags, only carry-ons, Ben and Alix walked past baggage claim when they got to JFK, went outside, and hailed a cab at the curb. Faye had sent her mother a text while they were on the plane, saying how much she appreciated their coming down to help settle her in and make her feel comfortable. She said that it meant a lot to her, and to thank Ben for her too. Alix relayed the message as they drove into town. They didn't stop to buy groceries, there was enough to throw something together for dinner that night. When they walked into the apartment, it was eerily quiet without Faye, even though she hadn't stayed there for long, and Alix had been there without her, after the first threat.

They each made a sandwich with what was in the fridge, which wasn't much. He had a ham sandwich, and she had turkey, and there were some apples in a bowl for dessert. They ate without talking, as Alix thought about Faye and missed her. And after they ate, they wandered into the living room. On every front, the war appeared to be over, and life had to go back to normal, whatever that was now.

Alix looked at Ben reluctantly, as though she had an announcement to make. 'I guess I'll move back to my place tomorrow. I've trespassed on your hospitality for long enough.' She had been there for several weeks, since the threats had started, and Faye had been there for nearly two of them. It was a long time to be staying at someone else's place, although he insisted he liked it, but she did have a home of her own to return to.

He looked crestfallen when she said it, and sat down next to her on the couch. He seemed disappointed, which surprised her. 'I was hoping you'd stick around for a while.'

'I don't have a good excuse,' she said wryly and laughed. 'No one's trying to kill me. I'm not getting death threats, there's no flood in my street, no broken water main, the heat is working. Looks like I'll have to go home,' she teased him. They were all the standard reasons for staying at a friend's apartment. 'I don't have an abusive ex-boyfriend I'm afraid of, and I'm not being evicted,' she added two more reasons, and he laughed.

'Could we just invent something? Like you want to move to Brooklyn and would like to check it out. Or your next-door neighbor is a hooker, and you don't like the look of her clients, who keep ringing your doorbell by mistake.'

'I like that one!' Alix brightened. 'Let's go with that. The hooker story.'

'What about just staying here for a while because we have a good time together, and you're good company and I like you?'

'I have a perfectly good apartment, though, which I like. How do I justify just letting it sit there and not going home?'

'Is someone keeping score?' he asked her. 'Is it anyone's business and do we care? You don't answer to anyone, and neither do I.'

'I'm not sure what I should tell Faye.'

'It makes me happy when you stay here,' he insisted. 'You're such great company. I have someone to talk to at night who listens to my stories, and we can talk about our day.' They were all the reasons people lived together, but not usually as friends at their age.

'I might cramp your style,' she reminded him, assuming he had some form of love life. They'd never discussed it.

'There's nothing to cramp,' he said without embarrassment. 'I haven't had a date in six months, and it was a disaster. Besides, I'll worry about you if you go home. What if the threats start up again?'

'If they do, I'll let you know.' She smiled at him, and saw that he really meant it and wanted her to stay with him. 'Are you serious?'

'Yes, I am. I've been thinking about it all week, and I don't want you to go back to your apartment. I want you to stay here.'

'For how long?' Maybe he only meant another week or two.

'As long as you want,' he said grandly. 'We can leave it open-ended and see how it goes.' She looked puzzled as he said it, and she wasn't sure she understood the invitation, although she thought she did. And what he was suggesting was a little bit naïve. She thought they were both too old for roommates, and they were used to their own space and could afford it. They didn't have to share an apartment so they could share the rent, which was the prime reason for most young people, which they weren't, or romance, which didn't apply to them either, since they were only co-workers and friends. But she had to admit there was some merit to the plan, but maybe not enough.

'Let me get this straight.' She looked him squarely in the eye before she asked him the next question. 'Are you volunteering as a roommate or a body-guard, or a little bit of both?'

'All of the above, and maybe some extras thrown in,' he said, seeming shy for a minute, which was unlike him. This was new territory for them, and he had taken her by surprise. She hadn't expected him to want her to stay, and she had been plan-ning to move back to her place the next day.

'What extras?' she asked, frowning at him.

'You know, whichever ones you want.'

'Ben!' She looked at him and started laughing. 'What is going on here?'

'I told you, I don't like labels. You can be what-ever you want, with or without a name. Roommate, best friend, girlfriend, partner in crime, whatever you feel like that day.' It was the closest he could come to describing what he had in mind with her, which was hard for him to explain after their being work partners and pals for four years, but for him, something had changed, and he was having trouble putting it into words.

'Are you propositioning me?' She stared at him, half kidding, and he couldn't tell if she liked the idea or not, which unnerved him, but he was in it up to his neck now, so he kept going on the path he was on.

'Actually, I was thinking that could be part of it. I like that idea, if you like it too.'

'Are you serious?' She was stunned and hadn't expected that from him.

'I am. I've been thinking about it since you moved in. I realized around Day Two that I didn't want you to leave. Well, maybe Day One, to be honest. I like living with you, you're nice to have around, and so is Faye.'

'So are you. I just never thought of us that way before. I figured we'd be work buddies forever, although my mother thought I was crazy not to start a romance with you.' It was actually the first time she had ever thought about it, when her mother said something to her about what a great guy he was and how good-looking and why wasn't she sleeping with him. But Alix didn't think it was an option for either of them, although she had liked staying with him too.

'So what do you think? What part of the plan

appeals to you?' He had offered a number of options, and they all sounded good to her. She was smiling at him, and he leaned toward her on the couch with a spark in his eye she had never noticed there before. He thought the negotiations had gone on for long enough. He kissed her as they were sitting there, and took her in his arms, and a little while later, they found their way into his bedroom, out of their clothes, and onto his bed, and then Alix stopped him for a minute and whispered to him in the dark before they went any further. None of this had been part of her plans for that night, but she liked it, a lot, and him, more than she had ever expected to, or realized she did, and they already knew each other so well, which made it even better.

'Where's the gun?' she whispered to him between kisses.

'Why? Are you going to shoot me?'

'I don't want to bump into it and set it off.' She had never slept with a man who kept a gun at his bedside before.

'I took the bullets out and locked it up, after you scared me to death and I almost shot you that night. I figured I was better off fighting a burglar with my bare hands than shooting you.'

'Good. Can we leave it locked up forever?'

'If that's what you want,' he whispered, far more interested in making love to her just then than talking about his firearms.

'Good . . . thank you,' she said, and then they

lost themselves in their passion and discovered whatever they hadn't known about each other and never suspected. It was the beginning of a whole new dimension between them, without labels. In an odd way, what happened that night was because of Tony Clark and the threats she had gotten while digging about him. As they lay in bed afterward, breathless and spent, Ben smiled down at the woman he had fallen in love with somewhere along the way. There were no words for what he felt for her, and they didn't need them. They had what they never even knew they wanted, and had waited four years to find together. And when he fell asleep next to her, she kissed him, and realized for the first time that she loved him. And then she curled up in his arms and fell asleep too.

CHAPTER 16

A week later, Alix and Ben were still going over the last details of the Tony Clark story, and at Felix's request, she had asked for an interview with Megan Clark in California, at her parents' Santa Barbara estate, and been refused. Mrs Clark was not speaking to the media. But Alix had been granted an interview with the newly appointed Vice President, and she had flown to Washington with Ben. The White House press secretary had set the condition that the newly disgraced Vice President was a taboo subject, and Alix had agreed to it. She was more interested in the current Vice President's views on a variety of subjects than dwelling on Tony Clark. People wanted to move forward, although in circles where they knew him, the shock waves were still being felt about the criminal activities of the ex–Vice President weeks later. No one could fully understand how he had been so astoundingly dishonest and no one had noticed. He had played his game well, and had a vast array of masks to hide behind. The most disturbing aspect of course was the tragic murder of Bill Foster. The rest was just a variety of games that involved unthinkable amounts of money. But Bill Foster had lost his life, Olympia her husband, and his children a beloved father, which was far worse than anything else was or could have been. And Clark's wife, Megan, and her children were casualties too.

As always, Alix did a good job with her interview of the new Vice President, and Felix praised her for it when she got back to the office the next day. She and Ben were sitting in her office going over their expense accounts when Felix walked in. He was down to two antacids at a time these days, instead of the handful he had been gobbling at once in recent weeks. Alix had begun to worry that he would choke on them. They had all come through the Clark affair with flying colors. Their coverage of every aspect of it had received the highest ratings, and the top brass at the network were extremely pleased.

'It must feel good to be back in your own apartment,' Felix said to Alix while he stopped and chatted with them, and she nodded and said something vague and unintelligible, which he didn't notice, and Ben laughed at her when Felix left and went back to his own office.

'When are we going to tell him?' Ben asked, curious about how she wanted to handle their new situation at work. It wasn't obvious to anyone yet and there was no reason why it should be. They hadn't said anything to Faye either, although Alix had admitted it to her mother in a recent phone call, and she was pleased. She wanted them to visit that summer, when Faye was there. Faye was planning to stay with her grandmother during her entire summer holiday from school, until September. Alix had told her mother that she didn't know what their plans were and they'd probably be working, but maybe they could take a week or two off at some point. Isabelle hoped they would.

'I thought you didn't like labels,' she reminded Ben when he made the comment about when they were going to tell Felix about them.

'I'm starting to like the idea better than I used to.' He grinned at her and stole a kiss while no one was looking.

'If you do that here in the office, we won't have to tell them,' she said, smiling at him. She felt young and happy, and was enjoying living with him. They got along well, and they went for long walks by the water on the weekends, and cooked dinner together at night. They had taken a ferry to Fire Island and walked on the beach. They were doing things that neither of them had taken the time to do in years, and suddenly they made the time to do them, and for each other. Life together, with or without labels, was feeling very good to both of them.

Alix had also been part of several debriefing meetings with the Clandestine Service of the CIA, about her meeting with the informant in Tehran and what he had told her. She went over it in detail with them, confirming the names of the four Saudi Arabian oilmen Tony had done business with, according to the same source. She divulged everything she knew from her contacts in the lobbies, and she met with the Director of National Intelligence. She had given them all her information before the grand jury hearing, but went over it with them again to make sure she had left out no details, no matter how minor or seemingly insignificant. She wanted to do all she could to strengthen the case against Tony Clark and confirm every shred of evidence she had, in case they were able to prosecute him, which was unlikely. It didn't change the fact that he was gone. Pelham had told her that a local informant in the Middle East had confirmed that Tony had recently been seen in Bahrain, but he had nothing to trade with now. He had no power base, only past information, most of which his Saudi contacts already knew from earlier meetings with him. He had become obsolete overnight when he was no longer Vice President. And CIA sources on the ground said he was based in Jedda in a small house he had been given. He was irrelevant to the Saudis now, and the CIA senior staff wondered if at some point the Saudis would kill him. It was a distinct possibility, although from a large amount withdrawn from one of his offshore accounts before his escape, they suspected he had paid them protection money. But whether they would respect that or not, no one knew or could predict. They were as ruthless as he was, and just as smart.

Alix was heavily praised for her cooperation, and

John Pelham thanked her again after their meeting with the director.

'How is Olympia Foster doing?' she asked him, anxious to know about her, but not wanting to bother her.

'I spoke to her a few days ago. We've had debriefing sessions with her too. I think she's doing better than she was when all this started. I think Clark had a choke hold on her. I'm not sure how he did it, but she seems more relaxed now than when we first met with her. People like him do strange things to people. He's a bad guy, but being trapped in Jedda with limited resources is not going to be a pleasant life for him. And I'm sure his gas and oil pals aren't happy with him either. They probably didn't know he was taking payoffs from the lobbyists too, and they thought they had an exclusive with him. And the assassination of Bill Foster put them in a bad light. That's what happens when you play dangerous games,' John Pelham said cynically, with no sympathy for Tony. 'Sooner or later you get burned. It all comes back to haunt you eventually.' It already had for Tony, and he was by no means entirely safe where he was, and had nothing left to bargain with. He was at their mercy.

After Pelham thanked her again for her help, he said he hoped they would work together again sometime, and she thanked him for the bodyguards for her and Faye. They told her that the FBI agent who'd been shot at Duke was doing well and back at work.

'And you look well taken care of to me,' Pelham said, smiling at Ben. He knew all about Ben's Navy SEAL history, they had checked him out very closely in the beginning, and he was impressed by some of Ben's missions. He had had a distinguished career with the SEALs and been decorated several times, before switching to network TV.

Alix hoped she'd have the opportunity to see Olympia again sometime, but it didn't feel right to intrude on her at the moment. It was all too recent, and the media had hounded her for a while, knowing how close she had been to Tony, and particularly when the news came out about her husband's murder. She had declined to comment, which everyone agreed was dignified and typical of her. Alix thought of her often, and wondered what she was doing. She hoped that Tony's disappearance had freed her and that she wasn't sad about it. His fleeing to another country in order to avoid prosecution was the best thing that could have happened to her. There would be no public reliving of the past in a trial.

The only time Olympia had been seen since Tony fled was at a campaign dinner for her brother. She had made a rare appearance to show family solidarity, although it had been obvious for years that they weren't close. But she had posed for photographs with him.

She had had dinner with her father-in-law at her home, and visited Josh again in Iowa. And after looking thoroughly at the catalogs of several law schools, and visiting both Columbia and NYU, Olympia made a careful decision, and enrolled in a master's program at Columbia that would bring her up to speed on recent legal developments, and would allow her to concentrate on the legal structure of nonprofit foundations, which was what she thought she wanted to do, and where she wanted to focus her interest. She was starting school in September. Josh was proud of her when she told him. And Charles Foster was delighted that she'd taken his advice. But when she told Darcy on Skype in Africa, she was stunned.

'You're going back to school, Mom?' She was beaming on the screen after her mother told her the news. 'What made you decide to do that?' She had been reclusive for so long since their father had died, that it was hard to imagine her leading a real life again. It was all that they had wanted for her. And now she had gotten there on her own.

'Your grandfather suggested it.' She gave him the credit for it. 'But I decided it was time for me to stop hiding in the shadows forever.'

'What about the second book about Dad?' Darcy asked, worried for a moment.

'I've put it aside for now. I'm not sure I have enough material for a second one, and maybe the world doesn't need another book about his principles and ideals. There are others on the political scene who are more current now, it's their turn. I think Dad would understand.' Darcy had tears in her eyes as she listened to her mother. It was music to her ears, and would have been to her father's too. She felt sure of that.

'I think Dad would want you to be happy, Mom. You've been sad for a long time.' Olympia nodded in agreement with her, and she realized now that Tony had worked hard to keep her down. He had wanted her silent, out of touch, and out of sight, so she didn't divulge anything Bill might have told her about him, and to make her seem unbalanced and irrelevant if she did speak up. He had convinced her that she would never recover from the trauma and shouldn't even try to. She had believed him for a long time, and he was possessive of her. Tony had damaged her almost as much as her husband's death, he had brainwashed her and no one had suspected it, not even she herself. He had been masterful at what he did, on every front, and incredibly toxic for her. She felt like she had been freed from a cult now, and returned to herself. And her kids could see it too. She was back.

'I'm thinking of going back to school too, Mom,' Darcy confided to her mother after Olympia's big announcement. 'I want to get a master's, at either NYU or Columbia too. I've already applied and I'm waiting to hear. I'm coming home in August.' Olympia was startled to hear it. She'd been planning to stay in Africa for another year. 'Maybe we can go to school together. If you don't mind, I was hoping to live at home for a year.' Olympia was thrilled to hear it, it was the best news she'd had in months, but was definitely a change of plans for her daughter. There had been no hint till now of this change of plans.

'What about your French doctor over there?' Olympia asked her, and Darcy looked wistful for a minute. She had just turned twenty-three, and with her mother turning over a new leaf, she liked the idea of living at home for a while. 'Did something happen with him?' Olympia inquired gently, and Darcy shrugged and was slow to answer.

'He's a wonderful person, Mom, but he's ten years older than I am, and we want different things. I don't think he wants to settle down for a long time, and he grew up in Africa. This is home to him. I think I'm just ready to come back, and he thought it was a good idea.' Her lip trembled as she said it, and her eyes filled with tears, and Olympia wished she could take her in her arms, but at least she could do that in August, which would be soon.

'What about taking a trip with me later this summer? Josh and Joanna are going to visit your grandfather in France. Maybe we could meet up with them.' Darcy's face lit up at the suggestion, and Olympia promised to call Josh about it too. Even a week or ten days together would do them all good. They hadn't done that since their father's death, and they used to take a trip together every year. It was time to pick up old traditions and revive them, and start new ones. Olympia mentioned that she had already rented a small house in the

Hamptons in July and had been spending time there on her own.

'I'd love that, Mom,' Darcy said, her eyes shining.

They talked for a while longer, and Olympia promised to talk to Josh about a trip, or maybe extend the rental in the Hamptons, or both. There was lots to look forward to now. And then before they hung up, Darcy asked her mother about Tony, and if anyone knew where he was. Olympia hesitated for a moment and then answered her, although she really didn't want to give her news of him, or even think about it herself.

'Apparently he's been seen in Bahrain and Saudi Arabia,' she said simply. 'They believe he's living in Jedda.'

'Do you think he'll ever come back?'

'No, I don't. He'd be crazy to. He'll go to prison if he does.'

'What about his wife?'

'I'm sure she'll divorce him, or maybe she'll try to go over to be with him, but I doubt it, given everything we know now about what he did, and not just to us.' There was so much more.

'It's so weird. It's like he died. Everyone is saying terrible things about him. It's like we didn't even know him,' Darcy said, still shaken by it. But her mother sounded firm and clear.

'No, we didn't know him,' Olympia confirmed. 'I think Dad's the only one who figured him out at the end.'

'I don't think I'll ever understand what happened,'

Darcy said sadly. It was the biggest disillusionment of her life so far, and maybe would be even in the future.

'I don't think any of us ever will. People like him just aren't human. They have no conscience or empathy for others. That's what being a sociopath is all about. It's all smoke and mirrors, fakery and lies.'

'How sad,' Darcy commented, and her mother changed the subject to something more pleasant. But at least she could talk about him now without feeling sick. At first, she nearly fainted every time she thought of him and what he'd done to Bill. But she was stronger now.

They ended their call on Skype a few minutes later, and Olympia called Josh that night about meeting in France with Darcy, and he loved the idea. He and Joanna were excited about their trip. And he was surprised too to hear that his sister was coming home.

'What happened to her big romance with the French doctor?' he asked his mother.

'I'm not sure, it sounds like it might have played itself out. He's a lot older, and he probably realizes she's young for him. She wants to live at home for a year and go to school. It sounds heavenly to me.' And his mother sounded wonderful to him, which was the best part. He felt like she had disappeared for six years. And now she'd come back to them. He had almost given up hope.

★   ★   ★

Things fell into place easily after that. Olympia extended the house in Bridgehampton and told both children they were welcome there whenever they wanted. Olympia was excited about school in September. It made her feel young again, thinking about it. Darcy was accepted at NYU for the program she was interested in, and being Bill Foster's daughter probably helped her get an exception for late admission, along with the work she'd done in Africa.

And they picked a date for all of them to meet in Paris for a week, on Darcy's way back from Africa, after Josh and Joanna stayed with Charles in France. Olympia suspected Darcy would miss her French doctor, but she'd be busy with school in the fall. They would have lots to do. New chapters had begun for them all.

CHAPTER 17

Alix had just come off the air after reporting a new sex scandal in Washington, and hurried back to her office to change her dark blue Chanel jacket for something softer and more feminine. Ben was taking her out to dinner at a new restaurant they'd heard about. Their life together was turning out to be fun. She took her jacket off, and as soon as she did, Ben took her in his arms and kissed her and started to unhook her bra, when they heard the door open and jumped apart like guilty children, as Felix stood staring at them both. He hadn't had the vaguest clue about what was going on with them.

'Don't let me stop you, children. I love porn in the office. How did I manage to miss this? Is this something new, inspired by what goes on in Washington?' He looked amused more than annoyed, and felt stupid that he hadn't guessed before. They were adults and could do what they wanted, and it had been a long time since they'd been on the road. He wondered if they were just bored or were having a serious affair.

'Sorry, Felix,' Alix said, blushing, as she slipped back into her jacket.

'No worries. You're adults, and it's none of my business.' And he liked them both. He had always wondered why nothing had ever sparked between them. He thought they were well suited to each other, which was why they worked well together. 'Far be it for me to interrupt your lovemaking, but do you have time for an earthquake in Beijing? They had a 7.2 half an hour ago, and there's a hell of a mess there. I figured I'd get you both on the midnight flight. You can always join the mile-high club, just don't get arrested in Beijing.' He was teasing them mercilessly and Alix looked embarrassed. Ben had thicker skin.

'How bad is it?' he asked the producer, focusing on the earthquake in China.

'It's too soon to tell, it sounds like a lot of casualties so far. It could get better or worse. International rescue teams are heading there now, and all the media who can get there. We just booked you on the flight.' Alix glanced at the monitor on her desk, which was on mute, which was why they hadn't heard it, and saw the first shots come up from handheld videos that had been taken with cellphones, as was often the case now. Someone always got on-the-scene shots before the press got there. She turned on the sound and you could hear screaming and buildings crashing, and the terrible rumbling in the ground. The quake had been a short one, but had done a lot of damage, and you could see people running through the streets and children crying.

'We'll go home and pack,' Alix said primly, and Felix grinned at them.

'Don't get me wrong. I love you both, and I'm all in favor of whatever it is you're doing, as long as you're both happy about it. We don't want any casualties here,' he warned them, and Ben nodded.

'Neither do we,' he assured their boss.

'Good. Then go cover the news and come back in one piece. Take care of each other,' he said gently, pleased by what he had discovered.

'We always do,' Ben answered, as Felix waved and left, and Alix groaned and looked at Ben. She was mortified to have been caught by their boss, like two kids making out in the office.

'How embarrassing.'

'It could have been worse,' Ben said, laughing at her. 'I was about to take your bra off when he walked in.'

'We shouldn't do that in the office,' she said sternly.

'Remind me of that next time,' he teased her. They'd been having fun together, and with no major event to cover at work since the vice presidential crisis, they'd had plenty of time off.

'I guess there goes our dinner,' she said regretfully, and he looked at his watch. They had to leave for the airport in three hours.

'Well, it's back to combat boots for us,' he said, and she smiled at him. 'It'll feel good to get on the road again. It's been nice here, but I've missed it.'

'Me too,' she admitted.

'And think of the money we're going to save them,' he added.

'How?' She looked puzzled.

'One hotel room now instead of two. They should give us a bonus.' He called for an Uber car, and she followed him out. Felix sent them a long email briefing them, which they read together on the ride to Brooklyn, and they both went to pack when they got home. Ben finished first, and made them something to eat, and she was wearing her heavy boots when she joined him, jeans, and her army surplus jacket in case they had to go straight to work when they got there, which was likely.

'You're the only woman I know who looks good in clothes like that,' he commented. 'And now it's going to drive me crazy knowing the sexy underwear you wear under them. I never knew that before.'

'Well, now you do.' She kissed him. He had made an omelet for a quick dinner, and they left for the airport right on time. The network travel service had sent a town car and driver for them, and traffic was light. They got to the airport in time to check in and go to the lounge. Alix watched the news, and they showed the same footage from Beijing again. And then she called Faye in France at her grandmother's to tell her where they were going. Alix still hadn't told her about their romance, she wanted to be sure of it before she did, but Faye knew that her mother was still living at Ben's apartment. Alix was surprised she hadn't asked about it. She wondered if maybe she didn't want to know. They chatted for a while until Ben and Alix had to board the plane, and Alix said she'd call her from Beijing if she could. More than likely communications there were down and might be for a long time.

They were on the plane a few minutes later and settled in, and Alix looked at him with a broad smile.

'What are you so happy about?' he inquired with a grin.

'Us. This has been really nice so far.' She said it as though she expected it to end any minute, but nothing had happened to worry either of them. They got along even better than they had before, and sex had added a whole new dimension to their lives.

'You heard what Felix said,' he reminded her, as a flight attendant handed them both champagne.

'About what?' She looked blank and took a sip of the champagne.

'He told us to join the mile-high club,' he teased her, and she was horrified.

'Don't even think about it, Ben Chapman. We're working. How can you say something like that?'

'Because I'm crazy about you,' he whispered and kissed her, and she kissed him back and smiled.

'Behave yourself.'

'That's no fun.'

'Then watch a movie, sleep, eat, do something.' He kissed her again, and the plane took off a few minutes later, and they circled New York and headed for Beijing. And it felt great to be on the road again with him.

The situation in Beijing was worse than they'd expected. When they arrived, they joined a large international press corps exchanging information, sharing locations they'd scouted, and translators, since almost no one spoke English or anything other than Chinese, even in the hotels. Several buildings had collapsed, which pushed the death toll and casualties even higher, and there were trapped bodies and injured children; paramedics and rescue teams. The Red Cross was there in force, a Swiss team with rescue dogs, Israelis, Americans, Germans, British, French, it was a whole community trying to help, and it was a week before anyone in the press corps came up for air. They were all exhausted, and Alix had caught a bad cold with a cough from all the plaster dust in the air, and the stench of decaying bodies was starting to overwhelm them all. It had been hard work physically and mentally since they'd arrived, and Alix hadn't been able to contact Faye all week, all the cellphone towers were still down. The Chinese army was helping, and a spirit of humanitarian unity and compassion was felt by everyone and bonded them all. Ben and Alix had been sleeping in the back of a British military truck for days. Everything the rescuers and locals needed had been flown in.

They were there for two weeks in all, and stopped for a weekend in Hong Kong on the way home. It was a relief to get away from the heartbreak in Beijing, with thousands dead, people maimed and injured, children orphaned, and homes and businesses destroyed. The city had suffered terrible losses, and those helping them had done a terrific job.

They had dinner at L'Atelier de Joël Robuchon on the first night there, and it made the time they'd spent in Beijing seem even more unreal. Hong Kong was so sophisticated and civilized and seemed totally removed from what they'd just experienced for two weeks. Alix's combat clothes were caked with dirt, and she had them cleaned at the hotel. She even went shopping with Ben, and felt guilty after what they'd seen that she was being so frivolous, but the fabulous shops were hard to resist. Ben bought her a beautiful jade bangle, which the shop owner said would bring her luck. It was the first gift he'd ever given her, and she slipped it on her arm and declared it her lucky bracelet from now on.

Once they were in Hong Kong, Alix was able to reach Faye. She said she had been worried about them, and watched all the coverage on TV, and she'd seen her mother several times. It was old hat to her, but it allowed her to see that her mother was alive and well. She was enjoying her time with her grandmother, and sounded relaxed.

'Are you sick?' she asked her. 'I saw you sneezing and coughing a few days in,' Faye commented.

'I caught a cold. There was so much dust and pollution in the air, I coughed the whole time I was there. I'm better now. We'll be home tomorrow,' she told her daughter, but Felix made a liar of her. He called them at midnight and told them they had to go to Cairo in the morning. There had been a bombing there, and a cabinet minister had been killed.

They were in Cairo for four days, and then headed home. They had been away for almost three weeks, and it felt like a century to both of them, when they landed in New York. It had been a long but fruitful trip.

They were lying in his bed that night after they showered, and Alix was already half asleep. She looked over at Ben next to her and thought about how lucky she was to be with him and have him in her life.

'I hope no one has a tsunami or starts a war tonight,' she said sleepily. 'I'm too tired to move or get on another plane.'

He pulled her close to him and held her. 'We'll do it next time,' he said seriously, and she glanced up at him.

'Do what next time?'

'The mile-high club,' he said sounding serious and she groaned.

'Stop it, no, we won't . . .' And then as an after-thought, she added, 'I love you, Ben, whatever we are . . .' The labels were irrelevant, they loved each other, it was all that mattered. The rest was all details. And it had been a very good trip. Felix was going to be very pleased.

CHAPTER 18

O lympia's trip to Paris with her children had been perfectly organized and orchestrated by her and Jennifer. They were booked to stay at the relatively new Peninsula Hotel on the Avenue Kléber, which was said to be fabulously luxurious, with beautiful rooms and suites, great food, impeccably trained staff, and a fleet of Rolls-Royces with drivers outside, waiting to take them wherever they wanted to go, just like the Peninsula in Hong Kong.

And Olympia wasn't disappointed when they saw their rooms. They had a lovely view of Paris rooftops from their windows. There was a holiday atmosphere to the trip. It was the first time Josh and Darcy had traveled with their mother in six years. And she couldn't wait to explore Paris with them, they hadn't been there in ten years. And part of the beauty of Paris was that nothing changed. The Eiffel Tower sparkled on the hour at night and looked beautiful. The sky was lavishly romantic and picturesque in pinks and mauves at sunset. It stayed light till after ten o'clock at night. The Arc de Triomphe and several other buildings had been cleaned. The Place de la Concorde was dazzling. The bookstalls were plentiful, the Louvre and its pyramids were unchanged. The open-air cafés were appealing, the walks along the Seine peaceful, Notre Dame, Sacré-Coeur, the Madeleine. They walked from one end of Paris to the other, and went to great restaurants at night. Olympia wanted to spoil her children and spend every moment she could with them because she had been out of commission for so long. It was the perfect place to celebrate her return. Joanna proved to be a good addition. And they'd enjoyed their time with Charles before that.

Darcy was sad about the end of her romance with the French doctor, but realistic about it. The ten years between them mattered, and he loved Africa as his home, since he had grown up there. At twenty-three she wasn't ready to settle down in Africa for the rest of her life, and she wanted to go home. She was ready. And he had told her he didn't believe in marriage, and wanted to have children one day without any official bond between them. They were culturally too different, whatever their difference in age. She loved him, but it was obvious to both of them that the relationship would never work long-term. She had spent a wonderful year in Africa, but now there were other things she wanted to do. Josh and Joanna were excited to be there, and spent a day driving in Normandy, which gave them a taste of the French countryside, while Olympia and Darcy went shopping.

The week went by too quickly, and they had dinner on the last night at a magnificent restaurant with lovely gardens called Apicius. The women had done some shopping on the Avenue Montaigne and the Faubourg St-Honoré and had returned with a few treasures, which gave Josh a chance to wander in the Bois de Boulogne, since he hated shopping. It was a trip they all knew they would remember forever. It was a celebration of life in exquisite surroundings, and they vowed to take a trip together every year, just like they used to.

'Let's do Rome next year, and Venice,' Darcy suggested, and Josh suggested Spain or Norway or Bavaria. They were talking animatedly at their last breakfast together before Josh and Joanna flew to Chicago. And Olympia and Darcy were flying home to New York. They were all sorry to see the vacation end. Josh and Joanna had promised to come to New York for a weekend.

And once back in New York, Darcy was thrilled to be home, in her own bed and her own room, and she could sense that the mood of the house had changed. The study her mother had hidden in for six years and used as a refuge from the world, with Tony's encouragement, still looked the same, with their father's photographs and mementos, but all the papers and research for her second book had disappeared. She had decided not to do it, and a stack of her books for law school classes had arrived while they were away and were sitting on the desk, waiting for her to look at them. She was excited to be starting school.

They drove out to Bridgehampton to spend a few days there. Darcy had already contacted some of her old friends and made plans with them, which Olympia encouraged her to do. By the end of her first week at home, she had seen several of them. They dropped by and Olympia's house had come alive again. It felt like a different home than the tomb it had become while Olympia had buried herself alive there.

And when she and Darcy had time, they went to museums, saw exhibits, went shopping, and made plans for their weekends at the beach. Olympia still hadn't contacted her friends from the years she had been married to Bill, and didn't want to so soon after the revelations about Tony Clark, but she was happy surrounded by Darcy and her friends, and she and Jennifer talked about how nice it was to have them around. And they enjoyed the house in Bridgehampton.

Olympia went for long walks on the beach and was at peace. It had been a happy, lively summer with her kids. She was finally getting over the shock of all she'd discovered about Tony. She was just grateful to be free of him, but her father-in-law felt he deserved more severe punishment for his crimes and was sorry he hadn't been brought to justice in the States. But Olympia was acutely aware that a murder trial would have been agony for them all.

Charles spent a pleasant weekend at the beach with Olympia and Darcy after he returned from France, and then left for Washington to visit some friends there. He still enjoyed keeping his finger on the pulse of Washington politics, and was aware of everything that went on. He told Olympia before he left how proud he was of her for going back to school, and she gave him full credit for encouraging her to do so.

'I hope I'm like him one day,' Darcy said in admiration of her grandfather, and then Olympia went back to the city for some meetings with Bill's attorneys about the estate, and she left Darcy at the house in Bridgehampton with her friends.

After the meeting, she did some errands for things they needed at the beach. She went to a hardware store and was pushing a cart full of flashlights, batteries, a small tool kit, and other practical items. She was searching for insect repellent spray when she bumped into another woman with a cart, and was startled when she saw it was Alix. She was purchasing some things for Ben's apartment that he kept promising to get and never did. The two women looked at each other for a long moment, and Alix smiled at her.

'I didn't want to bother you, but I've thought about you so often and hoped you were all right. How have you been?' Alix asked her warmly. Olympia looked healthier and more alive than when Alix had last seen her. She had a tan and was wearing jeans and espadrilles, and she seemed more relaxed than during the terrible time when the CIA had been building their case against the Vice President, with her help.

'I've been busy.' Olympia smiled at her, and Alix was struck again by her grace and beauty. She still had that magical quality to her, but she seemed more accessible and more human, and she appeared happier. Alix hoped that was the case. She had really liked her, even though they didn't know each other well, and Olympia had trusted her and liked her too. 'My daughter came home from Africa. And I took my children to Paris recently. It's the first trip we've taken together since . . . in a long time,' she stumbled over the words for a minute and decided not to say 'since my husband died.' 'And I'm going back to law school in the fall. I'm hoping to go to work after that.' Her eyes were bright as she said it and Alix smiled.

'You have been busy! And the book?'

Olympia shook her head and looked serious when she answered. 'I came to the conclusion that one was enough. It was eating me alive.' Alix nodded and was glad she had realized it before it did. 'I saw your broadcasts from Beijing about the earthquake, you were terrific, as usual,' she said kindly. 'And something else you did in Washington, I can't remember what it was. I'm a big fan.'

'Thank you. I'm a big fan of yours. I'm glad you've been so busy.'

'How's your daughter after what happened at

Duke?' They had kept each other's cellphone numbers, but never used them after that. Neither woman felt comfortable imposing, although they had liked and admired each other when they met. But their acquaintance dated back to a terrible time.

'She's all right. She's recovered surprisingly well. She's in France for the summer with my mother,' Alix told her. 'I'm going over soon with a friend to see her. She keeps saying she wants to do a semester there, but she hasn't organized it. Maybe spring semester. She just finished sophomore year.' It was nice catching up on their lives and families. They had met during one of the hardest times in Olympia's life, but it was also the end of an era. And Alix could see that when Tony had left her life, the healing had begun. She looked whole now, and at peace. Alix was glad to see it. They talked for a few more minutes, and then they both went back to their shopping, and Alix waved to her on the checkout line when she left the store. They didn't offer to get together, or promise to have lunch, or even call, but it had been a nice chance meeting for both of them that closed yet another chapter. Alix was happy to have seen her, and Olympia seemed pleased by it too. Alix couldn't wait to tell Ben about it that night.

'She looks like a real person now,' she said, 'not a ghost. That bastard almost destroyed her.'

'He destroyed himself,' Ben reminded her, 'and wherever he is now, he must bitterly regret everything he lost, every hour of every day.' But they'd never know if that was true or not.

'I hope so,' Alix said, looking thoughtful, but relieved that she had run into Olympia. She smiled thinking of her, and wished her well with every fiber of her being. She deserved to be happy. She had earned it.

Despite Felix grumbling about it, as he always did, Ben and Alix had signed up for two weeks of vacation in August. They were going to visit her mother, and Faye had been with her for two months by then, and was having a terrific time. Her grandmother and Gabriel had taken several short trips around Europe with her. She loved being with them, and had made several friends in the village, some of whom she had gone to school with as a little girl, when she lived there. And one of them had a brother she was dating, who was two years older and studying political science in Paris, but was home with his parents for the summer.

Alix and Ben could hardly wait to get to Provence. They were planning a couple of short trips too. They'd covered several stories back to back for the last month, and they were tired, but excited to see Isabelle, and spend time in France with Faye. Alix was embarrassed that she hadn't explained her relationship with Ben to her daughter. It was obvious that they were living together and had been for several months, Faye knew her mother hadn't moved back to their apartment, but all Alix had acknowledged was that they were roommates and good friends, and it was comfortable staying with Ben, and nothing more. She kept meaning to tell her but hadn't found the right time. She or Faye was always busy. And Faye had left for France as soon as school was over. Alix wanted to at least tell her by Skype or in person, not by email or text. But she never found the right moment. Faye had stayed with them for a few days before she left for France, but Alix had stayed in the guestroom again with her, so there was no obvious evidence of her mother's romance with Ben. It was a crazy situation that didn't make sense even to Alix and complicated their lives.

'Why are you hiding it from her?' Ben asked Alix frequently and felt awkward about it too. 'She's not a little kid. She's a nineteen-year-old woman. You had her when you were only a year older.'

'I don't know how to explain us,' Alix said, feeling stupid every time she said it, but it was true, she didn't.

'We love each other. Isn't that enough?' was his simple answer, and Alix knew he was right. Her mother knew about them and had no problem with it. And Faye wasn't shocked by her grandmother's relationship with Gabriel, when he traveled with them, or spent the night on weekends. She thought it was nice that her grandmother had someone in her life. Alix had promised herself to say something to her when they got to Provence.

Otherwise they couldn't sleep in the same room, which would ruin the vacation for them.

'What are you afraid of?' Ben finally asked her on the way to Provence, trying to figure it out. It was the only thing about Alix that made no sense to him. She was an honest person, and morally courageous, with strong beliefs. She was a good mother, and had integrity. And she was happy in her relationship with him. It seemed ridiculous to keep their romance a secret.

'What if it doesn't work out with us? Look at the mistakes I've made in my life. I slept with a boy I hardly knew when I was her age, got pregnant, married into a family that hated me, was a widow four months later, and his parents wanted nothing to do with us, so she was cheated out of grandparents and lost her father at three months. I never had a father to give her. And I left her with my mother for the first five years of her life, because I was too busy doing my own thing, and preferred it to taking care of her. What kind of credentials do I have for relationships? What if she asks me if we're getting married? Neither of us believe in marriage, and I'm happy the way we are and so are you, and at our age it makes sense. But what kind of example am I setting for her?'

'Your credentials are that you're a human being and a good person, and I think you're a great mother. And you're allowed to make mistakes. You were a kid when you had her, and it was probably the right thing to do to let your mother take care of her for a few years. And you're a prize-winning reporter for chrissake, you didn't just have a little job. I think you'll wind up with an Emmy one day. And you deserve it. The stories you cover, and how you cover them, make a difference in the world. You're the white knight in a very dark world, like when you went after Tony Clark. You saved Olympia Foster and the country from a corrupt Vice President. And I thought you were insane when you said he killed Bill Foster, but you were right. So what are you apologizing for? Does it really bother you that we're not married? Is that the issue? Does it mean that much to you?' He was asking her honestly and would have married her if it was important to her, but he'd never said it to her.

'No, I'd prefer not to. I don't want to screw up what we have or change anything. I just don't know how to explain it to her. I don't want her to think I'm a slut.' He smiled at what she said. 'And I can't promise her we'll be together forever. Nobody knows that. One of us could die, or we could get tired of each other. I want to believe in happily ever after, but I don't know if I do. How many people do you know that that works for? Not very many. Only a lucky few.'

'Maybe we'll be one of them,' he said hopefully. He was optimistic by nature.

'I'm not sure marriage improves the odds of that happening,' Alix added. 'I guess all my life I've done whatever I wanted, regardless of what anyone thought. I do what I believe in, and that applies to us too. I believe in you, Ben. I love you. I admire you, I think you're the best person I know. But what if you get tired of me a year from now, or bored or fed up? Then what? I tell her today that you're the love of my life, and a year from now, oops, I guess not. What kind of lesson is that? What kind of shining example am I then?'

'You're teaching her about life, that people love each other and you try like hell to make it work. And sometimes shit happens that fucks it all up. You fall flat on your face, and then you pick yourself up and dust yourself off and you go on and you try again. Maybe that's the best lesson of all. Look at us. You made a stupid mistake when you were twenty, but you got her out of it, which was a fantastic gift. I thought I had a real marriage, and our son died, and the whole thing fell apart, and now here I am with you, and I love you more than I've ever loved anyone in my life. And look at Olympia Foster. She had a great marriage, and their best friend murdered her husband, and it damn near killed her. You say she's up and running again, her kids are okay, and she's going back to school in the fall. Maybe the lesson is that you try and try and try and keep trying, and loving, and doing the right thing. Other people don't always play by the rules, but you still have to do it right, and do it with your whole heart. Isn't that what we're doing?' He made it all sound so obvious and simple. Alix loved him for that.

'I guess it is.' She smiled at him. 'Maybe all I need to tell her is that I love you and we hope it will work out. Maybe that's enough.'

'I think so.' And then after a minute, he turned to her and asked a question. 'Do you want to get married?'

'Not really. I'm too scared it would screw it all up.'

'I don't think it would, but I'm not dying to get married either. I don't think it's necessary if we're not going to have children.'

'Then let's not get married,' she said clearly. 'But I'd want Faye to get married if she has a baby,' Alix said, and he smiled.

'She might not. She's got her own ideas, just like you do, and she'll do whatever she wants, no matter what you tell her.'

'I don't know what I believe anymore,' Alix said honestly. 'I believe in marriage, just not for me. But I hope she gets married one day.'

'That might be tough to sell if you don't want it for yourself. Why don't we wait ten or twenty years, and see how it works out? If we still like each other twenty years from now, we'll get married. Is that a deal?' He grinned at her.

'Maybe. Ask me in twenty years. I'll think about it in the meantime.'

'You're just a coward. Or maybe you don't love me enough to marry me.' He was teasing her.

'Look at my mother, she doesn't want to get married either.'

'It must be hereditary,' he concluded, 'or some kind of family curse. The women in your family are phobic about marriage.'

'So are you,' she reminded him. 'I think my mother is afraid Gabriel will die if she marries him, like my father did.'

'That's crazy. You really think that's why she won't?' Alix nodded.

'She told me so once. She's convinced he'll keel over and die as soon as they leave the church.'

'That's sad,' Ben said, thinking about it.

'She's happy the way she is. And so are we.'

'Just tell Faye that. That's all she needs to know. She doesn't need to know all the complicated crazy stuff that goes on in our heads, of what we're afraid of and why. I never wanted another child because I was afraid it would die like Chris. That's foolish too. I love Faye and she makes me realize I would have enjoyed having another child, but I deprived myself of that, out of fear. We cheat ourselves sometimes.'

'Now you have Faye,' Alix said and he smiled.

They arrived at Isabelle's house half an hour later, and Isabelle and Faye ran out to greet them and threw their arms around Ben and Alix, and the four of them went into the house together. Gabriel was coming to dinner that night. And Alix was delighted to see her mother and to be with Faye again. She had missed her.

Ben left Alix's bags at the top of the stairs to avoid making a faux pas of which room he put

316

them in, which reminded Alix that she had to say something to her daughter so she could unpack her bags in the room she planned to share with Ben. Faye had Alix's usual room, which was too small for both of them, although it was a pretty room.

'Let's go for a walk,' Alix said to Faye when Isabelle went out to pick some lettuce and vegetables for that night, and Faye looked surprised.

'Is something wrong, Mom?' Faye wondered if something bad had happened, but she grabbed a sweater and followed her mother.

Once they were walking, Alix looked at her seriously. 'I have a confession to make. I've been living with Ben, not just as roommates, since you went back to school. I love him, and we're happy together, but I can't promise you it'll work forever and we have no plans to get married. Does that sound terribly immoral to you?' Alix looked solemn and worried, and Faye laughed at her.

'Oh, for heaven's sake, Mom. I figured that out when I stayed with you before I came to France. Your stuff was all over his room, and his bathroom. I think he's the best. I love him, and if you're happy with him, that's good enough for me. I don't care if you get married. He's nice to you, and to me. I hope it works out for you, and it works forever, but if it doesn't, we'll survive it together. You and I are forever. What you do with him is up to you.'

'Simple as that?' Alix looked at her in amazement.

She was a remarkable girl, and so mature. She'd been through a lot in her life.

'Simple as that. Is that okay with you?' Faye smiled at her mother.

'It sounds perfect to me.' They had their arms around each other when they walked back to the house, and both of them were smiling. Faye went to help her grandmother in the garden, and Alix bounded up the stairs and carried her bags into Ben's room. 'It's all worked out,' she said, beaming at him.

'You told her?' Alix nodded and reached up to kiss him. 'What did she say?' He looked worried.

'That we're idiots, and she figured it out when she stayed with us before she came here, and she said she loves you, she's happy for us, and she doesn't care what we do.' It was all he needed to know.

'Wow. That sounds easy.' He kissed Alix harder then, relieved by what she'd said. 'She's a terrific kid.'

'So are you,' Alix told him and meant it. 'So now we can live in sin forever and it's fine with her.' He laughed at what Alix said. He would have loved to make love to her to celebrate it, but he was afraid someone would hear them, it was a small house, and it seemed safer to wait until that night.

Ben and Alix unpacked and went downstairs. Ben took a bike ride into the village, and Alix helped her mother get dinner ready, while Faye set the table, just as she had done as a child. And

Gabriel arrived with wine from his cellar, and they spent a wonderful evening together. The two men sat outside afterward under the stars, while the women cleaned up the kitchen and joined them a little while later. They talked for a long time about life and politics, medicine, and people, and when they were tired they went to bed. And the next morning, they all met again for breakfast, and then Faye went off to see her friends, and Ben and Alix went for a drive, and checked out the local farmer's market and came home with baskets of fruits and vegetables and cheese and bread for Alix's mother.

The time went by too quickly. It was the perfect holiday for all of them, and before they left, Isabelle told Alix something that she hadn't expected and shocked her. She said that she and Gabriel were thinking of getting married, and Alix looked at her, surprised.

'Why?'

'Because I love him, and I want to. And at our age, why not? I think I'd like to be his wife, legally, I mean.' She seemed happy about the idea, although she hadn't before.

'I thought you were afraid he'd die if you got married, like Daddy.'

'He convinced me that was ridiculous, and I suppose he's right. He's in good health, and he's not working in war zones like your father.'

'When are you going to do it?' Alix asked her.

'Sometime when it feels right to us. There's no hurry. We won't make a big fuss. We'll just do it at town hall and go away for a few days, for a honeymoon, maybe to Italy. I'll let you know if I do it. But it sounds like a good plan to me.'

Alix told Ben about it that night, and he looked surprised too. 'You know what that means, don't you?'

'What?'

'That your mother is breaking the curse on the women in this family being afraid to get married. Watch out!' he warned her. 'It could happen to you!' He was teasing her, and she laughed.

'Well, not anytime soon.'

'I think it's a nice idea, if that's what they want to do, and have the right attitude about it,' he said sensibly. 'I like him a lot, and they're good together.' Alix nodded in agreement. Things seemed to be simpler and simpler in her family these days. Her mother was getting married after being widowed for more than thirty years. Faye was growing up, and she and Ben were happy living together and didn't need more than that. It all seemed very easy to her.

The next day she and Ben drove back to Paris, and spent a night there before they flew back to New York. The vacation had been idyllic, and Faye was staying for another week with her grandmother before she came home. She was going back to Duke for a semester, but applying to spend the spring semester at the Sorbonne, and was excited about it.

It had been a relaxing holiday interlude for both

of them, and Ben had enjoyed it as much as she did. They looked tanned and relaxed and healthy when they boarded the flight to New York, wondering what was in store for them when they got back. There was never any way to predict where they'd be sent, or what they'd be covering, or how dangerous or interesting it might be. But as long as they were together, they knew that they'd have a good time working on the story, and it would turn out well. It was all they needed to know. And they enjoyed their personal life now too. Neither of them was coming home to an empty apartment, or ruled by their losses of the past.

When they landed in New York, they got in a cab to Brooklyn and he kissed her. 'Welcome home.'

'I love you,' she said and smiled at him as they headed into the traffic leaving the airport and Felix texted them both.

'You're leaving for Tokyo tomorrow. Okay with you? Government scandal. Welcome home.'

Ben grinned as he read the message and put an arm around her. 'Sounds like fun,' he commented. And she laughed. Their life had never been better. They had everything they wanted for now.

CHAPTER 19

Olympia and Darcy started their master's programs on the same day. Darcy had an early class and took the subway to NYU before Olympia had to leave for Columbia. She had a last cup of tea with Jennifer before she did, and said she felt like a kid leaving for school with her books and her computer, wearing jeans and flat shoes. Jennifer smiled at the image, and once in her classroom, Olympia was relieved to see that there were some students older than she was in the seats around her, and there was a palpable feeling of anticipation in the room before the professor walked in. Olympia thought it was the most exciting thing she had done in years. And she couldn't wait to tell Darcy about it that night, and hear about how her classes had gone at NYU.

When the professor walked in, Olympia sat up straighter in her chair and paid close attention to everything she said. She was one of the most prestigious professors in the school, and Olympia was thrilled to be in her class. She had read two of her books in anticipation during the summer.

Her life was full and busy, Darcy was home and

would be living with her for the year, and she had survived everything that had happened to her.

She glanced over to her left and saw a young girl looking at her with interest, wondering what she was doing in the class, and why she had come back to school. Olympia was curious about the stories of each of them in the class, what they had done and had to overcome in order to be there. You could never tell about people, and she was sure that most of them had interesting stories to tell. She would have liked to know them all. And for now she wanted to get through the next year, learn everything she could, and get ready to work again. She had so much to look forward to.

Alix was working at her desk the week after Labor Day, after their trip to Japan a couple of weeks earlier. Faye had already gone back to Duke after a perfect summer in Provence, and Alix had decided to give up her apartment in the city. It seemed a waste to keep paying rent if she didn't live there anymore. She and Faye had discussed it and she said she didn't mind if her mother gave it up, now that she could have the guest room at Ben's to herself.

Ben thought they should get a bigger place in Brooklyn eventually, but they were fine where they were for now, and they liked the neighborhood. But they wanted more space for when Faye was home. Ben's apartment was a suitable bachelor pad, but a little crowded for the three of them.

Alix was talking to Ben on her cellphone when Felix walked into the room, and looked like he had something important to tell her. He was smiling broadly. She told Ben she'd call him back in a few minutes and hung up as Felix slipped into the chair across from her.

'What are you so happy about?' she asked him.

'You're getting an award for your work on the Tony Clark story, for outstanding reporting, and your cooperation with government agencies.' Felix looked at her proudly. 'A special Edward R. Murrow award.' It was the most distinguished award in TV news.

'How do they figure that when he wound up in Saudi Arabia?' she asked modestly, surprised by everything he had said.

'That wasn't your fault. You still did an outstanding job, and you deserve the award. There's a dinner in your honor in two weeks. We're announcing it on the six o'clock news tonight.'

'Thank you,' she said shyly. She didn't feel right getting an award when he hadn't been brought to justice and never would be. It seemed like a botched affair to her. But it had been a piece of incredibly complicated and convoluted investigative reporting, and at least he was no longer Vice President. She had contributed to that.

'And I think we're sending you to London this weekend for an event at Buckingham Palace to honor the queen. You're getting pretty fancy. Don't wear your combat boots to that one.'

324

'I'll remember not to.' She laughed.

'Everything okay with you?' he asked her with a fatherly expression.

'Better than that.' She smiled at him. She looked happier than he'd ever seen her, and had for several months.

'You and Chapman doing all right?'

'Yes, we're happy,' she confirmed.

'Good. Keep it that way. I'll let you know about London tomorrow. And congratulations for the award. It's a big deal, you know.'

'Thanks, Felix.' She smiled at him as he left her office, and then she sat thinking about Tony Clark again, and what a strange, stressful time it had been, putting all the puzzle pieces together until the last one fell into place. And wherever he was, she hoped he was paying for his sins, and not enjoying the good life. It wouldn't have been fair, although sometimes life wasn't.

And then she picked up her cellphone and called Ben again, to tell him about the award. Other than Faye, he was the best thing that had ever happened to her. She felt lucky and grateful for her life, with work she loved, a man she loved, and a terrific kid. It didn't get better than that.

Tony Clark woke in the morning as he did every day, with his lungs straining in the crushing heat, and his skin so dry it felt as though it was going to split open. He got up and put his djellabah on with nothing under it, and walked from his bedroom onto the terrace where they served his breakfast. He had learned to speak a few words of Arabic by then. Two male waiters brought him his first meal of the day, and steaming tea. He had lain in bed listening to the call for prayers that he heard five times a day. It would be time for the midday prayers soon. He had come to hate the sound of them, they were a constant reminder of where he was now, and everything that had happened. And then the day would drone on. He would have liked to read a newspaper, a real one, like *The Washington Post* or *The Wall Street Journal*, but they wouldn't let him have them here, and he couldn't read Arabic, so he couldn't read the local paper. But what did it matter now? The news didn't matter here. Nothing did. He wasn't part of the world anymore. He had ceased to exist when he came here.

They didn't let him have his computer, but he had seen CNN a few times since he'd been there. He had seen the new Vice President sworn in, which made him feel sick, and the statement the President had made about him. They were fools, all of them.

He lived in the small house they had given him, which was part of the arrangement he had made with them. He had expected it to be bigger, but they had lied to him. He was of no use to them anymore. He lived in purgatory now, or in limbo, waiting for something to change, or something to happen, and knowing that it never would again.

He was a man who had lost his life, his dreams, his world, and everything he had once built, and now he existed here in the heat, as it seared his lungs, watching time pass, listening to the call to prayers, and counting the moments like grains of sand, until his life would finally be over one day. He could hardly wait for that day to come. And if they tired of him, it might be soon. Whatever he had paid them in the past, they could always change their minds and kill him. He was well aware of that and in some ways, it might be a relief.

In the meantime, all he could do now was remember how his life had once been and would never be again. He never thought of the people he had hurt, but only what he would do to them if they let him come back one day. The hope of revenge kept him alive. There was no doubt in his tortured mind, it was their fault that he was there and that everything had turned out so badly. Even Olympia had betrayed him by not marrying him, and clinging to the memory of Bill.

One of the serving boys brought him another cup of the perfumed tea, which he hated with every ounce of his being. And now his existence was a living hell he felt certain he didn't deserve. And cruelest of all, they had forgotten him. He was a ghost, just like Bill. It was Bill's fault. If he hadn't threatened him, none of this would have happened. It could have been so simple, and almost was. Thinking about it, as he did constantly, Tony concluded that Bill had deserved to die. They all did. And then he took another sip of the tea he detested, and closed his eyes in the breathtaking heat and wished, as he did every moment of every day, that he were dead too. Bill was the lucky one, and had won in the end. It wasn't fair. Tony knew that he had deserved so much more than all of them. Bill with his unrealistic lofty ideals, as though he were a saint of some kind. Olympia with her weakness and willingness to let him control her. The President, who had betrayed him and exposed him. The lobbyists he had paid well. They had made a mockery of him. It was all so wrong, in his mind. He knew he was the better man, and he cursed and hated them all, even the Saudis who would probably kill him one day. But the joke was on all of them, because he no longer cared. He laughed in the deadly heat as the call to the midday prayers began. And to think, he had paid them for this, to be a dead man.